T0348687

The
YOUNG
SAMARITAN

J. SCHUYLER SPROWLES

The Young Samaritan

©2024 J. Schuyler Sprowles

BookBaby

All rights reserved. No part of this publication may be reproduced, distributed, or transmitted in any form or by any means, including photocopying, recording, or other electronic or mechanical methods, without the prior written permission of the publisher, except in the case of brief quotations embodied in critical reviews and certain other non-commercial uses permitted by copyright law.

ISBN: 979-8-35093-110-5

eBook ISBN: 979-8-35093-111-2

To Isabel and Emma, my beautiful grands.

Yea, though I walk through the valley of the shadow of death,

I will fear no evil; **Psalm 23 vs. 4 (KJV)**

TABLE OF CONTENTS

AUTHOR'S
NOTE

There are a number of occasions in the telling of this work of fiction where I have used the words of Jesus. Although it may not be in the biblical context as presented in the Gospels, I have taken the utmost care to use His words in the most thoughtful manner and hopefully in the spirit the Gospel writers intended. In each case where I adapted a scripture passage where Jesus has spoken, I have made reference with a footnote. Throughout this story there is dialogue between Jesus, His disciples, and the main character, Joshua. My purpose in these conversations has been to bring to life the extraordinary time when Jesus walked the earth. In doing so, I have drawn on numerous well-established Gospel accounts as a point of reference to place the reader in the midst of these remarkable events.

PROLOGUE

Uncertainty and upheaval had plagued the people of Samaria for centuries. From the Assyrian bloody conquests to the sacking of Jerusalem by Babylonian King Nebuchadnezzar, Samaria was perpetually on the verge of cataclysmic warfare. After Nebuchadnezzar's destruction of Solomon's Temple, the best of Judah's survivors were taken as slaves to Babylonia to build his statues and temples.

While Samaria had long served as the capital of Israel and a valuable passageway to Jerusalem, following the forced exile of Judeans to Babylonia and the decimation of the temple, Samaria fell into irrelevance and insignificance. Intermarriage between Samaritans and sojourners from throughout the region created a community of mixed-race inhabitants. While many continued to follow the Jewish faith, the practice of idol worship was intermingled with a devotion to Greek Gods to form a pagan melting pot, along with allegiance to the one true God, Yahweh.

With the end of Nebuchadnezzar's reign, the Judean slaves were freed. Many returned to their homeland to rebuild Jerusalem and their temple. Samaritan efforts to join in the rebuilding were rejected by the people of Israel and Judah, as Samaritan religious practices were distained as impure. Resentment over the fact that Samaritans were not part of the great exile of Jews to Babylonia deepened the fissure.

As pilgrimages and ritual animal sacrifices in the second Temple resumed in greater numbers, the Samaritans were considered pariahs and feelings of hatred and unforgiveness were common against them. It is against this background of centuries-long tumult that the story of the Young Samaritan begins.

1

JOSHUA

The night was still warm in the grassy foothills beyond the village of Sychar. Young Joshua lay on his back perched well above his family home gazing into the endless blanket of stars shimmering across the night sky. This was Joshua's favorite time, for only in the stillness of the late night could he truly be alone and dream. Staring at the brilliant heavens filled him with such wonder that it wasn't until the song of a lone bird alerted Joshua to the slowly approaching dawn and the inevitable dreariness of the day ahead.

His thin body ached from head to toe as he made his way downhill to the family homestead. The magic of Joshua's intimacy with the night was long gone as the gloom of a fog shroud dawn enveloped his thoughts as he trudged to the back door of his home. Looking up from the stony Samaritan soil, Joshua saw the sickening sight of his so-called "stepfather" as he cursed and stomped his way toward him. Soon this family intruder who was now unimaginably married to his mother was blocking his path.

They were standing face to face, forcing Joshua to abruptly turn his head as Langer's stale wine breath and ripe body odor encased the two of them.

"Where have you been, you little waste of a boy?" croaked Langer, as his watery bloodshot eyes looked down upon Joshua's bowed head. "Three goats broke through the pen last night because you can't build a decent gate to hold them. Were you up on the hill again with your head in the clouds pretending to be more than the worthless boy you are?"

Joshua looked up with his chin shaking and screamed at Langer, "I was hoping for the day you fall down dead and the ravens and worms feast on your rotting flesh." The intensity of his outburst surprised the young boy and his shoulders now tightened in fear.

Langer swiftly dropped to one knee and pulled Joshua by the cloak close to his face and wheezed into his ear, "Watch yourself, my dear boy, you just might find a viper sliding down your neck one night while you stare into the heavens. Just like the vipers who struck down your father, they may be coming for you next. They can smell weakness all over this land." Following his threatening words, Langer shoved the boy away. As Joshua gathered himself, vigorously wiping tears from his face before running to the back door, he heard Langer call from behind, "After your mother's done treating you like the baby of the house, I expect to see you in the pen fixing the gate that these stupid goats so easily broke through." Keeping his head down while he ran ahead, a lone thought crossed Joshua's mind: *What would happen if I left home?*

Joshua was immediately greeted with shrieks of delight from his three younger sisters. The twins, Talia and Tamar, with their baby sister, Leah, in tow, all fell into Joshua's arms for a morning embrace.

"Good morning, my sweetest boy," said his mother, Zina, with her back to Joshua and the girls as she pulled steaming barley rolls from the stone oven. The heavenly smell of freshly baked bread and the warmth of the crackling fire from the age-old hearth soon lifted the predawn chill from Joshua's bones.

As the crushing despair from his ugly encounter with Langer receded, Joshua felt the love of his family enter his heart. Taking his usual seat at the end of the sturdy oak table where Joshua had eaten for as long as he could remember, he quietly watched his mother busily preparing thick slices of hot bread dripping with goat butter and placing them on a long iron platter. Reaching for a handful of giant figs from the large clay bowl filled with fresh fruit, Joshua ate in silence as his sisters giggled and teased one another at the large table.

"Have you been crying, Joshua?" asked his mother as she finally sat next to her daughters and looked at her son's anguished face for the first time. "What has happened, boy? Tell me."

"I hate him mother . . . more than I've ever hated anything in my life! How could you have wed such a horrible man?" cried Joshua. "I miss father so much. Why did he have to die, mother? Why?" As the tears flowed, Joshua pulled himself from the table and yelled at his mother, "It's all your fault!" Knocking over his chair, he ran away from the family he loved. Joshua pulled back the thin fabric screening the small chamber serving as his bedroom and collapsed on his bed of straw.

The girls and their mother sat motionless. Their early morning joy of just moments ago had completely vanished as they now listened to Joshua's quiet sobbing from the other side of the cloth doorway. Mercifully, sleep soon overtook him. For a short time at least, Joshua was at peace.

2

FAMILY

The sun's mid-morning rays pierced through the tiny open space above Joshua's bed, causing him to stir. Still clinging to the last vestiges of a dream, Joshua heard his mother's soft voice. "I miss him too." Slowly opening his eyes, he squinted into the face of his mother seated next to him on the bed.

"I'm sorry, mother, I didn't mean what I said about you."

"I know you didn't, dear boy. Your father was such a wonderful man and he loved us all so much, but I worry the most about you." Gently combing Joshua's hair with her fingers, she said, "Father would want us all to stay strong as a family and he would look to you for that strength. Not a day goes by that I don't think about how hard this is on you, Joshua, but even in this sadness, we must carry on. I believe that is what your father is saying to us now."

Rising up from his thin bedding, Joshua told his mother, "I know father would never have wanted Langer in this family, yet he is here and everyone in the village seems to accept this. It just feels so wrong. He is so cruel, mother."

"He is a frightened and weak man, Joshua. We will talk about this again and I will tell you the whole story. But now you have work to do. And one more thing, my dear son: I will never ever let any harm come to you from that man. With every bone in my body I make that promise to you." With a firm kiss on Joshua's forehead, his mother rose from the sleeping pallet with a firm order to get to work.

After a long drink of fresh goat milk, Joshua headed out the door in search of the three goats that had slipped out in the night. As he hiked up the hill in the heat of the day with his walking staff and a coil of rope, he felt confident he would soon capture the wayward goats, as they seldom ventured much further than the very spot where Joshua lay gazing into the night sky not so long ago. After the confident and reassuring words of his mother, he felt ready to take on the day's challenges even if that meant another encounter with Langer. Sure enough, just fifty or so paces ahead were his escapees standing side by side chewing on clumps of tall grass that spiked around the scattered rocks. They looked unperturbed as each made soft noises and allowed Joshua to gently tie the three of them together before feeding them each a juicy fig and leading the easy-going runaways back down the hill. As the small barn and tiny goat pen came into view, Joshua again reminded himself to not let Langer spoil his sunny mood no matter what happened.

The other twelve goats welcomed their wayward companions with a steady chorus of baas as Joshua opened the gate to usher them in. He immediately spotted the small hole under the side fence where the breakout occurred and smiled to himself, knowing the rest of the herd had not shared the same need for adventure last night. Joshua immediately went to work filling in the gap and driving a stake into the narrow space. While completing this task, he felt a shadow cover the brightness of the midday sun over his head.

"I see it didn't take long for you to go crying to your mother, baby boy," wheezed Langer. Joshua kept working and did not turn to face him. "Look at me when I talk to you, boy!"

"Leave him alone!" cried Talia.

"Don't talk to our brother like that. You're not his father and you never will be," shouted Tamar. The twins stood their ground behind Langer, each holding a basket of fresh eggs for market.

Slowly turning around, Langer bent down to face the girls. "Can't you see I'm trying to make a man out of the boy?" barked Langer before walking away.

"Why should he ever listen to you?" shouted Talia. "You're just a mean man that doesn't belong here," added Tamar as Langer disappeared into the barn.

Turning to face the twins, Joshua vowed to kick Langer in the crotch the next time he tried to push him around. Their brother's words drew laughter from the twins as they each gave Joshua a tight hug before running off with their filled egg baskets.

Joshua spent the rest of the day shoveling goat waste scattered about the pen and inside the barn to be used later to fertilize the grape vines, fig trees, and vegetable garden. Many seasons ago, Joshua's father taught him everything about caring for the goats, from how to earn their trust when it came to milking chores, the importance of shoveling their dung, to always keeping their straw fresh and never forgetting to fill their water trough. The goat chores were now second nature to Joshua, but today he terribly missed the times when his father would walk by the pen and call out to him, "Those goats look better under your care than they ever did with me, son."

The thought of his father gone forever was so hard for Joshua to accept. Especially at times like this when the day's chores were done and he vividly remembered the two of them walking side by side back home with the setting sun crowning the Samaria foothills. As Joshua made his way to the house alone, he forced himself to recall the words of his mother at his bedside. *Even in this sadness we must carry on. I know that is what your father is saying to us now.*

Stepping inside, Joshua took in the aroma of turnip and potato stew simmering in the large clay pot over the fire. "Joshua's home," cried Leah as she sat at the big table watching her mother prepare the evening meal. Soon Talia and Tamar bounded out of their chamber all smiles, clothed in their favorite bright blue tunics, which accentuated their pitch-black hair and dark emerald eyes. Joshua's mother and little sister Leah shared the same ebony hair, striking eyes, and glowing white skin as the twins. If Joshua didn't know any better, he would swear he came from a different family, but the vivid memory of his father's long curls of hair, brown as the Samaria soil, was just like his. Their matching deep olive skin tone and brown eyes left little doubt to any villager passing by that they indeed were father and son.

Taking their usual places around the table, Joshua's mother ladled out steaming bowls of stew to all the girls before placing the largest serving in front of Joshua. The bread prepared that morning was quickly divided among all the family as a large clay pitcher of goats' milk was passed around the table. Before lifting a spoon, their mother called for a moment of silence to honor the memory of their father and to offer thanks to the one God who guided them through times of joy and times of sorrow into a future that only Yahweh knew. Every night that their mother spoke these words before the meal, Joshua harbored bitter thoughts of how this God could take his father away from him at a time when he needed him the most.

As he allowed his mind to dwell on the unfairness of things and why his mother prayed to such a powerless God, Joshua's attention was diverted to the twins who appeared to be conspiring with one another. Finally, Tamar spoke up while suppressing a smile, "Joshua said he's going to kick Langer in the crotch!"

"My goodness, Joshua, is that true?" inquired his mother as she too held back a smile.

"I sure am!" declared Joshua. "I'm going to kick him so hard there that he'll fall flat to the ground and won't get up for days, even while the chickens peck his ugly face!"

After a momentary pause, little Leah started to giggle and soon the twins joined in. Even their mother couldn't hold back. Looking around the table at the hilarity of it all, Joshua himself had to laugh at his own expense. It was, after all, a very amusing thought that this thin boy they loved so much would be so bold as to kick the man they despised so hard that he would fall to the ground in agony.

As the evening meal clean-up chores were nearly completed, Joshua's mother called him aside. "I think tonight may be a good time for you and I to have that talk about Langer and why he's here. I owe you that explanation and much more about our family."

After a quiet moment between the two, his mother ushered her young son out the door to make his nightly rounds checking on the goats and Lulu, their beloved donkey, and the many chickens huddling in the barn.

"If you happen to see Langer, just tell him I will leave his plate of food by the steps leading up to the roof, like always, but don't linger and please don't listen to anything he says. Do you understand me, Joshua?"

"Yes," Joshua softly replied and headed out the door.

As he quickly circled the family property, Joshua looked forward to tonight's talk with his mother. Did his family have secrets, he wondered. Were there fierce battles fought defending his family's land? What happened to everyone? Why did he only know of his mother's brother who lived alone on the far side of the village? These were some of the many thoughts spinning in Joshua's head when he spied Langer sitting on the bare ground, braced against a barn wall. He seemed barely awake, although he occasionally lifted a large leather pouch to his lips. Slowly walking past Langer's crumpled figure, Joshua heard his chilling words faintly from behind. "Your time is coming, boy."

Joshua walked on, but Langer's ominous warning nearly stopped him in his tracks. His mother's pleading to not listen to Langer seemed powerless now as renewed fear nearly overtook him amid his late-night chores. It angered Joshua to be so weak that words alone could have such a crippling effect on him.

Where he now headed would surely ease his troubled mind. Just entering the tiny corral belonging to this sweet animal, who was more family pet than working donkey, brought a sense of calm to Joshua. Calling to Lulu with inviting kissing sounds slowly coaxed her out of the small stable and into the welcoming arms of Joshua. As she nuzzled against the side of Joshua's face, he fed her a large fig and turnip. Gently stroking her soft crown, Joshua stared across the moonlit valley below and felt the peace that always came to him with Lulu in the stillness of the night.

As the breeze from the distant Great Sea to the west cooled the night air, Joshua and Lulu broke their gaze across the land and slowly turned back toward her stable. Satisfied that her water and barley straw were good for the night, Joshua gave Lulu a soft kiss above her nose and received a wink in return. With the evening chores now complete, Joshua headed back up to the family residence, anxious to have that talk with his mother and hopefully learn more about how they came to be in their situation and why Langer had come to stay.

3

LANGER

Stepping inside, Joshua first viewed their table lantern turned to its highest flame, casting a golden hue throughout the family's main room. A steaming clay mug of warm wine seasoned with honey and spice was placed before Joshua's usual place at the oak table. Directly across sat his mother, who sipped her own mug of warm wine. Although her face displayed a faint smile as she gazed at Joshua taking his seat, she appeared to Joshua to be lost in faraway thoughts.

"Is everything all right, mother?"

"I'm fine, Joshua, but like you, I just get very sad at times. What helps me in times like this is knowing that our God is with us, even at our very lowest."

"I wish father was with us instead of God, and I really wish Langer was dead," said Joshua with his head hung down staring at the table.

"I know you do, my dear boy, but we can't change the past. That does not mean you should not know about our family's past and how we came to occupy this land that has been so good to us since the time of your father's grandfather."

"But what about your family, mother? Were they always here too?" asked Joshua.

"No, my family came from lands far across the Great Sea. They brought with them spices and seeds and many coins to trade with the Jewish people in the north and the south. For the longest time, the Roman guards allowed my people to walk free among the people of Israel and not be taxed, but in time that changed. Soon the people from the land of my birth raised families with the Jews of Israel, and over time the Roman guards regarded us all as Jews. The Jews of Israel, however, did not feel the same way. In fact, they despised all the Jews who married foreigners, whether they came from across the Great Sea or from Egypt in the south. But it was here in Samaria that the people of our kind found shelter and peace. Although our great God, Yahweh, was worshiped in Samaria, so too were the many gods of my ancestors and the mysterious carved figures from other lands."

"But what about father and you?" asked Joshua, now captured by his family story.

"Your father and I were not even in this world yet. But your grand-father was, and he was the one who tended to all the land we live on today. Back in those days there were many sheep and grapevines, but your grand-father's family could do very little because he did not own the land."

"But if my grandfather did not own the land, who did?" inquired a wide-eyed Joshua.

"This, my son, will be a very difficult truth for you to accept. But it is time for you to know that the land we live on has always belonged to Langer's family," said his mother, now on the verge of tears. "I know this is hard, Joshua, but all of this property that has provided so much to our family is in Langer's family name." His mother sat with her arms folded on the table and leaned forward as she carefully watched for her son's reaction to the earthshaking disclosure.

After a long silence, Joshua sadly spoke. "In my heart, I knew there was something more. I just didn't know what, and now you tell me the worst thing of all."

As the evening wore on, his mother told the tale of how Joshua's grandfather greatly improved the profitability of the land. A well was dug, the vineyards tended to better than ever before, fruit trees and vegetables were planted and thrived. Soon goats and chickens were a common sight on the land. His mother explained how Joshua's grandfather would pay the Langer family a particular sum each growing season. But as time marched on, the Langer family grew smaller, and many moved on. Before long, with none of Langer's family around to say otherwise, the village considered Joshua's grandfather and his two sons to be the true owners of the land.

Joshua learned that his mother and father met in the village amid a busy trading season. His mother and her brother, Cyrus, were alone in the world, and just getting by helping vendors sell their goods. It was not long after meeting that Joshua's mother and father wed. The wedding was well attended by villagers throughout the land. Even the main rabbi of Samaria was there to bless the marriage, although he had serious misgivings about the well-liked young man marrying a non-Jew. But these were challenging times for the people of Samaria, and the elders of the village were eager to celebrate the success and happiness of one of their own.

At the start of their marriage, the household was filled with family from both sides. But shortly after Joshua's birth, his grandfather passed on, his mother's brother returned to the village to work as a cobbler's apprentice, and his father's brother was tragically slain one night in a violent exchange with a Roman guard over a tax dispute.

Despite the challenges of living under the dark shadow of Roman rule and the perpetual cloud of suspicion cast upon the so-called "Samaritans" by many of the people of Israel, Joshua's family thrived. As Joshua's family grew and the land continued to bear fruit, the villagers looked upon this family as the best of them.

Fondly looking back on the days after Joshua's birth, his mother smiled as she recalled how the villagers came to celebrate each of her children's births and to always lend a helping hand to tend the land. "Those were very good days," said his mother as she stared across the room.

"Why couldn't things just stay the same, mother?"

"Nothing ever does, Joshua. One day a very haggard-looking man came to the village, declaring to anybody who would listen that this property known to all as our family's was really his land. At first no one paid any attention. He was filled with wine on most occasions, so it was easy to cast him aside."

"Langer," said Joshua with all the bitterness he could muster.

"Indeed, it was," confirmed his mother. "But in the inns late at night where many of the village elders would gather, this stranger of low degree began showing a very old lambskin with writing on it that declared his family as the true owners of this property. One thing led to another and before long Langer began showing up here late at night. As you might expect, your father was very angry and each time Langer dared to show his face, your father would treat him very roughly and force him off the land."

"Why didn't father just kill him?"

"I'm proud to say that your father was not that kind of man, and you are not that kind of boy either. After a last awful confrontation with Langer, there was peace for a long time. And then as we all know, the worst thing in the world happened. Your father was struck down by that horrible viper lurking under the rock he was trying to remove from our barley field."

Silence fell upon Joshua and his mother, with the only sounds coming from the dying embers of the hearth as they both stared at the flickering flame of the table lantern. His mother then said with more sorrow in her voice than Joshua had ever heard, "Our family will never be the same again, and I worry about you most of all, Joshua."

"Why did you have to marry Langer?"

"I didn't have a choice, my son. During our family's grief, the same rabbi who married your father and me came to our home. He spoke to me alone as we walked in the fields. He promised that our family could remain on the land, but I had to consent to an awful agreement, that Langer and I be wed. He assured me that Langer will sleep in our rooftop tent until my period of mourning ends. As I sobbed, the rabbi explained to me that since I was never formally recognized as a Jew and without a male heir that was of the age, we could not remain on the land. He was also holding the skin that proclaimed Langer's family as the rightful owner. We were trapped."

With great sorrow, Joshua's mother recounted the fateful day. "As the rabbi and I returned to our homestead, I could see that many villagers were waiting for us, and there standing amid them was Langer. All I remember from that day was seeing you and the girls looking so sad and bewildered. I dimly recall the rabbi signaling Langer to come forward and stand next to me. A few words were uttered by the rabbi, and it was finished. There were no cheers from the villagers, only silence."

"I'm so sorry, Joshua. I don't know if you can ever forgive me, but my hope is that someday you can. Please, please remember that whatever happens to us, we are in God's hands, and he will lead us."

With his head hung low over the table, Joshua quietly replied, "I think God is only with Langer now."

Just then a terrible thought occurred to him. "Could Langer throw us out, mother?"

"I suppose he could, Joshua, but I don't believe that will ever happen. I'm sure you have noticed that Langer knows nothing about tending this land, and the people of our village will never help him if they know he has driven us off."

"Little Leah knows more about caring for this land than Langer."

"You could be right."

After such a grim discussion about how unfair life had become, the thought of Leah knowing more about this land than Langer evoked a tiny chuckle from each of them as they rose from the table. Before entering her chamber, where all the girls were fast asleep, his mother turned to Joshua, kneeling before the hearth and adding kindling to the low-burning blaze. "It's going to be all right, Joshua, I promise you."

4

RUN!

Joshua awoke with a start to see his mother sitting beside him on his straw-covered pallet. Her face was drawn and smudged with dirt and Joshua saw fear in her eyes. The chamber was dark with only the hint of dawn leaking through the square space high above his pallet.

Still half-asleep, Joshua raised his head bracing on both elbows and asked, "What's wrong mother?"

"It's Langer, he's gone mad." Her voice and hands were shaking, and she was on the verge of panic as she tried to explain the impossible circumstances to her son. "He returned last night full of wine. He was threatening to kill you and demanding that you come outside to face him like a man. I pleaded with him, Joshua, but he was not listening to me. Then I made a promise that he seemed to hear."

"What did you promise him, mother?" cried Joshua.

"That you would leave tonight and not return . . . ever."

"How could you do this, mother? I love you more than anything else in the world, but you have chosen Langer over your own son," said Joshua through sobs.

"My dear beautiful boy, I am choosing that you live through the night."

Clinging to Joshua tightly, she began to heave deep sobs as her terrified son sat limply on the straw pallet. She pulled herself away and ordered Joshua to dress quickly.

"I can't leave, mother. I'm afraid. I don't know where to go!" he shrieked.

Shaking his narrow shoulders, his mother addressed her son with more fury than at any time in his young life. "Listen to me, Joshua. You have to leave now, or he will kill you," she screamed.

"The girls have packed my warmest tunics and a blanket into a barley sack, and you will find enough food in there to last until you get to the village. They're waiting for you at the door. Go to my brother's home and wait for me there. I will come to you as soon as I can," she promised. Feverously kissing his face, she hugged him with all her might one last time. "Now you must go."

As he passed through his chamber into the large main room, Joshua saw his sisters waiting at the door with his scarce belongings. They were in tears as his mother guided Joshua to the door with her outstretched hands tightly on his shoulders.

Before stepping outside, she whispered into his ear, "He will be out there, my son. Please do not say a word to him, no matter what. When I finally drop my hands from you, run for your life and don't stop until you are far away."

They slowly opened the door together. Joshua was the first to appear, holding the packed barley sack against his chest. His mother followed closely behind, still clutching Joshua's shoulders. Then came the twins with their little sister, Leah, in between. Talia and Tamar were gripping Leah's hands and looking terrified as their eyes searched for Langer in the darkness. The twins then spotted him as he slowly emerged from one side of the barn.

"There he is, mother," called the twins.

"Do not say a word, girls," their mother pleaded as she continued to walk steadily ahead with Joshua still in her grasp.

Out of the corner of her eye, their mother saw Langer moving forward and staring directly at Joshua. It was then that she released her grip and screamed, "Run, Joshua, he is coming for you!"

Dropping Leah's hands, Talia and Tamar immediately charged at Langer and soon overtook him. They suddenly jumped on his back and frantically pulled at his hair while pounding their little fists into Langer's head. The twins' assault brought Langer to a halt. Roughly shaking the girls off his back, he turned and furiously lunged toward them. In the same instant, their mother came from behind and, with great force, pulled Langer by the back of his filthy tunic to the ground.

Panting as she hovered over Langer, Zina bent down close to his face and uttered a solemn promise. "If you ever lay a finger on these girls, I swear to the heavens above, I will beat you to death with my bare hands."

She gathered her daughters and headed for their home as Langer raised himself from the ground and shuffled his way toward the stable. Before opening the door, Zina turned and faced the vast western valley and yelled into the cheerless gray dawn, "We love you, Joshua," followed by many deep sobs. It took the girls some time to coax their devastated mother back indoors. Eventually, she succumbed to their pleadings and forced herself to face the hard new reality that awaited once she went through the door. Now it was just Zina and her girls living in what she had always thought of as her forever home. Now an unrecognizable strangeness was sweeping in, and her faith was surely slipping away.

Once inside, the twins and their mother went about their early dawn routines in silence. Not even little Leah said a word. Despite their broken hearts, the day was fast approaching and there was work to be done. The thought of Langer now being the only male living on this property was too much to bear for Zina. But, one thought began to worm its way into her unsettled mind; this loathsome man, who seemed so incapable of carrying out any useful function, was one hideous step at a time slowly taking over their homestead.

5

ALONE

Joshua heard every sound that echoed behind him as his legs pounded forward into the vast valley. He heard his heroic little sisters leaping onto Langer with all the fury they could muster, and he ran harder still, but now a slight smile creased his face. Later he heard his mother declare her everlasting love with so much sorrow in her voice that it brought Joshua to his knees. He turned to face his distant home perched on the hill he knew so well. It was laced in morning mist and barely visible from so far away. Remaining on his knees, he cried out, "I love you, mother, I love you, Talia, I love you, Tamar, I love you, Leah." He then lay upon his scarce belongings of clothing and food exhausted, afraid, and, for the first time in his life, completely alone.

As the sun rose over his distant home, Joshua tried to rest. The filled barley sack that his mother nervously packed through so many tears now served as a pillow. The fresh scent of Zina's tunics brought sweet comfort to Joshua along with a sharp longing for home. It was barely the beginning of his unplanned and frightful exodus. Slowly a restless slumber overtook the troubled boy, who a short time ago was running for his life from the only world he ever had known.

The brightness of the midday sun jolted Joshua awake and for a moment his unfamiliar surroundings of brush and rocky soil disoriented him. Quickly the painful reality of his circumstances came rushing in, bringing him abruptly to his feet. Looking back towards home, he could faintly see a thin column of smoke rising from the rooftop. The urge to pick up his barley sack and head back was overpowering, but he needed to relieve himself and satisfy his sharp hunger. Joshua would then make his way back home.

As he emptied the barley sack onto the ground, five silver coins tumbled out. Joshua's thoughts immediately shifted to how this considerable sum could be put to his use in the village. He would purchase more food, of course, but perhaps potent wine as well. His mind drifted to the past journeys into the village, sitting in a cart full of freshly picked vegetables with his father holding the reins as he guided Lulu along the narrow roads, making stops along the way. Often, he would see boys not much older than him, weaving on the roadside as their cart unsteadily rumbled past while his father sadly shook his head. Joshua wondered if they were drunk on wine. Maybe now he would find out for himself what that was like. He also remembered the incredible aromas of freshly cooked meat on long sticks above smoky fire pits. Yes, Joshua thought, he looked forward to sitting with men by the fire as they feasted on delicious chunks of smoldering meat.

Chewing on the hard barley loaf and a portion of goat cheese his mother so hastily packed last night, Joshua wondered what his family was doing. No doubt his mother was tending to the grape vines and watching over Leah. Were Talia and Tamar gathering their eggs and now taking care of his goats? And what of Langer? Was he asleep in the rooftop tent that formerly belonged to him? Probably so. He vividly recalled how terrified everyone was not so long ago. While packing everything back into the barley sack, Joshua arrived at a decision. He would continue to the village as his mother requested. If he walked at a brisk pace, he might make it there by sunset.

As the day wore on, Joshua realized that he would not arrive in the village until well past sundown. With the sun beginning its western descent along the distant ridgeline, Joshua squinted as he vainly fought against the sun's blinding rays. The weight of the barley sack was taking its toll as Joshua's arms increasingly felt the strain of holding all his belongings. He needed to stop more often than he expected to rest and wipe the stinging sweat from his eyes. On each occasion, he would eat a single fig or carrot to ward off his growing thirst and hopefully lessen the load of his cargo.

Every time he resumed his journey, Joshua paused for a brief look back in the direction of his distant home, no longer visible. He wondered if his family was thinking of him as much as he dwelled on them. He was comforted by the notion that somehow their thoughts reached across this vast land and linked them together. Turning to face the blinding sun sinking deeper into the western skies, Joshua forged ahead upon the strange ground, with each step taking him ever further into an unknown world.

He vowed to himself not to rest again until he reached the ridgeline that stubbornly remained well ahead. He realized the blinding sun would soon disappear behind the horizon after tormenting him for so much of the day. Joshua looked forward to the comfort of approaching dusk. As the sun slowly slipped behind the ridge, he was immediately overtaken by the cover of shade and a sense of relief from the unrelenting brightness.

The birds of prey who had accompanied him for so much of his journey were now dark silhouettes as they soared against the fading blue skies. Joshua wondered what these large, feathered creatures thought of this stranger traveling so slowly across their familiar hunting grounds. Was he a predator to be feared, or was he prey? Surely from their vantage point atop the world, they had witnessed many battles for survival where the strongest beast overtook the weak. Joshua knew in his heart he was not yet strong, nor was he nearly brave enough, but he dreamed of the day he would be just like his father, a strong and courageous man.

In that moment, Joshua came to a halt and nearly collapsed as he realized that he was utterly alone. He slowly raised his head to the darkening sky and recalled how his mother would often pray to the heavens in a language he did not understand and to a God he knew nothing of. Gazing at the first stars of the evening, Joshua prayed to his mother's God:

I don't know if there is such a thing as you, God, but my mother really believes you're out there somewhere. So, I'm asking that you tell her how much I love her and my sisters.

And if you are as powerful as my mother says you are, please keep my family safe from Langer, who is the worst man in the world. And if you really are out there, I want you to know that I'm more afraid now than I've ever been in my life and I know my mother would want you to protect me, at least until I become a man like my father. And why did you take my father away? That's why I can't believe you are a real god. But if it makes my mother happy to talk to you, then maybe sometimes I'll talk to you too. And please, please remember to tell my mother that I miss her more than anything.

As Joshua resumed his walk, he saw that the ridgeline was now not far away. Would the village be on the other side? As he picked up his pace, his heart began to soar with anticipation.

6

THIRST

As Joshua at long last topped the summit of the ridge, he wearily dropped his barley sack. Staring into the faraway horizon, he observed the sun sinking entirely from view, leaving behind bright streaks of apricot against the darkening skies. Joshua's eyes fixed on the valley below. He felt empowered by the sight before him. Spread out in the distance stood the mighty village of Sychar. Although he had been there several times in the past, it was always from the safety of the cart with his father holding the reins as Lulu led the way. This time was far different, for he had made the journey on his own and he couldn't help but feel proud of this accomplishment.

The question now facing Joshua was what to do next. As he consumed the scarce remains of his food supply, he felt chilled by the night air against his sweat soaked tunic. But most of all, Joshua thirsted. His last drink of cool water was from his home well before his world turned upside down. Pushing his exhausted body, he began his descent into the teeming village. Joshua had a singular purpose—to quench his overpowering thirst.

He recalled seeing a well in the village on an earlier visit with his father. He remembered the many tired-looking faces as they held their clay pots and waited in silence for their turn at the well.

As he approached the outskirts of the city, he heard a cacophony of noise emanating from the crowded roadways; a mixture of barking dogs, crying children, drunken laughter and angry men yelling into the night. As he proceeded along a twisted path leading to the center of the village, Joshua continued his desperate search for the well. Now fully engulfed by strangers who barely noticed him, Joshua felt even greater loneliness than on his journey through the barren wilderness.

Overcome with his urgent need for fresh water, Joshua nearly fell to the ground as he reached out to a gathering of villagers on the side of the road. With one arm holding tightly to his barley sack, he tried to hail for help, only to find that his severely parched throat prevented him from speaking above a gravelly rasp. Apart from one aged woman, the others quickly dispersed.

The lone woman bent her shawl-draped head close to the dirt road and peered into the strange boy's face. What she observed immediately drew her back. Seeing blisters on his face frightened the woman. Is this boy a leper, she thought. Raising herself up, she examined the boy further. His weather-beaten face had the look of the nomads who roamed the barren wilderness and on rare occasions wandered into the village seeking food and water.

Staring back at the woman through eyes barely able to open, Joshua managed to get out one word through his chapped lips. "Water," he croaked. Bending lower, the woman felt him weakly grab her shawl as he again struggled to speak. "Water, please water," pleaded Joshua. The old woman now understood. This frail boy lying at her feet with the grievously burned face was suffering terribly of thirst.

The woman tried in vain to pull the boy's limp body up to walk, only to fall hard to the ground beside him. Placing his feverish head in her lap, she wailed in the middle of the road. "Someone help me, please," she cried. "This boy is suffering in my arms. He must have water now, or he will perish!"

At first, her cries for help went unheeded as numerous villagers ignored her as they proceeded past the old woman and the boy she was cradling. But soon her repeated pleas for help bore fruit. As the old woman's mournful voice echoed into the night against the stone walls of nearby dilapidated buildings, people eventually opened doors and tentatively crossed the road. Soon a large cluster of villagers formed a circle around the two. Then several men and women broke from the crowd to run back into buildings and quickly return with full cups of water, as they urgently tried to aid the suffering boy.

Joshua choked as the water gushing into his mouth was more than he could swallow. Looking up, he saw a sea of curious faces peering down. He felt a gentle hand stroking his hair much like his mother often did while he lay on the comfort of his straw bed at home. Propping himself up from the ground on both elbows, he grabbed hold of a cup and began fiercely gulping, stopping only to extend the empty cup out for more.

"You need to slow down, son, or all that wonderful water will come out of you like a fountain." Turning to the side, Joshua saw the old woman sitting on the ground next to him. He realized she had been the one crying for help and holding him so tightly in the road.

The woman's kindly face was draped in a faded blue shawl that touched the ground. Joshua couldn't help but notice that her tattered clothing was covered in dust.

"I'm sorry for bothering you, but I am so grateful that you helped me. I don't know what I would have done without you," said Joshua as he continued to sit in the road and drink the water provided by the villagers.

"You can thank these good people who came when I called. This precious water is theirs," explained the old woman as she began to raise herself off the road with immediate help from the circle of villagers who remained clustered around Joshua.

Looking up at all the strange faces, Joshua started to express his gratitude, but was immediately interrupted by questions from the villagers.

"What is your name? What are you doing here?"

"Where did you come from? What do you want from us?"

"Where are your mother and father? Are you alone?"

"Do you know where you are? Who sent you?"

"Did you come with a tribe to steal from us?"

"Stop!" interrupted the old woman. "Let the boy speak."

Several of the male villagers helped Joshua to his feet and tried to dust off his soiled tunic as he told them all how thankful he was for their water. No sooner had he spoken these words than a look of panic overcame him. Frantically searching the ground, Joshua cried out, "My barley sack is gone! Who has taken all my possessions?"

"No one has, son. All your belongings are safe with me," said the old woman as she pulled the thin sack from her garment and handed it to Joshua. "Now, who are you, son? I think we all would like to know more about the boy who collapsed here on the road. Can you tell us your name?"

"My name is Joshua."

The old woman proceeded to softly ask questions on behalf of the curious villagers who remained clustered around Joshua. "Where did you come from, my dear boy?"

Pointing to the dark void behind him, he said "I am from the hill country to the east. I have been walking alone since before the last sunrise."

"So, you are one of us," declared the old woman.

"Yes, ma'am. I have lived in Samaria my whole life, but all I know of this village are the times when I rode with my father in our vegetable cart."

"Who is your father?" asked a villager in a slightly urgent tone.

"My father's name is Benjamin, but he is dead."

A nervous chatter broke out among the villagers. "This boy comes from a great family," said one of the onlookers. "But there is much sadness in that homestead because a man named Langer has taken over their land!"

"You have run from home, haven't you, Joshua?" said the old woman.

"I am running from Langer. My mother is very afraid that he may kill me if I stay, and I fear she's right."

"But what will you do now, Joshua? Our village is poor, and the tax collectors take nearly all of what we have," lamented the old woman as her fellow villagers sighed in agreement.

"I am on my way to see my uncle who has lived in this village most of his life. But I am not sure where he lives. His name is Cyrus. Do you know him?"

"We know your uncle, Joshua. He is a good man, but he is very ill and rarely leaves his tiny sandal shop by the old Jerusalem Road, a half-day's journey from here. But now you must rest and fill your stomach. Tomorrow is another day. Tonight, you will stay under my roof," declared the old woman.

"But, Mother, you have no room," said one of the villagers.

"I will make room. This boy is tired and hungry and has traveled far to our village! The least we can do is feed him and make him comfortable for one night. Tonight, the Lord has put him in our hands. Tomorrow, we will return him to the Lord and pray for his soul."

7

MOTHER

The villagers began to move across the road. The old woman could be heard making several demands.

"Can someone bring hot soup and bread for the boy? I will keep the water you have all generously provided and return your cups in the morning. This boy also needs a bath, and his tunic is filthy. One more thing, can anyone loan Joshua a small pallet to lie on? It is only for tonight, but our Lord is watching over us and we must please him."

As the villagers responded to her requests, Joshua had a question for the old woman. "I heard one of the villagers call you mother. Is he your son?

"They all call me Mother, Joshua, and you can too, my son."

In that moment, Joshua knew he was in the presence of true goodness and, for tonight at least, he would be taken care of. The small group of villagers escorted Joshua and the woman known as Mother through a darkened doorway and ascended a narrow stone stairway. Tiny clay oil lamps placed along the way provided the dimmest of light to guide their way. A single mouse went unnoticed as it nervously skittered past the villagers on its way down the steps. Arriving at the top step, Joshua peered ahead into a long roofless passageway lit only by the countless stars of the night sky. On either side of the passageway, Joshua observed openings to rooms extending into the darkness. In a few rooms, pale light could be seen flickering from open doors.

As the old woman and boy proceeded along the passageway, many of the villagers drifted away to their own rooms, but not before vowing to return to Mother's room with many of the items she requested. Now it was only Joshua and Mother walking together. In the middle of the passageway was a large pot hanging from an elaborate wooden fixture above glowing embers. As they passed the apparent cooking station, Joshua detected the faint aroma of spices and vegetables which flooded his mind with fond memories of home.

Entering the darkness of Mother's room, Joshua's eyes slowly adjusted to the barely visible flicker of flame coming from a nearby table. Mother lowered herself to the lamp and adjusted the wick and at once the tiny space was illuminated. Taking it all in, Joshua could see that the only furniture in Mother's space was a narrow table with many cracks and two chairs. Next to the oil lamp rested a crude wooden carving of a star. Against one wall lay a thin, covered pad of straw that served as Mother's bed. The rest of her quarters consisted of open shelves holding several chipped cups and plates, in addition to an assortment of jars. Against the remaining wall was a small space to store her few items of clothing. High above the same wall stretched a long piece of brightly painted fabric depicting tiny figures walking under a bright sun. Looking down at Mother's cleanly swept floor, it became abundantly clear to Joshua that there was no place for him to sleep. Sensing Joshua's dismay with her humble quarters, Mother offered encouraging words as she took a seat at her table. "One of my friends will bring us a sleeping pallet. Please sit with me, Joshua."

"Like that man said on the road, you have no room here, Mother," protested Joshua while carefully fitting himself into the remaining chair.

"We have all the space you could possibly need, child. Your bed will be set up outside where the stars will watch over you."

Reflecting on his many nights at home, staring into the night skies, "I have always loved gazing at the stars," Joshua quietly replied as his weariness began setting in.

"Then you will feel right at home. I must warn you that we do have our share of rodents in the courtyard, but we also have many cats. You will hear them playing games in the night, but be assured, the cats always win," said Mother with a wink. "Let's enjoy a cup of sweet wine together while we wait for our friends."

Joshua could barely keep his eyes open as Mother rose from the table to retrieve two cups. She poured them each a small portion of wine from a jar and placed it back on the shelf. Returning to her seat, she urged him to take a sip to help with sleep. This brought a smile to Joshua's face as he was already well on the way.

Just then a woman appeared, holding a small bowl and cloth. She explained to Joshua that this mixture of olive oil, honey, and fig nectar would cool his burned face. She liberally applied the ointment to his forehead, cheeks, and lips. Soon another woman entered the increasingly crowded space with two steaming bowls of soup. Although the soup was decidedly thinner than what Joshua was accustomed to at home, the aroma and rich flavor enlivened his senses. As impossible as it seemed, one more woman holding what was a fresh cloak squeezed her way into the cramped space. Upon nudging herself beside the boy, she instructed him to remove his filthy tunic and wrap this clean cloak around his body. She further asked that he leave his soiled clothing beside the sleeping pallet.

Joshua was overwhelmed as he looked up at the roomful of women tightly gathered around the small table where he and Mother sat sipping their soup. Never had Joshua received so much attention. He marveled at all the care he was receiving due to Mother's pleas for support on his behalf.

As his exhaustion returned, Joshua could barely follow all the lively chatter and laughter filling the air. Mother and her friends seemed to be conversing all at once, while Joshua struggled to keep his head from falling into the empty soup bowl just below his drooping chin.

Upon seeing Joshua's weary state, Mother quietly dismissed her friends, who one by one silently departed into the darkness of the courtyard. The echoes of shuffling feet and two men softly addressing one another could be heard outside, prompting Mother to inform Joshua that his sleeping pallet had arrived. "Let's have a look, shall we?" suggested Mother as the two rose from the table and ventured into the darkness just outside her tiny quarters.

Joshua ached with desire for sleep as he approached the welcoming sight of the straw-filled sleeping pallet positioned in the middle of the courtyard alongside the embers of the cooking fire. Before returning to her room, Mother reminded Joshua to remove his dirty tunic and to wrap his body in the fresh cloak before lying down. Handing him the cloak, Mother bid him good night and said tomorrow he could bathe. She also pointed out that the brightly painted clay pot near the pallet would serve his needs.

Joshua watched as this tiny woman, known simply as Mother, slowly made her way back to her quarters. Within moments, he was stretched out on the straw mat staring up into the endless canopy of stars with the clean cloak wrapped loosely over his thin frame. The night sky felt especially close to his gaze tonight. The skittering rodents and stray cats had already begun their nightly dance, but Joshua never heard a sound.

But for an occasional twitch, Joshua slept soundly while the night sky sparkled above. Soon, the sense of an approaching dawn was in the air. It was in the thin space between the darkest of night and the slightest hint of the coming dawn when Joshua was awakened by what he thought was the soft shuffling of feet. Raising his head, still heavy with sleep, slightly above the straw mat, he saw before him the dark outline of numerous kneeling figures with bowed heads and folded hands. Facing the solemn group in the same kneeling posture was the unmistakable outline of Mother.

Joshua strained to keep watching but sleep easily overtook him again until well into the brightness of a new day. He awoke to the sound of sandals slapping against the stone floor as the residents of this unusual place continued to pass by his straw pallet. Not yet ready to draw attention to himself, he continued to lay in a sleeping pose while peeking through half-closed eyes at the bustle of activity swirling about him. Soon the irresistible aroma of fresh bread prompted him to sit up and face this strange new world he found himself in. Joshua recalled the kneeling image of Mother and the residents in the night. Was I dreaming, he wondered, or did I really see them praying like his own mother often did late at night?

Amid his pondering came the welcoming voice of Mother. "Well, look who finally decided to greet this magnificent new day of our Lord!" In her thin and worn hands, she held a filled platter of grapes, boiled eggs, and steaming bread, which she set beside Joshua's pallet. "I will let you eat in peace and when you're ready, come see me. Your tunic is clean now, but still a bit wet. Let it dry further in the sun. Just wrap yourself in the cloak for now."

"Why are you doing all these wonderful things for me?" asked Joshua.

"Because the Lord delivered you to us," replied Mother, as if the answer was obvious. "Eat your meal and do not be shy about using the clay pot, nobody here is watching you that closely." She then turned away and slowly walked back to her tiny quarters.

8

COMMUNITY

Joshua, wrapped only in a thin cloak that barely covered his body, felt self-conscious as he sat across from Mother. "You look rested, Joshua," said Mother as a warm smile creased her wrinkled face. "My friends have gathered some things that may be useful to you in your travels." She then handed over an old wine sack with a large strap attached. "This is for water, Joshua. You will never last long without a full water pouch as you painfully discovered last night." Reaching down to the floor, Mother picked up a large bag by the strap and placed it on the small table. The bag was made of animal skin. "I'm afraid that barley sack of yours won't last much longer." Inside the bag Joshua could see the extra tunic and blanket that his mother had hastily packed along with a fresh bread loaf and pieces of fruit. Extending his hand into the bag, he tried to feel for the coins without drawing Mother's attention. Just as he began to touch the coins, Mother spoke up. "All the coins are there, Joshua. Don't you worry."

"I'm sorry, Mother, I should have known better. Please don't think poorly of me."

"I think only good things about you, Joshua. You are now alone in the world, just like me and my friends, and you are learning how to survive," assured Mother. "Just remember that our Lord watches over us no matter what happens." Sensing that Joshua had something on his mind, she asked, "What is it, Joshua?"

"I saw you and the others in the courtyard before dawn. Why were you all gathered at such a lonely time?"

"We were praying, son, as we do each morning in the stillest part of the day. You say it's lonely, but we feel the Almighty draws closer to us at that time to hear our prayers."

"What did you pray for last night, Mother?"

Reaching across the table, Mother closed her fingers around Joshua's hand. "You, my son. We were giving thanks to the Lord Almighty for delivering you to us in your time of need. We believe all things happen for a reason. It is not for us to know the reason why, but we must honor the hand of God when it is laid upon us."

"But why would God bother you with me?"

"Remember, Joshua," said Mother with a gentle smile, "It is not for us to know the reason why, only to obey Him when He calls. Just look at what he has accomplished. He saved you from perishing in the road, He fed you, and gave you shelter."

"No, Mother it was you who cared for me," protested Joshua.

"No, my dear child, it was God. We are merely His hands."

Lost in his own thoughts, Joshua sat in silence as Mother made herself busy tending to things in her tiny living space. Soon a woman appeared holding Joshua's dry cloak in her hands and a small towel. Mother and Joshua thanked her, but before leaving, she turned at the door and provided a brief blessing. "May our Almighty God watch over you on your journey and keep you safe."

Quickly turning to face Mother with a look of surprise, Joshua asked, "What journey does she mean?"

"Your journey, my son. Where it will take you is known only to God. But it is clear, you have already begun."

"Didn't I tell you I was going to my uncle's house? I will live there and wait for my mother to bring me home," said Joshua.

"Your uncle is a good man, and you should see him. But Cyrus is very poor just as we are, and he will be unable to care for you. I believe your mother knows this about your uncle, but your life was in danger, and she knew you had to leave at once." Mother rose from the table and paced her small room as she attempted to explain the painful circumstances Joshua was now facing. "Better she sends you to a member of your family than into the wilderness without a destination."

"But she will come for me, I just know it," said Joshua as tears filled his eyes.

"And what then, my son? Will this man Langer welcome you with open arms? I think not. I'm so sorry, Joshua. I know you love your mother and I have no doubt about her love for you. But sometimes great love calls for great sacrifice."

"What if I stay here with you and your friends, Mother?"

"I'm afraid that cannot be, my son." Returning to her chair, Mother folded her hands against her chest. "We are the poorest of the poor, Joshua. Our husbands and wives have long ago perished. Our children left us behind and we seldom see them. We live to take care of one another as best as we can. This crumbling building is all that we have. But our mighty Lord watches over us and keeps us under His wing."

"Does it ever feel like this mighty God has left you behind?"

"Never," replied Mother. "He is with us always." Sensing Joshua's next question, she answered. "How do we know this, you may ask. Because we speak to Him, dear boy, and He speaks to us. Someday you will experience this yourself and I pray that day will come soon." A brief silence settled over the two before Mother pulled herself up from the table and announced, "Now, my dear boy, I believe it is time to bathe this smelly body of yours before the foul odor surrounding me never leaves my room," she said with a hearty laugh.

Returning to the courtyard still wrapped in the thin cloak, Joshua observed that his sleeping pallet had been removed and in its place was a stone tub sitting on top of a low platform supported by four iron wheels. As he approached, he saw steam rising above the hollowed rock. Casting his eyes in all directions, Joshua saw only a few chickens strutting about and on occasion one of the residents of this unique community would pass by. Remembering Mother's words that nobody would be paying any attention to him, Joshua let his cloak fall and quickly slipped into the clear, warm water.

Immediately Joshua relaxed into a state of total bliss as he settled into the soothing water that smelled of herbs. Never could Joshua recall a time when he had been the beneficiary of such royal treatment, but he knew full well it would soon come to an end. As his bath began to cool, Joshua saw that the once clear water had slowly transformed into a grimy pool of sediment. Swiftly stepping from the tub, Joshua dried off using the thin towel he was provided and jumped into his freshly cleaned tunic. Upon his return to Mother's room, he was greeted by all the women who came to his aid the night before. Although clearly crowded tightly together in the small space, Joshua could see that they were all smiling as they faced him.

"They've come to say their goodbyes and wish you well on your journey," said the voice of Mother, hidden from view behind the cluster of women.

Although Joshua remained perplexed as to what journey these kind women felt he was about to embark on, he went along with their assumptions and expressed how thankful he was for their care and generosity. "I know not what the days ahead hold for me, but I am certain of one thing, your love has saved me," he declared.

As Mother's friends drifted away, they each paused before Joshua to offer a brief blessing and place a kiss upon his forehead. Soon only Joshua and Mother remained. Stacked on the table were all his belongings tucked tightly into his new pouch along with the water container. "I believe the time has come for your departure, my dear boy," said Mother as she rose from the table.

"I know it has, but before I leave, there is something I must do," said Joshua as his hand dug into the pouch. He then pulled out one of the silver coins that displayed the bust of Caesar and slid it to Mother's end of the table.

"I cannot accept this, my son. You were placed in our hands by the grace of God and not for a price," insisted Mother as she slid the coin back to Joshua.

"And your God is now using my hand to place this coin with you," he replied while sliding the coin back to Mother. "Please keep this for my sake and in the name of God."

"You say your mother provided you with this coin?"

"She did."

"Then I will accept this gift in the name of one mother to another," she said with a faint smile. Moving close to Joshua, she placed the strap of the pouch containing all his belongings over one shoulder and the strap holding the water container over the other. With all her strength, she gave Joshua a final hug and whispered in his ear, "May the Lord bless you and keep you." Stepping away, Mother then turned her back and softly spoke. "Please go now, Joshua. There are two men waiting for you in the courtyard who will escort you to the village well and guide you to your uncle."

9

THE WELL

The first thing Joshua noticed as he walked through the village were the dogs. Looking hungry and hot as they panted in the midday sun, the dogs were aggressive and did not appear to belong to anyone. The men who escorted him, while old and very frail, were unconcerned by the dogs. They seemed to Joshua to be at peace with the world. This was in sharp contrast to the somber-looking men and women they passed on the road. As they trudged onward toward the well, Joshua detected vacant stares on the faces of many standing in their open doors. The broken-down buildings along the way looked to Joshua like they could come down at any moment. Occasionally, donkey-led carts filled with various goods would rumble past, leaving a cloud of dust in their wake. Joshua was reminded that he once sat beside his father in their cart as they traveled this road. He wondered if the drivers considered Joshua to be one of the poor villagers, or did they even think of him at all as they rolled by?

"This is the poorest part of our village, Joshua," said one of his aged escorts as he swept an arm over the road in front of them. "The people here are watching you with curiosity and maybe some suspicion since you are a new face to them. You must be very careful, son, and never let go of this bag you carry."

"The rich neighborhoods are no better," declared his other frail escort. "You are young, Joshua, and on your own; therefore, they will try to outwit you at every turn. The well is just ahead and there will be no crowds there in the heat of the day. Fill your water vessel and keep moving. Your uncle lives off the Old Jerusalem Road some distance from here. If you don't wander about, you can be there before the sun sets."

Before heading back to Mother and their communal friends, they each laid a hand on Joshua's shoulder and offered a final word of advice. "It is best that you do not linger in the village for long. This is no place for a boy such as you." Looking into his tender face, the aged villagers waited to meet Joshua's eyes before delivering their blessing in unison, "May our Almighty God watch over you and keep you safe." With a final nod, the old men turned and began their slow walk home.

Joshua remained where he was and just watched as his escorts trudged further away into the dust and din of the Samaritan village until they became indistinguishable from the other travelers on the road. Again, he was alone, only now he stood as a stranger to all who glanced his way. Before self-pity overtook him, Joshua forced himself to ponder his next actions. He turned to face the well just ahead and cautiously proceeded forward.

Joshua was wary of more dogs who were drawn to the scent of food coming from his bag. Joshua slowly approached the low stone wall surrounding the small opening to the well. Peering down into the open space, Joshua saw only darkness. Unlike his well at home, there was no chain or bucket hanging from a rack to lower into the water.

"It fell apart," said a woman reclining under the shade of a palm. Joshua saw the long coil and bucket lying next to her along with pieces of wood scattered about. "I believe someone was unable to draw water and went into a rage."

"Is the well dry?" Joshua asked.

"It could be," said the woman. "It often happens when the days are long and hot."

"Surely there are other wells."

"Yes, but you must give the tax collector who waits at the well what he wants, and I don't wish to visit him today." Approaching Joshua with the bucket dragging behind, she proposed they work together and try to raise fresh water from the very bottom.

"If you hold on tight to the very end of the chain, I will lower the bucket down," said the woman.

Setting down his sack of belongings and his water pouch, Joshua proceeded to wrap the chain around his wrist and leaned back as the woman slowly lowered the bucket into the dark hole. Judging by her appearance, Joshua thought the woman to be about the age of his mother, but the lines on her weathered face made her seem older. Like many villagers, Joshua could see that her garments were thin and frayed as he observed them flowing freely in the sultry midday breeze. Displaying a hopeful smile, she glanced back toward Joshua. He returned her encouraging look with one of his own. This woman, thought Joshua, was alone in the world and his heart went out to her.

Soon there was barely any chain left to drop down. "I'm afraid this well is as dry as the ground we stand on," lamented the woman.

Pretending not to hear her, Joshua bent half of his body into the well and waited.

"Young man, if you fall into this hole, I cannot save you," she cried.

With his voice echoing against the walls of the deep well, Joshua called back. "I know something about wells. If the bucket is low enough, the water should gush in. You just must wait sometimes."

Before long, the echo of a tiny trickle of water could be heard from below, causing the woman to lower her head next to Joshua and whisper, "That's the sound of water, young man, I just know it."

After straining for a considerable amount of time, the woman and Joshua carefully raised the full bucket to the top of the well and placed it on the ground as water splashed over the rim. Without warning, the woman grabbed both of Joshua's arms and began joyfully dancing around the bucket and crying out for all to hear. "We did it, we did it!"

Much to Joshua's relief, the woman finally released his hands and dropped herself to the ground. Playfully, she dipped her fingers in the bucket and splashed Joshua in the face several times before sending him off to retrieve her two clay water jugs which sat under the nearby palm. Watching as the woman filled both containers, he realized there was barely enough water remaining to fill his vessel. Holding the bucket in the air, Joshua had to fend off a panting dog with his foot before filling his water pouch. While concentrating on the last drops slipping from the bucket into his possession, the dog suddenly reappeared and in one swift motion, used his teeth to pull off one of Joshua's leather sandals before running off.

Joshua could only look on as the dog ran across the road before slipping behind a broken-down structure. Turning to the woman to express his dismay at losing a sandal, he could see that all the joy from their victory at the well had vanished. She struggled to slip a long pole through the top of each water jug and with loud grunt hoisted the heavy burden atop her thin shoulders.

Looking to either side, the woman drew closer to Joshua and in a solemn tone told him, "It saddens me that you are alone and so ill prepared for what lies ahead. Wherever you intend to journey, you must never stop looking over your shoulder. Never forget that the world you find yourself in is a frightful place." Without another word, the woman turned her back to Joshua and with both arms slung over the pole to balance her heavy cargo, she slowly drifted into the village. Only then did it occur to Joshua that he didn't know her name. While gazing at the road ahead, he felt something drop at his feet. Looking down, he saw his sandal and sitting beside it, the panting dog.

10

JOURNEY

Squatting down to one knee, Joshua could feel the dog's hot breath against his face. Stroking his back with one hand, he felt hard knots under the skin and signs of recent wounds where blood matted his thin gray fur. "You're all alone out here too, aren't you?" said Joshua as the dog continued to feverishly pant. Talking to the dog felt natural to Joshua and made him think of the many one-way conversations he had with Lulu and his treasured goats back home. "I shouldn't be doing this, but I'm going to give you some of my water."

Joshua retrieved the empty bucket and poured a small portion of his water into the bottom. In the time it took to close the pouch, the dog had licked the bottom dry. Against his better judgment, Joshua repeated the process two more times before announcing to the dog that there will be no more water. Reaching into his supply bag, Joshua broke off a small crust of bread and lowered his hand to the dog, "I have to leave you now, but here's . . ." The dog immediately snatched the bread from Joshua's hand before he could finish his sentence.

Sitting on the hot dirt and squinting up into Joshua's face, the dog continued his labored panting. As Joshua looked down at the pathetic animal, he wondered how much longer the poor creature would last in the endless heat or against attacks from the many aggressive dogs who growled menacingly whenever Joshua passed by. With a final scratch on the head, Joshua turned from the dog and walked away.

Vowing to himself not to turn around, Joshua forged onward, but could not stop thinking about the scraggly animal who stole his sandal, drank his water, and swallowed his gift of food whole. Slowing his pace until he could not bear to go further, Joshua came to a halt and turned around. There in the distance, sitting right where he left him, was the dog, panting as hard as ever. Realizing he was about to make a very bad decision but craving a companion, he called out, "Are you just going to sit there?" In an instant, the dog broke into a run and nearly knocked Joshua to the ground as he jumped onto his chest.

Walking side by side as if they'd been doing it forever, Joshua looked down at his new friend and said, "If you and I are going to be together, then I think I should give you a name." Then it came to him like a bolt of lightning. "Everyone I meet says I'm going on a journey, so I think I'm going to call you Journey. That sounds like a perfect name. Nice to know you, Journey. My name is Joshua." Reaching into his sack for a fig, Joshua bit it in half and handed one half to Journey who swallowed the fresh fruit in one bite.

Continuing along the road that would lead him to his uncle's house, the boy resumed his observations of the village around him. He saw signs he couldn't read in front of old wooden carts that barely stood upright with vendors shouting to all who passed. Some were selling produce and eggs, other vendors sold sandals and cloaks. As Joshua walked on, he observed a large pen containing live chickens and goats where several men had gathered to barter over price.

Looking around, Joshua noticed that he hadn't seen Journey for some time and wondered if he ever would again. *That's probably for the best*, thought the boy. *Why would a hungry dog want to follow someone like him anyway?* Joshua's gloomy thoughts were suddenly broken by the angry shouts of a woman. Turning to see what was causing the commotion, he let out a gasp! There in the distance was a hard-charging Journey heading straight for him with a steaming chicken dangling from his jaw. Falling farther behind was the angry woman futilely cursing and furiously waving her fist at the thieving dog as she gave up her hopeless chase.

Joshua marveled at Journey's speed as he flew past with a fierce look in his eyes while firmly clenching the cooked chicken in his teeth. Once ahead of the boy, Journey slowed his pace and turned off the road, disappearing behind a cluster of rocks, just as he did when he ran off with Joshua's sandal. *This dog*, thought the boy, *truly knows how to survive in the world.*

Shuffling onward along the route that led to the old Jerusalem Road, Joshua saw that the village was bustling with more activity. More traders were hawking their wares, donkey-driven carts were rattling past with more frequency, and people surrounded Joshua from all sides. *Never in his life had he known the feeling of being a stranger*, thought the boy, *but now he did, and it wasn't good.*

Moving to the side of the road and away from the clatter and confusion of the crowd provided Joshua with a certain measure of calm as he scanned his surroundings for any sign of the mischievous dog. Just ahead he noticed an old man hawking wine out of a small wagon by the side of the road. The only villagers who appeared interested in the vendor's product were several boys who looked to be not much older than Joshua. The boys were clearly teasing the old man as he repeatedly cursed in their direction and pleaded with them to leave him alone.

As Joshua continued to watch the boys taunt the old man, he suddenly felt a greasy substance drop on his sandaled foot. Looking down, he saw Journey proudly perched below and a drool-soaked piece of chicken resting on his toes. "I see you have brought me fresh game from your hunt." Moving the chewed meat off his toes, he squatted to eye level with the dog and stroked the top of his head. Journey's hot panting into Joshua's face carried the scent of roasted chicken meat. "Thank you for thinking of me, but I'm going to let you eat the rest," said Joshua as he used his toes to move the chicken leg closer to the dog.

The bickering between the boys and the wine vendor was still going on as Joshua stepped up to the wagon. Reaching into his bag, he pulled one of the four remaining coins out and displayed the silver piece in his palm before asking the vendor, "How much wine can we buy with this coin?"

The old wine merchant's eyes opened wide. He looked suspiciously at Joshua. "Are you with these thieves?" he asked.

"No, I am not."

"Then why do you say 'we' when offering to buy my wine?" asked the vendor.

"Because I may ask these boys to join me and then you can be on your way."

"Very well. I will then sell you both jugs of fine wine for that one silver coin in your hand. But you must promise that these nasty boys will never bother me again," said the old man. The boys looked on in silence as Joshua made his surprising offer, but all were now eagerly nodding in agreement behind suppressed smiles and smirks.

Observing the old man pull his empty wagon down the road, one of the boys spoke up. "You could have bought ten jugs of wine with that coin of yours, yet that old man calls us thieves. He, my friend, is the true thief," the boy bitterly declared. "My name is Demetrio, and that's Philipo and Ethan." The two boys offered sullen nods in Joshua's direction. Demetrio then asked, "Who are you, my friend? Why have we not seen you before?"

"My name is Joshua. I've come from a farm far to the east and I'm traveling to my uncle's home on the old Jerusalem Road. His name is Cyrus."

"We know the man you speak of. You should know that your uncle is not well up here," said the smaller boy named Ethan while pointing at his own head. "The only people he talks to are travelers from the old road who trade in food and water for repairs to their worn sandals."

"Philipo go find us cups and bread so we can celebrate with our new friend Joshua," ordered Demetrio. Philipo then ran off in the direction of the many vendors along the village road. "Don't return empty-handed," he added with a laugh.

"Why is this ugly dog by your side, Joshua?" asked Demetrio.

"I like him, and he seems to like me, so we stick together. I call him Journey."

"You gave this dog a name! Dogs don't have names here. They run wild and steal food and many like this beast of yours end up being food themselves," said Ethan, who drew further laughter from Demetrio.

The words of Mother, the old men escorting him along the road, and the woman at the well, warning him not to linger in the village, now haunted Joshua as he sat on the rocky dirt across from boys he hardly knew. With growing unease, he wondered what made him choose to be so reckless and buy wine with one of his mother's precious coins.

Joshua watched as Demetrio raised the full jug to his lips and promptly spit the contents on the ground. "This wine tastes like warm dog piss. You should find that old man and take your coin back, my friend," cracked Demetrio.

Following Demetrio's mockery, Joshua lifted the other jug to his mouth and took a deep gulp. The wine was sickening. It was all Joshua could do to hold down the taste of rotten fruit and dirt as the warm liquid passed through his lips. Gagging hard as he slammed the jug to the ground, he looked at Demetrio and said, "This wine is truly wretched, but I don't know, as you do, if it has the taste of warm dog piss."

Joshua's comment drew hysterical laughter from Ethan, as Demetrio gave their new acquaintance a cold stare. The awkward moment was quickly interrupted by Philipo, who was charging toward them while carrying an armful of goods close to his chest and yelling at the top of his lungs for everyone to get up and run. Soon they were all on their feet and in full flight while carefully hanging on to the full jugs of wine. With Journey by his side, Joshua stayed close behind the other boys, knowing that outraged vendors would be coming after them following Philipo's obvious theft. As the sun slipped lower in the western sky and the boys' shadows grew longer and distorted against the higher terrain, it occurred to Joshua that he had no idea where he was running, nor who he was desperately following.

The boys, clearly winded, came to a halt at the edge of a shallow canyon. Bending over with hands heavy on their knees, they gasped for air while looking behind for any signs of angry vendors in pursuit. Satisfied that no one was coming, they began a descent into the canyon with Demetrio taking the lead and Joshua in the rear. Walking in single file, their path led to the wide entrance of a cave. Stepping inside, Philipo immediately dropped to the ground his collection of bread, cheese, a bag of green olives, and four clay mugs. "Good work, Philipo," declared Demetrio. "The wine is terribly foul, but this stolen food will make it much easier to drink," he added.

Sitting on the damp earth inside the cave, Joshua looked out at the western-facing sky. The sun was making its way down to the mud-colored hills in the distance. In the background he could hear voices and occasional laughter coming from the other three, but he paid scarce attention. Joshua realized he would not be arriving at his uncle's home until well after dark. He stared at the jug of rancid wine at his feet and decided to give in to whatever awaited him as this day slowly faded into night.

Looking up as Joshua came to join them, the boys ceased talking and watched their strange new acquaintance drop the heavy wine jug to the ground. They kept their silence with eyes fixed on the travel bag that held the silver coins as Joshua placed it on the ground and lowered himself to the cave's floor. As the boys choked down full cups of the rotten liquid, they soon became engaged in lively conversation, including tall tales of encounters with Roman guards, near-death experiences with wild beasts, and even talk of lying down with young village women. Truth mattered little to these stories of bravery and manhood. As the night wore on, Joshua found himself laughing heartily at all the boys as they exaggerated their gagging while forcing down the awful wine.

The encroaching night cloaked the inside of the cave in complete darkness. Joshua could no longer see the expressions on the faces of his newly found friends as they rambled on with more talk and laughter. In his effort to keep pace with Demetrio, Ethan, and Philipo, his head grew heavy, and he seemed incapable of joining their conversation. At one point, Joshua rose to relieve himself nearby, only to crack his head on the low ceiling of the cave and fall hard to the ground. The sharp smell of dirt and the sound of distant laughter were his last memories of the night.

11

REMORSE

A cold wetness brushed against Joshua's face, followed by the sound of whimpering against his ear. In an instant Joshua's eyes fluttered open to see Journey's head up against his own as the dog purposely sniffed his hair and face. Panic immediately seized the boy. He at once raised his head off the cave floor and frantically searched his clouded mind for answers. *What has happened to me? What have I done? Why do I have such horrible pain in my head?* Just then the questions came to an abrupt halt and the answers became painfully clear. *The boys from the village, buying the bad wine, running through the field, and entering this dark cave.*

As his head mercilessly pounded, the deep remorse over his own actions gnawed at the core of his thoughts. Just then his gut began to roil, and it was all Joshua could do to turn his fragile body to the side and violently retch onto the cold earth of the cave. The foul stench of the rancid contents spewing out of his mouth brought on further heaving until the boy was totally spent and left gasping for air. Amid Joshua's agony, a horrible thought suddenly surfaced: *The coins!*

Unsteadily rising to his feet, Joshua spun in every direction, desperately hoping to see his bag undisturbed and sitting where he left it in the night. His heart sank as he peered into the faint light of dawn at the mouth of the cave. There in the tall grass just steps away were the scattered remains of his belongings. Lurching from the cave, Joshua frantically snatched up the clothing and blanket that his mother had so hastily packed for him on the night he ran for his life. A frightful night that felt so distant now. Trampling the grass as he desperately searched for the shoulder bag and water pouch Mother's friends gave as gifts to hold all that he owned, Joshua cried out into the still dawn.

Why am I such a fool?! How could I be so reckless?! I want to go home! Overcome with despair and hopelessness, Joshua dropped to his knees and began to sob. He deeply missed his family and the life he once had. The more he cried, the more his desire to return home grew. Amid his sorrow, Journey came up and licked his tear-streaked face. Rising to his feet, Joshua continued to scan his surroundings and then in the distance his eyes fell upon the shoulder bag. But for the strap clinging to a tall sprout of grass, his bag looked light enough to fly away in the early morning breeze.

Immediately dropping his recovered belongings, Joshua sprinted ahead with all the strength he could muster from his dissipated body. Knowing in his heart the coins would be gone, he still hoped for some kind of miracle as he tore through the grass. Reaching for the bag upon his arrival, he saw in one painful instant that the three coins were gone, only a small crust of bread remained. Not far from the empty bag, he discovered his water pouch. That too was empty. At that moment, Joshua knew with certainty that he was in danger, and he began to panic.

Joshua's head pounded with such ferocity that he could barely see as he made his way back to the cave to retrieve his sparse belongings. His mind raced with thoughts of dying. Visions of serpents and wild beasts attacking from behind prompted him to wildly search the ground in every direction. Cold sweat dripped from his brow and his craving for water was intense. Adding to his agony was the sudden churning of his bowels, forcing Joshua to immediately strip off his soiled clothing and squat in the high grass.

Casting his eyes above the swaying grass, Joshua observed the birds of prey gathering in numbers as they circled the sky. *Is this what you wanted, God of nothing?"* he cried. *"To see my mother's son die in a field! She believed in you and for what? You took her husband away and replaced him with an evil man! But you weren't finished, were you? You sent her only son away to perish alone in this desolate field! Take me now, you God of nothing! My body is empty and all that's left is my rotting flesh for birds and beasts to feast on! I'm sorry, mother, but your God is not here. Someday, I hope you hear my voice in the wind and know that I loved you."*

Through much of the early morning, Joshua suffered as his young body continued to purge the poison of the rancid wine. As he weakened, his mind grew numb. Bone-weary, fatigue began to settle in. Never straying far from the cave, but choosing not to enter, he peered into its dark interior. He recalled fragments of the past night, evidenced by the dim shapes of the two discarded wine pots deep in the cave. Fighting off an overwhelming desire to sleep, Joshua gathered his remaining clean belongings and stuffed them into his empty bag. His soiled tunic lay in a heap near the cave opening.

With barely enough strength to remain standing, Joshua could see Journey's tail wagging in the distance as he romped through the tall grass in apparent delight. Pulling the straps to his bag and empty water pouch over his bare shoulders, Joshua pushed his soiled and naked body onward into the field. It wasn't long before the appeal of the soft grass overtook Joshua and brought the exhausted boy to the ground. He fell into a deep slumber as the green blades gently rippled around him in the breeze. Then came the rains.

Joshua did not hear the thunder of the approaching storm. As the wind and dark clouds swirled above, he lay undisturbed in the grass. It was the ferocity of the pounding rain that abruptly brought the boy to his feet. Racing to the cave for protection, Joshua quickly realized he wanted no part of the dark empty space. Stopping short of the cave opening, he tossed his bag of clean belongings inside and ventured back into the downpour. Urgently unlacing his water pouch, he held it in a waterfall that had suddenly formed over the cave. With the pouch now filled, he placed it firmly on the clay dirt where rivulets of water raced past. Returning to the falls to satisfy his thirst, Joshua luxuriated in the cold fresh water as it rushed through his lips and down his bare body.

Soon Journey returned and shook his soaked fur before dipping his head into the water pouch for a long drink. Once the dog's thirst was quenched, he slipped behind the waterfall and into the dryness of the cave to observe the storm from inside. Joshua remained under the falls as he watched the steady rain quickly refill the pouch and begin pouring over the sides. He stepped forward to tightly lace the pouch closed. Gazing out over the rain-swept field, he spotted his old tunic lying atop the rain-soaked grass. Bounding into the field to retrieve his clothing, he could sense that the rain had returned freshness to the once-soiled garment.

The rain had diminished to a faint mist as Joshua returned to the cave. The sun reclaimed the dark skies as vapor rose from the earth. The once surging waterfall over the cave was reduced to a trickle as Joshua dipped his head in for one last drink. From inside the cave, Journey slowly rose to stretch his front legs before stepping out to join the boy as he wrung water from his tunic before laying it on the grass to dry in the midday sun.

The sudden downpour cleansed the remorse of the night before from Joshua's mind. As he stood facing the wet field of grass and wild-flowers, the fresh breeze blowing against his bare skin sharpened his senses and lifted his spirits. Despite Joshua's recent misfortunes, for the first time since running from the only home he had ever known, Joshua felt truly alive. As Journey sauntered to his side, he knew he was ready to face whatever came his way.

12

MYSTERY

C lothing himself in the rain-washed garment, Joshua realized he must have left his sandals in the cave. Feeling the dread of returning into the darkness of the cave, his heart pounded as he slowly crept back into the cool void. Suddenly, sensing movement on the ground, Joshua froze in his tracks. There, only steps ahead, lay his sandals, but to Joshua's horror, barely visible in the dim light were a pair of vipers slowly slithering through the sandal straps.

Forcing himself to move, Joshua placed one foot behind the other, never taking his eyes off the serpents as they slid through and over his sandals. Finally feeling the sun on his bare shoulders, Joshua recognized with overwhelming relief that he had backed completely out of the darkness of the cave and into the light. Pausing only to retrieve his sack and his water pouch, he ran, never looking back.

With Journey now by his side, Joshua raced in the direction of his uncle's house until his pounding fear subsided. Stopping for a short spell to catch his breath, he forged onward with the sole purpose of reaching his uncle before nightfall. As the sun descended ever closer to the horizon, he knew it would be a race against time.

As the village of Sychar came into view, Joshua tried hard to ignore the injuries to his bare feet while trudging over stony clay. Soon he would be returning to the crowded village and again he would be a stranger. Familiar thoughts of despair and loneliness crept in as he drew closer to the village.

This was not home he was approaching, but merely a crossroad. One direction led Joshua back to the welcoming arms of his mother and sisters. His life, however, was truly in danger there if the loathsome Langer was present. Furthermore, Joshua painfully reminded himself that he no longer had the means to travel. There was no bread or fruit in his bag and no longer did he have the silver coins to purchase anything to survive. But for the fresh water in his pouch, his blanket, and a spare garment, he had nothing.

The other direction led to his uncle's house. An uncle he hadn't seen since he was a small boy. Would he even open the door to him? What if his uncle no longer lived in the dwelling along the old Jerusalem Road that Mother and the thieving boys pointed him to? Then what? Unsettling thoughts clouded Joshua's mind as he stepped into the chaotic sounds, ripe smells, and dusty streets engulfing the village of Sychar.

Amid Joshua's troubled thoughts, Journey approached from behind and leaned firmly against his legs as if to assure the boy that things would be all right, before bounding ahead in search of unknown treasures. Shuffling his bare feet along the congested road, as clouds of dust followed in his wake, Joshua gave little notice to the steady stream of villagers on foot and in donkey carts rambling past. The cries from vendors announcing their end-of-day bargains for produce took on a desperate plea as the shadows grew longer.

"Young man," beckoned a male vendor. Raising his voice above the chaotic din of the village, the vendor cried out once more, "I say to you, young man with bare feet . . . come to me."

Hearing a stranger's voice that seemed directed at him, Joshua turned to see a small and aged man with wisps of white hair atop his head, motioning with one arm for him to come to his table. "Yes, you, young man . . . please come," invited the vendor.

With great reluctance, Joshua moved in his direction, vowing to himself not to be lured into further misfortune. Stepping slowly to the nearly bare wooden tabletop, he could see that a fist-sized crust of bread and small cluster of dark grapes remained.

"Greetings to you, young man. My name is Abe and I wanted you to know of a long-held custom of mine. But first . . . may I know your name?"

"Joshua . . . and I have no coins and nothing to trade."

"Ah . . . well, then, it is clear that I have picked the right person," said the vendor as he pushed the bread and grapes to Joshua. "Please take, eat. I ask for nothing in return."

Staring at the offering before him, Joshua raised his tired eyes to the vendor. "Why do you do this for me?"

As if waiting for such a question, the kind vendor softly laughed. "This is my custom, dear boy. I give what remains at the end of a long trading day to the one who seems to need it most." Shaking his head, he added, "Watching you with your head down and dragging your bare feet as others passed you by was more than enough for me to call out to you."

With a nod of gratitude to the vendor, Joshua slowly ate the grapes one at a time. The flavor of each grape bursting in his mouth brought immediate relief as he slowly chewed the fresh fruit. "These are very good grapes," said Joshua as he continued to nod.

"May I ask where you are going?" inquired the vendor as he closed his stand for the day.

"To the old Jerusalem Road."

"Ah, the road of many mysteries . . . Well, then, farewell to you, my son." The old man turned to leave.

"Wait, wait," pleaded Joshua. "Why do you say the road of many mysteries?"

Continuing to walk away as if he didn't hear, the vendor finally stopped and faced Joshua. He raised his voice to be heard over the passing villagers, "There are strange souls out there who claim to do magic, but they lie. Many thieves roam the hills looking for easy prey. Wild beasts stalk the grasslands. But I have also heard that once in a great while, miracles may happen along that ancient road." Pausing to carefully consider his next words, the vendor then called out to Joshua once more. "You are too young, my son, to take this journey on such a treacherous road on your own, but if you must, you will truly need a pair of sandals for your feet and a weapon in your hand. Be well."

Joshua stood and watched as the generous vendor disappeared into the crowd. Gazing down at the old wood tabletop with the picked-bare grape stem and a small portion of bread, he solemnly pondered his next move. Just then Journey's snout slid over the table sniffing the bread, prompting Joshua to quickly snatch the loaf away.

Kneeling to eye level as he rubbed the dog's scruffy head, Joshua began another one-way conversation with his companion. "I was wondering where you went, you crazy dog. I probably shouldn't worry; you know this village far better than I do. I can tell from the smell of your hot breath that you've been eating chicken again." Looking down the road behind them, Joshua was relieved to see that there was no furious villager chasing after the thieving dog.

Joshua took a long drink from his pouch and poured a portion into his cupped hand for Journey to lap up before heading into the glow of the setting sun. Taking small bites of the bread as he walked was soothing to his empty stomach. Looking ahead, Joshua could see that the village was becoming less congested. Stone buildings teeming with villagers fell behind as he walked. The cacophony of voices faded. As darkness settled in, the sound of Joshua's bare feet shuffling along the now empty dirt road was all he heard.

Long gone were the streaks of sharp colored clouds in the west as brilliant stars now decorated the skies. A slight breeze ruffled his garment as he methodically forged ahead. The sight of Journey running about in the distance gave the boy comfort that he was not alone. The utter stillness of the night seemed to engulf Joshua and swept away his anxious thoughts. Soon he was captured by a feeling of peace.

As he took in the endless swirl of stars above, a faint howl could be heard echoing in the distance. Bathed in the soft glow of twilight, a single thought crossed Joshua's mind: *It is all connected.*

Unable to contain himself, Joshua released his own loud roar into the night and listened to the faint echo as it traveled into the void. "IS ANYBODY OUT THERE? MY NAME IS JOSHUA . . . I SAY . . . IS ANYBODY OUT THERE?" he cried. As the boy gazed across the darkness and listened for the slightest sound in return, Journey returned and gently laid the half-eaten remains of a hare at his bare feet.

Quietly laughing to himself, Joshua bowed down to pat Journey on the head in thanks for the gift. Then came a distant sound from the void . . . a sound that halted his breath . . . *Could it have been a voice? Was it possible the voice called his name?* Joshua stood completely still and waited, but nothing. Just as he assumed, it was the sound of his own voice, mocking him as it echoed back in the night. In the stillness it came again. It was clearly the far-off voice of a man crying out in the darkness. "Joshua, Joshua, is that you?"

The hairs on Joshua's flesh stood straight up. But for the breeze rustling through the grass, not a sound was heard. And then . . . the same voice returned. "Look for my light in the darkness, Joshua. I am holding my torch up high for you to follow. Come to me," cried the voice. Joshua wildly spun in every direction until he finally spied a tiny flickering flame.

"I SEE YOUR LIGHT," he shouted. "I AM COMING TO YOU!"

Running with all the strength he could muster, scarcely feeling the stony earth against his bare feet, Joshua did not stop until he saw the dark outline of a man holding a fiery torch high above his head. Cautiously moving forward, he could make out the features of the man's face in the flickering torch light. There before him stood a man with the longest beard he had ever seen. Through the thick gray whiskers, a broad smile creased his face.

"My dearest nephew, Joshua. I've been expecting you!"

13

CYRUS

Joshua was at a loss for words. As he stood before this tall, bearded stranger, he searched for what to say. "Is your name Cyrus?" he carefully asked.

"It is. I am your mother's brother and that makes me your uncle," he assured.

The two stood apart as shadows and torchlight danced on their faces. As they awkwardly stared at each other, Joshua, pointing to the darkness behind him, asked, "How did you know it was me out there?"

"Mother told me." Seeing the boy's confusion, he explained, "The woman who the villagers call Mother, who took care of you when you fainted on the road. She rode a donkey all the way here to see you. Although I do not know this old woman well, I do trust her. She carried with her a meager sack of dried fruit as a gift to you. I have stored it in my hut. She was very concerned you were not already here. I could see the worry on her face."

"Did Mother tell you why I was traveling to you?" asked Joshua as his chin began to tremble.

"She did indeed. I am so sorry, Joshua." Stepping before the boy, Cyrus wrapped his long arms around him in a consoling embrace. "I can only imagine how hard this has been for you. The world can be so terribly harsh and lonely." As Cyrus firmly held Joshua's thin body and gently patted his back, he felt the boy's quiet sobs against his chest.

The embrace was suddenly broken when Cyrus felt a large animal brush against his legs. Immediately jumping away in alarm, Cyrus looked down to see a wild dog actively sniffing his tunic. "Get away from me, you beast!" he cried.

Swiping the tears away with one sleeve of his garment, Joshua bent down to receive Journey with a cheery greeting while dodging the dog's fervent efforts to lick his face.

"This is Journey. He's my friend." Raising himself to face his uncle, Joshua added, "We have been traveling together."

"But he is a dog," said Cyrus with astonishment as he suspiciously stared at the panting animal.

"Do not worry. He will not bother you," Joshua assured. "The hares in the fields, though, should be on their guard."

As the two made their way a short distance to Cyrus's small living quarters, the boy listened to his uncle tell the story of how he came to live alone by the side of the old Jerusalem Road.

"I was never good around people," he explained. "It seems I was meant to be completely alone in the world. It terrifies me to enter the village and talk to others. Even children taunt me when they see the fear in my eyes, so I rarely make the journey."

Approaching a small hut built of clay and stone, Joshua was amazed that his uncle could live in such a place. "Where do you get water?" he asked.

"About a half day's walk from here there is a hidden spring. But I must be cautious, for often wild beasts are lurking in the brush."

"What kind of beasts?"

"All kinds large and small, but it is the lion I fear and admire most."

"Why the lion?" wondered Joshua aloud.

"Because there is no beast on this land that is wiser or fiercer. If the lion wants to take you, there is nothing to be done but surrender to his mighty fangs and claws," said Cyrus, pushing open the creaky door to his tiny home.

As Joshua stepped into the cave-like abode, he saw with dismay that nobody could possibly live in this overcrowded space. What little he observed in the torchlight revealed a wooden workbench filled with long sandal straps and bottoms, several tools, and a collection of clay jars set on the dirt floor. Pushed under the bench was the small bag that Cyrus indicated was from Mother.

"Where do you sleep?"

With torch in hand, his uncle ushered him back outdoors. He guided his nephew to the side of the hut where a tented roof served as an open-air canopy. A small stone fire pit glowed just beyond the overhead covering. Under the tented roof, Joshua observed a neatly arranged pair of tree stumps and a large, overturned clay pot that served as a table and chairs. Nearby, looking more like a big animal nest, was a pad of twigs and old prairie grass with old garments piled on top. *A bed no doubt,* assumed Joshua, for this strange man who lived all alone and far away from the unsettling influences of men and women.

What was my mother thinking, to send me to such a lonely place to be with a man who can barely care for himself? Joshua stood in silence as feelings of despair clouded his mind. Leaving the boy to his thoughts, Cyrus busied himself with stoking the fire pit and adding an armful of branches from a nearby pile.

"I know this is not what you were hoping for when your mother sent you to me. Your mother and I have not seen each other in many years. When the old woman came to me, she told me of the death of your father. She said you have three sisters, but I understand a stranger now lives in your home and claims the land belongs to him." Turning from the fire pit to face Joshua, he asked, "Is it true that the rabbi forced your mother to marry this man in order to remain on the land?"

Joshua solemnly nodded as he stared into the growing flame of the fire pit and pondered his bleak circumstances. Soon Journey walked in from the darkness seeking an affectionate pat on his side from the boy. He then padded in Cyrus's direction for further support, prompting his uncle to swiftly rise from the fire pit and step back from the approaching dog.

"He won't harm you. He just wants to smell your garment so he can know you better. He is a very friendly animal and not a wild beast," assured Joshua. As Journey sniffed the bottom of Cyrus's well-worn garment, he froze in place with eyes squeezed shut. He feared a savage bite on the leg at any moment, but none came. Slowly lowering a trembling hand to gingerly touch the top of Journey's bony gray head, the dog quickly responded with a soft lick to Cyrus's extended fingers. "I think he likes you, uncle," declared Joshua. A tentative smile broke through Cyrus's beard as the dog allowed him to gently stroke his mangy fur before again disappearing into the brush.

Listening as Journey noisily rustled in the dry grass beyond the firelight, Cyrus stood with arms folded against his chest gazing into the night. "I have never known a dog that I was not wary of before. This is truly a miracle, Joshua!" marveled his uncle.

The sound of Joshua dropping his few belongings to the ground broke Cyrus out of his reverie as he again spoke to his sister's son. "You look weary and hungry, my nephew, but I have little to offer. My bed of soft sticks and grass is yours if you wish. I live each day on what I gather in the field. There are wild berries and trees that grow fruit when the seasons allow. I have a trap that I set with the hope of catching a hare on occasion. The meat from a hare can last for many days. But I'm afraid those hares have been outsmarting me for some time now. So, I have learned to feast on the abundance of hopping bugs that never fail to keep my hunger away."

Seeing the disturbed look on Joshua's face, Cyrus opened a nearby clay pot and picked out two of the small delicacies of the field, placing them in his palm for the boy to examine.

"I roast them over the fire with the oil from wild olives until each bug is well charred." Placing one in his mouth, he offered the other to Joshua as he delightfully chewed. "Please, try one. You will see they are good."

Not wanting to appear ungrateful to his uncle, Joshua immediately dropped the blackened bug into his mouth and began to chew. A look of surprise lit Joshua's face as he gave his uncle nodding approval while crunching sounds came from his mouth. "This will never replace my mother's stew," he said with a grin. "But I must say, these bugs of the grass have a good taste to them. Do you have more?"

"I have a pot full of this food of the grass and there is an infinite amount in the fields beyond," said his uncle as he swept his arm across the darkness just outside the light of their fire.

Taking a seat on a tree stump, he invited Joshua to sit across from him on the remaining stump while placing the jar of cooked bugs on the makeshift table between them. "Please, eat as many as you like. We must feast on them now while the season is high, for when the nights become cooler, they vanish until the hot days return."

"What do you eat after the grass bugs are gone?" asked Joshua while reaching into the pot for more of the seasonal offerings.

"I always hope to trap a wandering hare, but as I said, they seem to be getting wise to my old ways." The fire pit cast a flickering light over the two as Joshua listened intently to his uncle tell the tale of his lonely life. "I live from day to day, my nephew. There are times when travelers along the road will bring their broken sandals to me for repair. I ask for any food they can spare in return for my labor. But my fear of people is getting worse, and I often hide from sight until they pass. Many days I search the road for bits of food that have fallen by the wayside from large tribes of pilgrims making their way to and from the great temple in Jerusalem. Still other travelers have taken pity on me and leave a portion of bread or fruit behind."

"Why are you so afraid of people, uncle?"

Silence followed Joshua's question. The crackle of burning wood was the only sound. Continuing his long gaze upon the fire, Cyrus finally broke his pause. "I have witnessed the cruelty of men most of my days. All the way back to the time when my sister and I were forced to fend for ourselves as children. Our mother and father disappeared one day and never returned. We heard they were killed by Roman guards, but we never knew for sure. Begging for food and seeking shelter in abandoned dwellings was how we lived from day to day. It was a hard life, Joshua. Your mother seemed to fare better than I did. She showed courage and protected me as best she could, but I was often prey to the worst instincts of men. Then your mother met a man who one day would be your father. He was highly favored among the villagers and in time they were married. I was truly lost without my sister to comfort me, and my cowardice only grew worse as time went on. One day my sister came to me after being gone for so long. I could see that she would soon have a child, and that of course would be you."

Captured by the story of his family, Joshua urged his uncle to continue. "Is that when you came to live with us?"

"It was indeed. I must have been a pathetic sight to her when she found me. She begged me to live on their farm. As you know very well, I did come to live with all of you for a time. And though I tried to fit in, I never felt that it was home to me. So, I returned to the village I feared, hoping against hope that somehow I would find my place in the world, but it was foolish of me to take such a journey. I will spare you the horrors I faced. One day an elderly sandal maker took pity on me and brought me to this lonely outpost where you and I now sit." Clapping his hands upon the top of his garment-draped legs, Cyrus turned from the fire pit to again face Joshua. "So, now you know the whole story of the strange man who is your uncle."

"Where is the man who took pity on you?" queried Joshua.

"He died a long time ago, and I buried him not far from where we speak. He was a good man who taught me my trade," said Cyrus, rising to add more kindling to the fire before returning to his seat. "It gives me no joy to tell you, my nephew, that these days we live in are so filled with despair. But you must never let the shadow of fear overtake you or coward-ice will have its way with you, as it has with me for most of my life."

A look of anguish darkened Joshua's face as he listened to his uncle's grim words and he pressed for further answers. "I do know something of the wickedness in men's hearts. It is why my mother forced me to flee from the only home I knew. But I must know why you call these days we live in full of despair. Is there no hope in this land? Are we all doomed to live in misery for the rest of our days?"

"I do not claim to be a prophet. I am just a man who has taken refuge alone in the wilderness away from all that I fear is evil. Although a wild beast may strike me down at any time, it gives me a measure of peace to live among them. For the beasts who roam the land carry no evil in their hearts. They kill to survive and see another day. Therefore, it is on this land that I have discovered a bit of courage, away from men and the darkness that enslaves them. But you ask, is there any hope to be found in this dread-ful land we roam? I look upon your innocent face and I say yes, there must be, for the sake of us all."

The sound of movement in the brush brought Joshua and Cyrus's immediate attention to the darkness that enveloped their dim firelight. "Journey, is that you out there?" cried Joshua. Soon the dog stepped into the light with another mangled hare dangling from his jaws. This one he dropped at Cyrus's feet before lying down near the fire.

Cyrus appeared awestruck as he rose from his seat, staring at his new four-legged acquaintance. "Day after day goes by as the hares laugh at my vain attempts to trap them. But this dog of yours is barely here one night and he brings before us such a prize as if it were nothing at all! My only regret is that he has torn away most of the flesh for himself while we sit feasting on bugs."

Watching Journey deep asleep by the fire brought on a series of yawns and stretches from the boy and his hermit uncle. Their intimate conversation continued long into the night and was good for both souls, but they were now bone-weary. Cyrus again offered his nephew the bed of twigs and grass and Joshua politely declined the offer. The boy then proceeded to lay out his only blanket near Journey and the warmth of the fire pit. Laying his head on the rolled up spare tunic, Joshua let out a sigh as he stretched his exhausted body over the length of his blanket from home. *It is good to be here,* thought Joshua as he listened to the soft flutter of the canopy in the breeze. He was nearly asleep when he heard Cyrus sit up from his bed of sticks.

"Joshua, are you still awake?"

"Yes, but I fear not for long."

"I almost forgot to deliver you a very strange message from Mother. I promised her that I would tell you."

"Please tell me."

"She said I Am is coming," Cyrus mumbled as he drifted off.

Joshua's eyes opened wide. "But who is I Am?"

He waited for Cyrus's reply, but soon only the sounds of deep snoring could be heard under the canopy.

14

THE ROAD

The bright rays of the early morning sun broke across the wet grass and rested upon Joshua's face, stirring him awake. Although not yet ready to rise, he gazed between the tree trunks and overturned clay pot where he and his uncle talked well into the night. Nearby, Joshua could see that Cyrus remained deeply asleep in his nest of sticks and old garments. What brought a smile to his face was the sight of Journey propped comfortably atop his uncle looking completely at home in this lonely outpost.

"Well, I see you have a new friend," said Joshua as the dog hopped off his uncle's chest to stretch his front legs and vigorously scratch the back of one ear. Seeing that only a few live embers remained in the fire pit, Joshua took it upon himself to add new branches from the nearby kindling pile. Soon a cloud of smoke filled the small living space under the canopy. The thick smoke drifted over Cyrus's slumbering body, prompting him to rise quickly in a state of panic.

"Fire!" cried Cyrus as he jumped to his feet still half asleep. Seeing his nephew's gray outline by the fire pit calmed him a bit. He now understood the cause of the billowing smoke. "My dear boy, you have added wet wood to the embers, and you will get nothing but smoke!"

Joining Joshua, the two worked to reduce the smoke rising from the fire pit and slowly added dry grass to the coals. Soon a small flame sprouted from glowing ashes. "Now we can add the small branches to our new fire, but not too many, for we have no need of a robust fire as the day grows warm," advised Cyrus to his young guest.

"Is there anything to eat this morning?" asked Joshua, hoping his uncle might have something to offer other than the charred bugs of the grass.

"Forgive me, dear boy, for not being a good host. I am so used to being alone that some days I don't feed myself until the sun has nearly set. Are you hungry now, Joshua? If so, I have eggs that the pilgrims have given in trade for fixing their sandals, and there is the bag of Mother's fruit stored in the hut. This talk of food so early in the day has made me hungry as well. I will prepare a feast of eggs and fruit. I have a jar of honey as well; that gives the grass bugs we dined on last night a wonderful flavor. You'll see," said Cyrus as he happily busied himself preparing their morning feast.

"I must find something for Journey as well. Although, I usually share with him whatever I have. My water pouch is also getting very low, and I can see that the dog is frightfully thirsty," said Joshua as he observed Journey heavily panting under the shade of the canopy. "I would be very grateful for any water you have to spare."

Cyrus paused from his meal preparations and gave Joshua an approving glance. "You are my nephew, dear boy, and whatever is mine is yours and that goes for your pet beast as well. This visit of yours has given me great joy and has even settled my fears for the wickedness that never lingers too far from us all." After a prolonged silence, Cyrus continued, "Go to the hut and you will find my large bucket of fresh spring water. There too you will see clay bowls and wooden spoons for our feast."

Throughout the coolness of the morning, Joshua and his uncle talked of many things over their cooked eggs and fruit as Journey sat between them, expecting handouts from each. Cyrus peppered his nephew with many questions of the family and the farm he left so long ago. Joshua, in turn, pressed his uncle for stories concerning the life he had chosen, away from people he dreaded. Yet just a stone's throw away from the heavily traveled Jerusalem Road.

"The men and women who make their way along the road are merely passing by," said his uncle. "Only on rare occasion will they approach my abode for they know of my sandal craft. They offer grapes and wine for my services, and we share a few words. The longer they remain, though, the more unsettled and suspicious I become, and I soon usher them away."

"What words do they share?" said Joshua.

"Some talk of wild beasts that roam the lonely hills, others warn me of robbers who hide in caves by day and prey on innocent travelers in the dark of night. Still others tell of prophets and fortune tellers who warn that the great temple in Jerusalem will one day fall and scatter the children of Israel far and wide. Some now tell of a great prophet in the North who will lead the Jews to victory." With a dismissive laugh, Cyrus looked at Joshua sternly. "These are mere stories, my nephew, from desperate men who seek something in return for their tales of fantasy and woe."

"But what if there is some truth in their words?"

"There is always a kernel of truth when devious men talk of future doom or glory. There is power in telling of the coming days. For we all seek a world free of the cruelty and wickedness that rules our land today, even if it means the world we know may come to an end."

"Do you think the world is coming to an end, Cyrus?"

"Not today, my nephew, not today. We will make the most of this day," said Cyrus, rising from his seat to take a long leisurely stretch. "I will craft a fine pair of sandals for those bare feet of yours and then we will search the fields for berries and ripe fruit from the trees."

"But what about Yahweh, Cyrus? Do you believe there is a God known as Yahweh as my mother does? Even the woman of the village who is called Mother says there is something greater than us all," said the boy while gathering the clay plates from their morning meal.

"Will this God find food for us today? Will he sweep the evil that possesses men's hearts away? I think not, young man," said Cyrus as he bowed low to stroke Journey's side and receive quick licks to his face. "Perhaps this animal will seize a hare for us today and we can roast the fresh meat on the fire. Will that good fortune come from the power of God or the hunting prowess of this dog?"

"Like you, uncle, I question if there is a God who watches over us. Where was this God when my father was brought down by the viper? How could such a merciful God let a wicked man like Langer take over our land and force me to choose between leaving home or face certain death at his hands? Still, I have these curious thoughts, Uncle Cyrus."

"What thoughts might you have now, nephew?"

"That this faraway God has somehow led me to you and maybe further still," said the boy as he gazed upon the old Jerusalem Road below. "Do you recall telling me last night about the message from Mother?"

Coming to a stop on his way to the hut, Cyrus turned to his nephew. "I do remember saying something to you, Joshua, but I was nearly asleep, so my words are no longer clear to me. What is it that you heard me say?"

"I Am is coming. Mother made you promise to deliver those words to me."

"Ah, yes, I do remember her telling me this before she mounted the donkey to ride back to the village. I asked her what these strange words could mean, but not another word passed her lips. She just slowly rode away. Who is I Am, Joshua? Do you know?"

"I have never heard such words. But I do believe it must be something glorious for Mother to travel all this way alone to tell me," he said while following Cyrus to his hut.

As Joshua entered the dimly lit space, the smell of musk and over-ripened fruit brought unwelcome memories of the rotten wine Joshua consumed just days ago. "I am going to make you a pair of sandals fit to be worn by royalty!" declared Cyrus as he eyed the size of Joshua's clay-encrusted feet. "Then we will walk the fields together with your pet beast by our side."

The sandals Cyrus made for his nephew were indeed of superior craftsmanship. Joshua had never experienced the simple luxury of such well-made footwear with straps that laced above his ankle. He was overcome with gratitude and hugged his uncle tighter than perhaps Cyrus had ever been embraced before. They spent the day trapping hopping bugs in a clay jar, picking berries from thickets of wild brambles, and picking the low-hanging fruit from a distant grove. It was a good day made even more splendid when Journey raced up to Cyrus with a freshly killed hare dangling from his jaw, eliciting a loud celebratory howl from the man who so feared the wild dog only the night before.

Many days passed much like Joshua's first day in the fields with his uncle. Cyrus tutored his nephew on the finer points of starting a fire, building a tiny flame into a steady blaze. On days they needed water, Cyrus would leave Journey behind in the hut, for fear that this now-treasured dog would become easy prey for larger beasts lurking near the hidden spring.

It was with great trepidation that Cyrus cautiously retrieved fresh water. Joshua learned the importance of stillness as they silently observed the brush-covered spring for any sign of movement before rapidly advancing to the waters while pulling Cyrus's rickety wagon of empty buckets behind. Once the buckets were filled, Cyrus threw caution to the wind and quietly slipped into the cool waters fully clothed with Joshua following suit. The two luxuriated in the briefest of baths. Then it was a heart-pounding race to safety with buckets of fresh water sloshing behind.

These were idyllic days for Joshua and Cyrus as their fondness for one another grew. But soon, Joshua's thoughts increasingly turned to his mother. Why hadn't she come for him as she promised, he wondered. In his own way, Cyrus tried to assure his nephew that one day he would see his mother, but perhaps not as he envisioned. Joshua found little comfort in Cyrus's words. On some late nights, Cyrus could hear his nephew softly crying before drifting off to sleep.

Listening to Joshua's restless whimpers under the gentle flutters of the canopy tore at Cyrus's heart. For reasons unknown to Cyrus, these plaintive cries felt like a disheartening sign that their precious time together was ending. As if to perish such melancholy late-night thoughts, Cyrus stretched his long arms out to provide comforting pats to Journey, who was always snuggled closely by his side atop the rough bed of twigs and soft grass. For this night at least, they all remained together. Tomorrow was another day.

Joshua's eyes were already open as the dawn's glow crested the eastern horizon. Arising from his own bed of sticks and grass, he saw that Cyrus remained soundly asleep with one arm draped across Journey's side. The sight of his uncle so closely bound to the dog he once feared never failed to bring a smile to his face. Joshua shushed Journey when the dog perked up his ears and cast a sleepy eye in his direction. Soon Journey returned to his peaceful sleep alongside a very still Cyrus who would not greet the morning for some time to come.

Joshua felt a sense of adventure as he quietly made his way down to the ancient road. For days, he had gazed from above as travelers from unknown lands unhurriedly passed by from either direction to destinations that remained foreign to the boy. Stepping upon the well-worn path for the first time seemed to connect Joshua to the innumerable people who had walked past this very point where he now stood. Could he ever make such a mysterious journey, he wondered.

As he stared into the hazy distance, he dared to envision himself along this lonely road trudging into an unknown future and leaving his sorrow behind. Amid such thoughts, a huddle of people approached from the north. Joshua grew excited as they drew near. But soon the band of travelers moved far off the road as if to avoid making any contact with the boy. The cluster pressed on to the south, never once raising their heads to view the lone figure of a boy by the side of the road as they made their way to the majestic city of Jerusalem.

Joshua recalled Cyrus telling him of the deep mistrust many held toward the Samaritan people. With his head hung low, a feeling of shame and hurt overtook the boy as he slowly made his way back to the good company of Cyrus and Journey. Although stung by the early morning rebuff, Joshua gathered a new sense of purpose as he returned to his uncle's remote dwelling.

For the next several days, Joshua repeated this early morning ritual, of quietly slipping away down to the ancient road while Cyrus and Journey remained fast asleep. Passing travelers who were willing to speak remained few and far between. Occasionally they would stop to engage the curious boy with his many questions of where they came from and where they were going. Their tales of Jerusalem with its glimmering temple on a hill and their strange stories of a mystic rabbi from Galilee who was followed by crowds of people as he roamed the countryside fired Joshua's imagination.

One early morning as Joshua made his way back to his uncle's encampment, his mind, as always, was filled with exotic stories of the people and places connected by the ancient road. Raising his head as he neared the crest, Joshua was startled to see the tall figure of Cyrus with Journey faithfully by his side staring down upon him.

"Did you really believe I was still sleeping when you noisily rose from your prairie bed each morning? Why did you try to keep such a secret, Joshua?" he asked softly.

"I did not want you to feel I was betraying you, Cyrus. I know how much fear you hold toward men. But I am different from you and can't help but wonder about the people I see passing below. The truth is I can't stop thinking about the strange stories they tell me. I know it was wrong not to tell you of my secret wanderings, but I beg you not to be angry with me."

As they returned under the canopy, Joshua took a seat on one of the tree stumps and began to eat a bowl of freshly picked nuts and figs. Cyrus, however, was restless and quietly busied himself with stoking the fire pit and feeding Journey a plate of charbroiled hare from last night's evening meal. Unlike most mornings, neither one spoke a word.

Finally, Cyrus broke the silence. "My dear nephew, I am not angry with you. You have given me more happiness in the short time we have been together than I have ever experienced in my lifetime. But I now fear you will soon be leaving me, and my heart is filled with sorrow." Turning to face his nephew, Joshua could see tears in his uncle's eyes. "Do you intend to leave me?"

"I believe the road calls to me, but I do not understand why. I feel that . . ."

Cyrus interrupted his nephew with a sharp tone. "Don't be foolish, dear boy. It is not the road that is calling to you, but the fanciful stories you have heard from the lips of many liars who travel this road. A road that only leads to more misery whichever way you trek."

After a long pause, Joshua placed his empty bowl on the turned-over pot and softly spoke while never raising his gaze to meet his uncle's eyes. "There is one thing that I am most certain of, and that is that I love you, dear Cyrus, with all my heart. I too feel the sorrow of knowing our time together may be ending."

Taking the remaining seat, Cyrus beseeched his nephew to stay. "But why leave, dear boy?! You are a mere child and there is real danger out there. You are safe with me. Together we can stand guard against the evilness of man and the wild beasts who roam the land. And what of your mother? She entrusted you to me. What do I tell her on the day she comes calling for you?"

Rising from his seat to face the empty road below, Joshua said, "Tell her I love her as I do you and I will return to her when I become a man."

"Oh, how I wish that was a promise you could keep, my dear nephew, but you cannot. For the odds are heavily against you." Cyrus began to pace as he continued to proclaim the ways of the world to Joshua. "If the evilness of man and the wild beasts who roam the wilderness were not enough to pull you back from such foolishness, please remember the biggest danger of them all. You, my dear boy, are a lowly Samaritan just as I am, and the land we live on condemns us. You cannot change what this world believes no matter how much you wish it were not so."

While stirring the glowing embers from the bottom of their fire pit, Joshua searched for the right words. "I do not seek to change the world. As you said, Cyrus, I am but a boy who is striving to be a man. But it seems the longer I remain here, the more I miss my mother. Therefore, I must move onto whatever lies ahead and leave my deepest sorrows behind."

Remaining seated, Cyrus's voice turned to resignation. "Although it troubles me deeply that I may be sending you to your death, I feel I cannot stop you." Sadly turning to Journey who lay at his feet, Cyrus asked, "But what of this dear beast?"

"I am leaving him with you, Cyrus. From the very beginning, it was clear to me that you and Journey are meant to be together. He loves you, Cyrus."

Cyrus held back new tears as he stroked the top of Journey's head while the dog sat contentedly beside him. "I believe I love him too. But how can this be, I have never loved a beast before?" After a long pause, Cyrus continued. "I promise to take very good care of him, just as he has taken care of me."

More stillness followed before Cyrus rose to his feet and took a long lazy stretch before announcing that there was much preparation to be done if his nephew intended to embark on such a dangerous journey. Just then Journey leapt up and began to bark incessantly. Someone was approaching.

15

A MYSTERIOUS VISITOR

"**M**ay I come up?" cried the voice from the road. "My cart has a broken wheel, and I can proceed no further."

Joshua anxiously looked to his uncle for approval. Slowly retreating to the far edge of their encampment, Cyrus offered his tentative consent with a slight nod. All the while Journey continued his frenetic barking, remaining at Cyrus's side to guard his frightened master.

"You may approach," shouted Joshua as he peered below upon a man dressed in a long flowing dark cloak that was ill-suited to the fierce heat of the season. He held a prominent walking stick as he worked his way up the short rise. "May we have your name?" asked Joshua.

"My name is Jeremiah. I come from Jerusalem." Raising his head to face Joshua, he continued. "I am traveling to Galilee to see my brother, who is gravely ill. I fear he may perish before I can be by his side."

Joshua stepped back as the stranger stepped up to the encampment. His lined face was dark from the sun and his eyes were sunk deep behind the bones of his cheeks and forehead. A bright necklace with a silver star dangled against his dark tunic. Although his expression was serious, it suggested no harm, nor did it offer any warmth. To Joshua, this man possessed all the mystery and intrigue of the ancient road below.

Speaking softly in a voice that Joshua barely understood, the man looked to Cyrus who remained standing far off. "Do you have any water to spare for me and my donkey? In my haste to leave the city, I'm afraid I did not prepare well for such a journey."

Hearing of the donkey's thirst, Joshua grabbed his half-filled water pouch and immediately ran down the hill to aid the animal. In his hand were three fresh figs. Seeing the donkey harnessed to the broken cart under the blazing sun upset the boy. After gently detaching the bit, he slowly brought the water pouch to the donkey. Stroking the animal's head, Joshua talked softly to the weary donkey as he consumed all the remaining water in the pouch. Comforting the animal brought a sense of calm, but also pain to Joshua as his mind drifted back to the quiet days of his farm that now seemed so long ago.

Before returning up the hill, Joshua walked around the cart and saw a paltry supply of feed for the donkey, a bushel containing a sparse collection of dried meats and fruit, and an empty water bucket. For someone taking such a challenging journey, the traveler was ill-prepared. In one corner of the cart, Joshua saw a small heap covered by a blanket. Gazing up to see if he was being watched and seeing no one, Joshua investigated further and raised the blanket. Underneath was a modest assortment of bedding material, but slightly protruding from under the pile was a tiny metal point. Curious, Joshua lifted the bedding. To his shock and amazement, lying across the worn boards of the wagon was a curved sword adorned by a silver and gold grip. The sword flashed against the bright sun as if it were alive. Joshua at once dropped the pile like he was holding a bag of serpents.

Joshua was immediately stricken by a wave of fear and intrigue. His eyes then locked on the stern face of the stranger from Jerusalem who was staring at Joshua from above.

Joshua's mind raced as he scrambled up the hill. *What would he say to the stranger? Would he tell Cyrus about the sword?* As he neared the top, his mind was set. He would say nothing unless asked. What Joshua also knew for certain was this: He wanted to join the man from Jerusalem on his journey north to Galilee.

Silence greeted Joshua upon his return to the encampment. It was clear to the boy that few words were exchanged in his absence between his uncle and the traveler. Journey paced nervously while Cyrus kept his distance. Anxious to break the quiet tension, Joshua, showing no awareness of the hidden sword, asked, "Has my uncle offered you any water?"

"I believe your uncle wished to wait until your return," offered the man.

"Well then, I will get a large mug of cool water from my uncle's hut." Turning to his uncle who remained on the far side of the encampment, Joshua spoke, "There are two broken spokes on one of the wheels of his cart. Perhaps with your tools and tacks you can fix the man's wheel and he can be on his way?" Cyrus silently nodded in agreement.

Returning with a full mug of water, Joshua continued to make up for his uncle's silence. "Our water supplies are quite low now, but I see that you and your donkey have none. There is a hidden spring a short journey from where we stand. I suggest you come with me, and we will replenish our water supply together."

Joshua's suggestion elicited a prompt response from Cyrus. "You cannot go to the spring alone with this stranger, it is far too dangerous!"

"My dear uncle, I will be fine, for you have taught me well how to retrieve water when no wild beasts are nearby. While we are gone, you can repair this man's cart. Please, Cyrus, do not worry about me."

Suddenly Journey began to bark again as he raced up the hill to the east. At once, Cyrus dashed to the hut and hid inside. Joshua spun around and saw with alarm that the stranger from Jerusalem was nowhere to be found. *What is happening?* thought the boy, as he stood alone under the canopy. *Has my mother finally come for me?* Joshua bolted in the direction of Journey's barking. Quickly coming alongside the still agitated dog, Joshua gazed in the distance toward the village. A pang of disappointment pierced his heart. It was not his mother who was slowly approaching atop a donkey, but rather the slumped figure of the kind old woman from Sychar who had taken such good care of him.

Although Joshua was disheartened to see that his mother was not coming for him, he was still pleased that the woman known as Mother was returning to Cyrus's encampment. Running to greet her while calling for Journey to calm down, Joshua was all smiles as he helped Mother down from the donkey.

"I am so happy to see you, Joshua. I was worried when I came before, and Cyrus had not heard from you. Where is your uncle? Is he hiding?" she inquired with a slight smile. Joshua nodded toward the hut. Mother placed a finger to her lips and quietly stepped to the door of the hut. Softly knocking, she gently offered a teasing question. "Is this how you welcome an old friend? Between you hiding behind the door and this barking beast who rudely greeted me, I'm starting to feel unwanted."

"You can never be unwanted, Mother," shouted Joshua with a smile as he sat on a tree stump petting the dog.

Puzzled, Mother looked back at Joshua. "Where did this beast come from?"

"His name is Journey, and he came with Joshua from your village," said Cyrus through a crack in the door. "Is the stranger still here?"

"What stranger? Cyrus, would you please come out of your hut? I do not wish to speak through a door any longer."

As Mother waited for Cyrus to muster the courage to emerge from his hut, she was suddenly taken aback as an unfamiliar man dressed in a flowing dark cloak stepped out of the shadows and stood next to Joshua.

"My name is Jeremiah," said the stranger addressing Mother who now edged away from the hut door with wide eyes. "I am from Jerusalem, and I am making my way to Galilee, but my cart has a broken wheel, and I can travel no further until it is repaired."

Fixing her gaze on the man's sunken eyes and the six-pointed star that dangled from his neck, Mother stepped closer. "Why does a man such as you have a need to travel to a place such as Galilee?"

"I have learned that my dear brother is deathly ill, and I desperately need to be by his side."

"I see," said Mother, now standing before him, raising her face to meet his eyes. "I am very sorry to have to tell you this, but I do not believe a word you are saying."

"No, Mother, I saw myself that Jeremiah has a broken wheel," said Joshua.

"I am not talking about his wheel, Joshua, I want to know the real reason this man from Jerusalem needed to leave such a glorious city so quickly." As her stare remained fixed on the man's eyes, Mother voiced her suspicion. "I believe you are afraid to tell us the reason. Am I right?"

With a mocking laugh, Jeremiah scoffed at Mother's accusations. "I am afraid of no one. If you must know the truth, woman, I will tell you." As he was speaking, Cyrus had quietly joined the rest, although at a safe distance. Journey pressed nervously against Cyrus's side. Mother stood firm before the man as Joshua paced by the fire. The canvas tarp fluttered noisily overhead as a gust of wind blew through the encampment, stirring dust clouds in its wake. All anxiously waited for the man's next words.

"Three days past I fled the city of Jerusalem. My people arranged for a cart and donkey, so I could quickly exit the city in the dead of the night."

As he spoke, Mother, Cyrus, and Joshua stood transfixed by his words. "I have killed three men. All deserved to die." Cyrus let out a small cry upon hearing the man's words and backed further away.

Jeremiah continued, "The men were all filthy gentile guards of Rome. The first guard tried to block me from entering our great temple. He demanded that I pay him a tax before going further. You must understand that I have never resisted paying such guards or the disgraceful tax collectors who do their bidding. I have succumbed to their corrupt demands all my life. But on this day, I arose with a new vow in my heart to never again bow in their shameful presence."

Jeremiah was now the one who paced as he provided his testimony while his dark eyes darted from Cyrus to Joshua and finally rested upon Mother. "This guard looked down on me with the hateful arrogance I had long ago grown accustomed to from these vile men. This time something broke through deep in my soul." As stillness prevailed over the encampment, Jeremiah spoke again in a raised voice. "It was the voice of the Almighty telling me that my time had come. I humbly pleaded with this guard to come down from his horse, so I could hear his orders clearly. Being the ignorant man that he was, he complied with my request and before both of his sandals touched the earth, I ran him through with my sword. Two more guards pursued me on foot: I hid and attacked from behind, separating their helmeted heads from their wretched bodies. In the chaos of the moment, men and women ran and cried while the blood of their despised conquerors drained in the street."

Never flinching as the man from Jerusalem delivered his testimony, Mother kept up her steady gaze. "I demand to know in the name of the Almighty Adonai who you are!"

"I am a proud warrior of Israel who will no longer kneel to the filthy Romans," roared Jeremiah, his voice echoing off the stone wall of Cyrus's hut behind them. "You stare at me as if I am a criminal. I swear to you that I am nothing of the kind. I am a soldier of King David and all the prophets who came before and after him." Lowering his head to be eye-to-eye with Mother, he softly added. "I will never bow to their pagan gods and in the name of our Almighty Adonai, I will never again cower to their commands until the day they hang me from a tree."

"I too am a proud woman of Israel, but I am a proud Samaritan as well and unlike you, I have not broken the Almighty's Seventh Commandment. You say you kill for a noble cause and perhaps this is true, but your people of Jerusalem treat us like rotted fruit that ravens pick at in the street. Why should we care what happens to you?"

"You speak of purity and Jewish law, which I understand little of. But the filthy foot of Rome grinds into your neck as well as mine. Of this I am certain," said the self-declared warrior.

Stillness enveloped the encampment following the verbal confrontation. Even the ever-present gusts from the far-off Great Sea seemed to still. Although Cyrus and Joshua nervously paced along the periphery, Mother never moved, remaining steadfast with her eyes fixed upon the man's haunted face.

Finally, Mother broke her stare and turned to face Cyrus and Joshua. "I trust this man who stands before us. Although he has killed, he is not our enemy but our true advocate. He will surely die one day as he wields his sword against the guards, but until that time comes, we must protect men like this for the sake of us all. Give him what he needs, so he can be on his way."

Stepping forward to face Cyrus and Mother, Joshua spoke with more iron in his voice than perhaps any time in his young life. "If Jeremiah will allow, I choose to accompany him as he makes his way north on the old road." Looking toward the warrior, Joshua observed the slightest glimmer of consent cross his face.

"No," cried Cyrus from across the encampment. "You will not travel anywhere with this man who lives by the sword. Can't you see, my dear nephew, that the Romans seek to kill this man for what he has done? Do you really believe the cruel guards will spare you when that day comes? I cannot bear to talk of this any longer for my heart is breaking." With those final words, Cyrus turned away to walk to the fields with Journey by his side.

"I have had dreams that this day would come," cried Mother to the slowly retreating Cyrus. "The mighty Yahweh is calling your nephew and Joshua has no choice but to follow him."

Coming to a stop, Cyrus continued to look away. "The Yahweh that you speak of has only brought hardship into our lives. Now you say I should just release this young man to his distant hand."

"His hand is not distant, my dear friend, for it rests firmly on Joshua's shoulder and I believe it will guide him into glory for us all."

Turning around, Cyrus looked only upon the man from Jerusalem. "Do I have your word that you will protect my nephew at all costs?"

"In the name of the Almighty Adonai, I will protect this boy with my sword and with my life. You have my word that this young man will not taste the bitter fruit of death while he is under my care."

"Then there is much work to be done and no time to waste if you are to stay ahead of your pursuers," announced Cyrus as he walked with purpose through the tall prairie grass back to the encampment.

Joshua was at once overtaken by a sense of dread. He looked to Cyrus for reassurance, but there was none forthcoming as his uncle looked away from his glance. Jeremiah appeared lost in his own thoughts while walking slowly about the encampment, staring at the ground. Only Mother looked his way and if Joshua had to guess, this kind and mysterious woman of Sychar was as frightened as he was.

16

I AM

As Joshua battled his second thoughts of taking such a perilous journey with a wanted killer, Cyrus poured all his doubts and nervous energy into repairing the sojourner's broken wheel. Using a combination of tacks and sandal straps, the wheel was more fortified than the other three. However, the man's donkey was struggling mightily in the unrelenting sun. After traveling such a great distance with little water or food, the donkey now lay on its side. Cyrus called to Joshua to immediately come down the hill with a bucket of water and more food for the exhausted and dehydrated beast. After much comforting from Joshua and consuming nearly all the water, the donkey sprung to life and stood upright looking ready to travel.

While Joshua cared for the donkey, Cyrus and the man from Jerusalem quietly made their way up the hill. Upon Joshua's return to the encampment, he saw that Mother was alone and appeared to be packing Joshua's few belongings for the journey that would soon begin.

"Where are the men? he asked.

"They have traveled to your hidden spring. You cannot journey far without ample water in your cart, Joshua."

"But there could be wild beasts hiding in the brush, and Jeremiah has probably not experienced such things in Jerusalem."

"I'm sure he has not, but this soldier of God is very familiar with killing. I trust Cyrus will know best how to retrieve the water with this man by his side. I have already prayed for the Almighty to watch over them, and I know my prayer has been heard."

"How can you be so sure of such things?" wondered Joshua aloud as he idly stirred the live embers in the fire pit.

Coming to the boy's side, Mother spoke. "The Almighty hears all our prayers, and we are in His hands, always. You must trust him, Joshua, now more than ever. As I told your uncle many days ago, I Am is coming."

"But, Mother, I know not what that means."

"You do not know the ancient story of Moses, my dear boy. It was the almighty Yahweh who came to Moses. He was alone tending sheep for his father-in-law when the voice of our Lord came to him through a fiery bush."

Joshua continued to slowly stoke the embers in Cyrus's fire pit. He quietly waited for Mother to proceed with her story, if for no other reason than to distract him from the growing doubts he was feeling about his impending journey.

"Moses was paralyzed with fear as he stood before the never-ending flame. 'Free my people of Israel who toil as slaves under the cruel fist of Pharaoh in the land of Egypt,' said the voice of the Almighty whose name could not be spoken. Moses cried out, 'But who do I say sent me?' 'Tell them I AM sent me.'"[1]

---

1 And God said unto Moses, I AM THAT I AM and He said, thus shalt thou say unto the children of Israel, I AM hath sent me unto you. Exodus 3:14 (KJV)

Mother stepped away from Joshua and returned to the task of assembling the modest assortment of dried fruit and bread she had brought from the village. "I believe in my heart that it is the same clear voice that spoke to Moses who now speaks to me in my dreams," said Mother. With tears in her eyes, she looked at Joshua as if begging for his understanding. "It is the most comforting voice I have ever heard, and it comes to me in the early dawn before I rise. 'I Am is coming,' the voice says and then I awaken."

"But, Mother, what does this have to do with me? The voice that whispers to you in the early dawn is for you. I do not hear such a voice," said the boy as he walked to the hut and opened the latch. Soon Journey pushed through and began sniffing the ground about the encampment. "He is trying to pick up Cyrus's scent. He does not understand where he has gone. I too am starting to wonder what is taking my uncle so long to return," said Joshua as he worriedly scanned the horizon in the direction of the hidden spring.

"They are in the Almighty's hands, Joshua, and that should be enough to give you peace," assured Mother.

Mother's words struck the boy as hollow, and he turned on her with a raised voice. "Was my father in the Almighty's hands when a viper struck him down in his own field? What of my mother and sisters who now live under the filthy hand of that bastard Langer? Tell me, Mother, in the name of the Almighty Yahweh, where were his golden hands then?"

Uncomfortable silence followed the boy's outburst. Joshua was first to speak. "I'm sorry, Mother, I did not mean to raise my voice with you."

At once, Mother raised her hand to stop Joshua from apologizing further. "It is all right to be angry with God, dear Joshua. We must understand that he is still telling our story. There is much written by the prophets of their anger with the great Adonai. In my life of poverty, I too have cried out to him many times and have not received an answer for my lamentations. But I now hear his gentle voice every dawn and . . ."

Joshua interrupted. "Please, Mother, not again. The message that I Am is coming has nothing to do with me."

Now it was Mother who raised her voice, "It has everything to do with you, dear boy, for I never heard such a voice until the night you fell into my arms in the road. It has come to me each dawn since then. And one more thing you should know: the voice is becoming louder in my head."

"Do you hear what you're saying, Mother? If I Am is indeed coming and this voice is getting louder, why do you continue preparing for me to depart? It is here that I belong, Mother. I no longer wish to leave with this man from Jerusalem. If what you say is true, I intend to greet this I Am myself and welcome him."

A knowing look passed between Joshua and Mother as they stared at one another in silence. Soon Journey broke the stillness as he leapt up with a start and dashed into the open field howling. Joshua quickly regained his stance and peered across the field. To his relief and unbridled joy was the sight of Cyrus waving his arm and pulling the wagon. The figure of the warrior trailed a few steps behind.

Returning to Mother, Joshua could barely contain his excitement. "What do I tell Jeremiah?"

"You tell him there has been a change in plans, and we pray that he has a safe journey on his own."

Joshua and Mother then shared a hearty laugh, perhaps for the first time. This aged woman and young lad were clearly on a journey together. Where it would lead, however, was unknown to them both.

17

A FEAST

Upon learning of Joshua's decision to remain, Cyrus let out a joyous cry and embraced his nephew in a tight hug. Jeremiah was unmoved by the boy's announcement and set about the task of loading his cart with extra water and provisions for himself and the donkey. Much of the dried fruit and bread that Mother had brought from the village was now in Jeremiah's hands. Joshua made sure the donkey drank deeply from the water bucket before placing it in the cart.

With a distinct shadow now alongside the donkey and cart, the man from Jerusalem reached under the stowed garments to retrieve his sword before taking a seat and grabbing hold of the thin straps that served as reins. He looked at Joshua who stood nearby. "What changed your mind, young man?"

Not knowing exactly what to say, Joshua remained quiet for a moment before speaking. "I'm told a powerful man is approaching soon and I choose to await his coming."

"Who told you such things?

Raising his eyes to the encampment, Joshua replied, "The woman who is known only as Mother."

"I see," said the warrior with the hint of a smile. "I would listen carefully to her if I were you." With a nod to Joshua, he turned his head, made a slight whistling noise to the donkey, and pulled away, leaving the boy standing alone in the road.

Joshua continued to watch as the cart stirred up dust in its wake. He then cried out words he had never spoken: "May the Almighty watch over you!"

Peering into the distance, Joshua saw Jeremiah raise his cloak-draped arm and point his fist to the sky. The boy stood alone on the road and watched the warrior's cart as it disappeared into the sunbaked haze. He now wondered if he had let his best chance to journey into a new life just slip from his grasp. The thought left him with a sense of melancholy as he turned from the road to make his way up the bluff to rejoin Cyrus and Mother.

Returning to the encampment, Joshua saw that Cyrus had made a bitter concoction of tea from the leaves and grasses of the surrounding field. "I prepared a mug for you, my nephew, please join us," invited Cyrus. Mother barely noticed Joshua as she sat in silence sipping her tea across from Cyrus, apparently uninspired by the taste.

Joshua sat on the ground between them, holding the hot cup in his lap. No words were exchanged as the three stared over the rising steam. Journey lay peacefully on his side, stretched out upon the cool, hard-packed earth beside Cyrus. "It seems odd to me, Cyrus, that we are having a hot drink in the heat of the day," said the boy.

"While you were helping our visitor below, Mother informed me it was time for her to make her way back home. Therefore, in her honor, I wanted us to enjoy a cup of my special tea before she departs."

"Is this true, Mother? Why leave now when the voice who calls to you seems so near? Please stay with us tonight and sleep on my bed," urged Joshua as he gestured to his bed of small sticks and soft grass. "In the cool of tomorrow's dawn, you will feel refreshed, and the donkey will be well rested for your journey home."

Cyrus rose from the wooden stump and excitedly declared, "Journey and I will hunt for hares, and I will prepare a great feast tonight with sweet wine and fresh fruit from the field!"

Raising her head from the steaming tea, Mother finally spoke. "Please bring my donkey out of the sun and tie him under here where he can cool. I have extra feed for him tied to a blanket and one more loaf for this feast of yours. But now I must find a place of privacy and I trust you two men can accommodate such a request. I wish to take a nap on your bed of sticks, Joshua, so I am well rested to help Cyrus with his feast." Looking squarely at Joshua, she continued. "We must keep our eyes wide open, young man."

As the sun made its incremental descent to the far horizon, Cyrus and Joshua busied themselves in preparation for the evening feast. Both were excited to host such an honored guest. Mother now lay atop Joshua's primitive bed with a thin blanket covering her shoulders and appeared to be fast asleep. Cyrus took to the field with Journey at his heels as the two set out for hares. Following a long overdue effort to clean the firepit and Cyrus's cooking tools, Joshua set out to gather kindling.

While collecting fallen branches from scattered shrubs and trees, Joshua's mind wandered back to home as it often did when he was alone. His heart ached for his mother and sisters. When would he see them again? What were they doing now? Why did his mother never come for him? "I miss you, mother," said Joshua aloud as tears blurred his vision. "I like my uncle Cyrus very much, and there is an old woman who seems to care a great deal about what happens to me. She says something is coming and she talks about God a lot, just like you. I feel so alone without you, mother. I hope you still think about me and that someday I can come home and be with everybody again." His words then broke into sobs as he dropped to the ground. Hidden by the tall grass waving above his head, Joshua cried his hardest and longest since leaving home.

Bustling activity greeted Joshua as he dragged a giant palm frond stacked with new firewood into the encampment. Mother had risen from her midday slumber and was arguing with Cyrus over the best way to prepare a dinner of cooked hare meat as they crossed paths with spices and dried fruit from the hut. "Welcome home, my nephew," said a cheery Cyrus with a wave. "Our mighty beast hunted down three hares today! He must know we have a guest tonight and are preparing a grand feast."

"If only your uncle knew how to cook the hare, we could all be at peace," protested Mother with a hint of a smile, watching as Joshua slowly dragged the pile of wood past her without a word. "What's wrong, my dear boy? You look deeply troubled."

"I fear my life is no more worthy than this pile of sticks I dragged from the field," lamented Joshua as he stared off beyond the old road below to the distant horizon where the dimming rays of the sun were consumed by soft orange clouds.

"But sticks can add flame to a cooking fire, warm your bones on a cold night, and, most important of all, bring light to the world when darkness surrounds us. May we all be as worthy as mere sticks. Do not fear, dear boy. Your time is at hand."

Joshua shook his head as he turned his gaze from the setting sun to face Mother. "I wish I could feel as you do."

"It is not what I feel, but what I know. Trust not in your feelings, dear boy, which come and go like the dust in the air." Placing her hand on his chest as he attempted to walk past, Mother spoke just above a whisper. "The voice came to me again just before I rose from my slumber while you and Cyrus were away. Please do not lose heart now, Joshua, for the time is at hand."

Placing his hand softly over hers, Joshua spoke no further of the voice in Mother's dreams. "I am so glad you are with us, Mother. Look at Cyrus. I have never seen my uncle happier than he is today."

Cyrus carefully skinned the hares using the cutting tools from his sandal repair trade. He appeared ready to break into song at any moment. Journey sat attentively beneath his master, ready to snatch any edible remains that dropped to the ground. Seeing that Mother and Joshua were observing his work, he cheerily called out. "We will have the greatest feast tonight with plenty of fat hare meat for us all. I will bring out the sweet wine that has been stored in my hut for such a night as this, and Mother if you wish to cook the meat according to your traditions, I will gladly turn the fire pit over to you. I believe the time has come, Joshua, for you to build a great cooking fire with the dry wood you have collected." Returning to finish the task at hand, Cyrus placed the freshly cut meat portions into a clay bowl well above Journey's reach. He then scraped all the hare remains onto a large palm frond and bent down to give them to Journey.

The festive meal could not have gone better. Mother's use of the many spices and oils that Cyrus had collected from sojourners of the Jerusalem Road completely transformed the hare. The meat that Mother slowly turned on long sticks over the fire pit until charred to perfection was a sensory pleasure unlike any Joshua had ever experienced. The freshly picked plums and figs that Joshua gathered while collecting dry wood were a perfect addition to the tender morsels. Few words were spoken as they gathered over one clay platter to slowly savor each finger full of the grand meal. Journey too partook in the feast, as Cyrus separated a generous portion for his companion and laughed heartily as the animal consumed his share in two rapid bites.

Announcing that it was time to serve his special wine, Cyrus set out three tiny goblets and a large wine sack atop the overturned clay pot table. Joshua and Mother shared a quick glance of concern, knowing how bitter Cyrus's midday tea was. Seeing the look of joy on his uncle's face as he filled the goblets made Joshua smile to himself. Cyrus was at ease among people he trusted, even if it was only for a little while.

Rising to make a toast, Cyrus lifted the goblet above his head. "This is for my beautiful nephew who has made me discover happiness after so many lonely years; to my one true friend, Mother, who is by far the best person in all of Samaria; and to this beloved beast who lays at my feet." Upon finishing the heartfelt toast, Cyrus consumed his tiny goblet full of dark wine in a single gulp, followed by a prolonged sigh of satisfaction. Cautiously raising the filled goblets to their lips, Mother and Joshua shared another look of trepidation before closing their eyes and quickly downing Cyrus's special fermented nectar.

The wine was not merely tolerable, but Cyrus and Mother claimed it was the finest they ever consumed. As for Joshua, compared to his mother serving an occasional cup of sweet wine back home and the rancid wine he drank with the older boys of Sychar, Cyrus's wine was glorious. From the moment it touched his tongue, each sip sparked his senses down to his gut.

"This wine is fit for a king or even the greatest rabbi in all the land," declared Mother. All agreed and proceeded to make more toasts and tell stories until the wine sack was thoroughly emptied.

As the night grew late, lively conversation began to slow, and a slight chill crept into the encampment, causing Mother to shiver. This prompted Joshua to add more dry branches to the fire pit. Looking at Cyrus as he stoked the embers, he observed his uncle gradually returning to his familiar pensive state. Soon no words were spoken as stillness prevailed within the tiny outpost. The low crackle from the fire pit and the occasional far-off howl of a beast were the only sounds to penetrate the night as Mother, Cyrus, and Joshua became lost in their thoughts.

Eventually Cyrus rose and silently shuffled to his well-worn bed of sticks and plopped down with a weary sigh. "It has been a long time since I have slept on the ground all night," said Mother with a yawn. "I fear that I will need your help, Joshua, if I am to rise from your unusual bed in the morning."

"It is my honor to help you, Mother. Please use my clean cloaks to soften the bed and keep warm through the night. I will now give you privacy and prepare to sleep on the other side of the fire pit," said Joshua, as he carried garments left on the Jerusalem Road under his arm to spread on the ground.

"Sleep well, my dear boy," said Mother softly as she gingerly lowered herself down to the bed of sticks. "We had a very good feast, didn't we?"

"That we did, Mother. It was truly a great feast," said Joshua as he lay on the ground and gazed into the moonlit vastness beyond. "I want you to know that I will never forget you, Mother, as long as I live." As Joshua's eyes closed, he hoped to hear a reply from Mother, but none came.

18

STRANGERS

It was in the utter darkness before dawn when Journey's howls penetrated the night. Joshua sat up with alarm and watched the dog nervously circling the encampment and incessantly barking. Looking across to Cyrus, he could see panic in his uncle's eyes as he stood. Glancing at Mother, Joshua saw that she remained asleep. He thought it was odd that she could sleep through such a disturbance. His attention to Mother was quickly diverted by a lone voice of a man shouting from the road.

"We mean you no harm," cried the man below. "I journey with other men. We are returning to our home in Galilee, but I fear a lion is stalking us. We saw your fire above and pray now that you grant us shelter till the morning light. We will then be on our way."

"Who is it that calls to us?" shouted Joshua as he looked down on the gathering of men, their upturned faces flickering in the light of their torch.

"I am Peter, a fisherman from the Sea of Galilee. I beg you to grant us passage above."

"Don't believe him, Joshua. These men lie and they intend to kill us," Cyrus frantically whispered from a distance.

Journey's barking erupted again as Joshua observed a figure steadily making his way to the encampment. "Who goes there?" shouted Joshua while backing away.

Joshua's heart pounded with fear as he watched the intruder step into the encampment. He remained barely visible in the light of the fire pit and his eyes were hidden by the hood of his cloak. "I am Jesus of Nazareth, son of Joseph and Mary."

"Please don't hurt us," pleaded Joshua. "We are poor Samaritans who have nothing but what the land provides us."

"I must tell you that the angels of heaven have carried home the old woman who lies atop your bed," said the man from Nazareth who remained hidden in the shadows.

Upon hearing the words, Joshua's knees nearly buckled. "No, no, no, Mother is here with my uncle and me. We had a great feast last night." Turning from the stranger who spoke such terrible words, Joshua frantically ran to Mother and dropped to her side. "Mother, please wake up, please, you can't leave me now. I can't bear to live without you." As he began to sob, he placed his hand over her cold fingers laced atop her chest and desperately hoped to feel the beating of her heart. "Cyrus, where are you?" he cried. "Please come now. Mother is dead."

Suddenly Cyrus burst into view where he had hidden in the grass. "What have you done to her?" he bellowed with eyes fiercely glaring at the stranger from Nazareth. He rushed to Mother's side. "Maybe she is just deeply asleep," Cyrus hoped aloud.

"She is truly gone, uncle. Feel her cold hands and you will know."

Kneeling to the ground, Cyrus firmly grasped Mother's hands into his and soon began to softly weep. While keeping his gaze upon Mother, Cyrus raised his voice and raged at the stranger who remained quietly standing nearby. "We were all happy until you came uninvited to our home, and now she is dead. Please leave us now, so we may be alone in our grief and give our friend a proper burial."

"This man is not to blame, Cyrus," said Joshua just above a whisper. "He merely told me that Mother was no longer among the living. I believe she died in the night while we deeply slept. I feel so sorry for her, Cyrus. She told me many times that something glorious was coming and now she will never know."

As Cyrus and Joshua remained on their knees before Mother's still body, a slight shuffling of feet could be heard behind them. Neither bothered to look as they continued in silence to gaze upon Mother's still face. Even Journey lay peacefully at Cyrus's feet. It was the heavy odor of sweat and unwashed garments that caused the boy to look up. To his surprise, he saw the faces of many strange men gathered around them. All remained quiet and seemed to share in the silent grief of Joshua and his uncle.

"We can help you bury your friend in a most honorable manner," said Peter, the stranger from the road. "We carry a small amount of spice and oil that will preserve her body and we are most willing to assist you in preparing a proper tomb. The teacher who we follow will also say magnificent words over your friend before you commit her to the earth."

"That is very kind of you, but it will not be necessary," said Joshua as he raised himself from the ground. "For I must return Mother to the people of her village. It is there where many will mourn this dearly loved woman and commit her to the earth."

"May we ask why you call your dear friend Mother?" asked one of the men. "Does she have many children?"

"I do not know how many children she gave birth to. What I do know is this: she has given new life to countless lost and forsaken people of her village, and to them all she is known simply as Mother." As he began to prepare for his return to the village, Joshua turned to face the gathering of men who all appeared weary and hungry in the gray light of the approaching dawn. "I do have a question for the man of Nazareth. But he does not look to be with you now."

"He has gone into the field to be alone," said one of the gathered strangers.

"Does he not fear the lion?" queried Joshua. The gathering looked at one another but said nothing. "I have one more question concerning this man from Nazareth. How could this stranger know Mother was dead when he was so distant from her and the night was so dark?" Again, Joshua's inquiry was met with silence from the weary men, who merely looked ahead. "Do you fear this man? Should my uncle and I be afraid?"

Finally, a voice spoke from behind the gathering. "There is nothing to fear from Rabbi."

"Who speaks?"

A man came forward. He was somewhat smaller than the rest and his eyes seemed to sharply penetrate through the gray mist. "My name is John. My brother James and I have traveled far with the man from Nazareth and we have seen many signs. For such a young man, you have many questions, and that is good. But our bones are weary now and we must lay our heads down in your encampment if you allow it. Before we rest, though, let us help prepare the woman you loved and called Mother for her final return to the village.

Quietly observing from afar this gathering of intruders crowded into his encampment, Cyrus listened carefully to each word spoken by them. He then retreated to his hut where considerable clattering and pounding ensued. Upon his return, Cyrus held a jar of oil and several thin garments which he set down before Mother's body.

"Why, these are burial cloths and a shroud," declared the man named John as he bowed down to inspect what Cyrus had brought. Carefully picking up the jar, he slowly breathed in the aroma and promptly cast his eyes upward to Cyrus. "This oil you possess is very precious. How did a Samaritan such as you acquire such treasured oil?"

"All I have ever owned has come to me from sojourners such as you who travel the road below. They offer to trade possessions if I make needed repairs to their well-worn sandals. But fewer come this way now, choosing to walk many days out of their way along the Jordan River to avoid any possibility of encountering lowly Samaritans," said Cyrus with a tone of bitterness in his voice. Walking up beside Joshua, he placed a long arm over his nephew's shoulder and spoke softly yet firmly. "We must prepare Mother's body, dear nephew, before you lead her on the donkey home to the village. Otherwise, she will not be presented to those that love her in an honorable state."

Joshua scanned the gathering of weary men as some lowered themselves to the ground. One of the larger men with a burst of dark hair that shot out from all sides of his head remained standing and approached Joshua. "I am Peter, young man, the one who spoke to you from the road. What your uncle says is very true. You must prepare this woman's body properly for burial before you journey with her. We can help you with this son, but we must act now."

Thus began the grim task. With Joshua distancing himself from Cyrus, Peter, and John, he looked on as the men knelt before Mother and removed her ankle-length tunic. Fragrant aromas drifted through the encampment as the men liberally applied the precious oil. The burial cloths were placed upon her entire body and around her head. All the while Joshua's thoughts ran from how absent of any dignity the end of life seemed, to how hopeful and certain Mother was that something glorious was coming to them both. Death was so dark and absolute, thought Joshua. The dreams of glory and wonder that Mother fiercely held were mere fanciful notions that had no place in this joyless world.

"The work is finished, Joshua," said Cyrus as he slowly stood from his labors. "But I must go to the hidden spring with John and Peter where we can wash, for we are now impure. You too must quickly be on your way, for Mother's body will slowly rot in the heat of the day."

Joshua remained motionless as the three men placed her fully wrapped body atop the donkey. The thin burial shroud was placed over her back and allowed to softly flow over her head before the men gently tucked the shroud under her waist. Spare twine from Cyrus's hut secured the body firmly atop the donkey. Seeing that the time had come, Joshua ran to the hut to fill his water pouch and fill the pocket of his tunic with fruit from last night's feast. There were no words exchanged as Joshua emerged from the hut and took the rope from Cyrus's hand. With his head cast down, he gently pulled at the rope and set out on the melancholy journey with Mother's body.

"I will be waiting for your return, my nephew," called out Cyrus as he stood alone watching Joshua and the donkey carrying Mother's body away toward the village of Sychar. Gazing at Joshua's slumped shoulders as he led the animal forward brought to his uncle's mind a sad sight of total defeat. "Please be strong, my nephew. You are far too young to give up now," uttered Cyrus to himself before turning away.

19

JESUS

Joshua barely heard his uncle's voice as he trudged through the knee-high grass. He paid little notice to anything at all as he loosely held the donkey's rope over his shoulder. Had he bothered to raise his head, he might have seen the figure of a man slowly approaching from the distance. It wasn't until he heard the high-pitched screech of a bird of prey flying overhead that Joshua came to his senses. Gazing at his surroundings, Joshua spotted a man walking in his direction. As they drew closer, Joshua could see that it was the man named Jesus. Seeing that their paths would soon cross, Joshua wondered what he would say to the encampment intruder who announced in the black of night that Mother was dead.

As the space between them closed, Joshua saw the man raise his hand in a friendly gesture. Coming face to face, Jesus placed his hands on Joshua's shoulders without saying a word and lowered his gaze to meet the boy's eyes. Stillness followed as the two stared at one another. "What is it you want from me?" Joshua nervously asked. "As you see, I am delivering Mother to her home."

"I merely wish to walk alongside you and your good friend as you enter the village," said the man from Nazareth as he dropped his hands from Joshua's shoulders. "Do I have your permission?"

"You are welcome to do so, but I am not sure why you wish to join me in this walk, for you never knew either of us."

"No one should be alone on a walk such as yours. I merely wish to lift your despair by offering you my presence and to walk beside the body of this woman who you so dearly loved."

Jesus stepped to one side of the donkey as Joshua resumed his walk with a slight tug of the rope. After some time passed, the boy looked over his shoulder to see this curious but harmless-looking man staring at the ground as he walked, whispering words that Joshua could not understand. Looking behind a second time, Joshua observed that Jesus was no longer speaking words to himself, but instead he rested a hand upon Mother's body as they moved ahead. Seeing Joshua glancing back, Jesus gave him a friendly nod accompanied by a slight smile.

Gazing forward as the distant village of Sychar came into view, Joshua's thoughts turned to the man who followed a few steps behind. He saw him as different from the other men he came with. Judging by his threadbare appearance, he may have been a slave at one time. He was clothed only in an inner tunic that was well worn and barely covered his knees. His skin was somewhat darker than the other men and he was thin, recalling his Uncle Cyrus's boney arms and legs. The face of this man from Nazareth seemed unremarkable to Joshua. His eyes lacked the intensity of the man named John, nor did he possess the look of strength he observed in Peter. What made the greatest impression upon Joshua, though, was the curly hair that framed Jesus's head along with his scruffy beard. In many ways, the hair was like his own, and the hair and beard were much like those of his deceased father. For that reason alone, Joshua felt a connection to this strange man. He provided a sense of dignity and honor to the solemn walk as he escorted the body of Mother, keeping his hand atop the shroud that covered her small form, as they entered the outskirts of Sychar.

Soon the barren land was interrupted by isolated ramshackle dwellings. Children dressed in near rags dully looked out from dark interiors at the sight of an unknown boy and man leading a donkey carrying a body covered by a thin burial shroud. As the small and solemn procession continued, the road became more crowded with villagers on foot as well as the familiar sight of donkey-driven carts rattling by. At first, the common sight of the deceased being escorted through the village drew little attention, but as the clamor in the street steadily rose, the level of curiosity did as well.

Soon children of all ages were running up to the donkey and quickly touching the body before dashing away screaming and laughing. Vendors began shouting questions at Joshua and the man from Nazareth. In time it became impossible to proceed any further as scores of villagers poured into the street surrounding them. Fear gripped Joshua as he turned to face Jesus. But Jesus was gone! Verging on panic, Joshua spun around frantically looking for Jesus. Then came the sound of his voice.

"We are escorting the body of a holy Samaritan woman whose spirit has been lifted by angels and delivered to a heavenly domain," declared Jesus as he weaved in and out of the gathered mob. "You have nothing to fear from us for we come in peace."

"Who speaks to us with such authority? We don't even know who you are," yelled a villager from the back of the mob.

"My name is Jesus. I am a Galilean, and this is my friend Joshua, a young Samaritan. I implore you to let us pass, so we may deliver the body of this holy woman to those who will deeply mourn and bury her." Jesus spoke these words as he paced before the pressing crowd. He did not raise his voice while speaking but delivered his message with confidence, speaking face-to-face to those blocking their way.

"Who are you, a Jew of all people, to tell us what must be done in our own village?" cried out another villager.

"I speak in the name of my Father who sent me," said Jesus in a bolder tone.

Stillness hung in the air over Jesus' last pronouncement. The hushed whispers of many villagers' questions could scarcely be heard. "Who did he say sent him? Why does his father matter to us?"

Joshua stood in rapt attention as he watched Jesus casually walk among the crowd of villagers. He was fascinated with how easily this man conversed with the restless gathering of Samaritan strangers. Before long, Joshua heard laughter coming from the villagers and observed many smiles as Jesus spoke to them. It was as if Jesus had somehow become their old friend. Gone was Joshua's fear as he saw a once-suspicious mob transforming into a gathering of joyful celebrants.

Soon the villagers went their own way as if the earlier chaos had never happened. With the road clear, Joshua resumed the journey to Mother's home. He was deeply comforted to see that Jesus had returned to the donkey's side and that his hand once again rested atop Mother's body. "What did you say to them to make them so joyful?" he incredulously asked.

Looking directly at the boy, Jesus replied. "They came to understand that there is nothing to fear." Keeping his gaze fixed, Joshua knew the man from Nazareth's message was meant for him as well. What would have happened if Jesus was not walking beside me next to Mother's body, wondered Joshua. Or what if it was his uncle that walked beside her body? Would Cyrus and he have fled for fear of being overrun by the villagers? Then he recalled what Jesus said, "There is nothing to fear." Amid his wandering thoughts, a huge question broke through above all the others. What if it was Jesus alone who the restless crowd was closing in on? Could the stranger from Nazareth have been the sole cause for such restlessness in the village street? What were they seeking? Did they even know?

With his mind nearly bursting with questions, Joshua spun around to face Jesus, but to his utter dismay, he was nowhere in sight. Unable to take another step, Joshua dropped his rope and paced around Mother's body. He carefully examined the road from where they'd come for any sign of Jesus. How he longed to see this man from Nazareth, but it was not to be. Abandoned by this near stranger who had promised to accompany him left Joshua feeling deeply resentful.

Staring at the forlorn scene of Mother's body draped over the still donkey in the middle of the empty road brought renewed sadness into Joshua's heart. As he stood under the hot sun taking in the now quiet village surrounding him, Joshua's despair nearly overpowered him. Recalling Jesus' last words before he disappeared, "They came to understand there is nothing to fear," made him think of Cyrus and how he was so overwhelmed by fear. Just then the donkey brayed and raised his head to the sky, as if to remind Joshua they still had work to do. Taking a long drink from his water pouch, he brought the pouch under the donkey's snout for an equally long draw of water. Retrieving the rope off the ground, Joshua resumed his lonely procession to Mother's home.

With fewer villagers congregating in the heat of the day, Joshua was able to see well down the road ahead. Soon two figures appeared in the distance. With tunics draped over their heads to screen their eyes from the brilliant sun, Joshua could not see the faces of these men who slowly approached him. As they drew closer, it became clear they were the same elderly men who escorted Joshua through the village so long ago.

"It is good to see you again, Joshua," said one of the old men as they stepped before him. "We understand that it is Mother's body you are returning to us."

"How could you possibly have known I was coming with her?"

"We heard of all the commotion involving a man and a boy delivering the body of a holy woman atop a donkey to her home and we believed it must be Mother, for we knew she came to see you," said the second old man as he gently touched the top of Mother's burial shawl. "May I ask when she died?"

Stepping to the man's side, Joshua too rested a hand atop the burial shawl. "Mother must have left us in the night as we slept. She, my uncle, and I enjoyed a wonderful feast before lying down for the night. Visitors came to our encampment in the darkness before dawn and caused quite a stir, but Mother did not rise. It was then that we learned she was gone. It was her plan to leave for home the next day. Little did I know she would return wrapped in burial cloth," said Joshua, as much to himself as the two men.

"She was very old, Joshua, much like my friend and I," said the man as he patted Joshua's back. "You have done well to bring her to us."

Not yet wanting to see the men go, Joshua added. "She spoke often of a coming glory, but now she'll never know."

"What if this glory you speak of did come to Mother in a dream before she died and is with her still?" offered one of them as he received the rope from Joshua's hand. "And what became of the man who was with you? Was he among the visitors who came in the night?" they asked. After walking some distance, the men looked back at the boy and waited for an answer.

"Yes, he was one of the visitors, but he vanished just before you arrived. Why do you ask?" shouted Joshua as they drifted further away.

"We had hoped to meet this man," he heard them say. "The villagers claim he spoke new words of truth and it gave them peace." The old men turned back to the road. "Farewell, my son," came the echoes of their final words as Joshua watched the fading vision of Mother's body slowly slip from sight.

20

FRENZY

It took some time for Joshua to determine what to do next. Feeling truly lost and again alone, he toyed with the idea of returning home. But how, he wondered. He had one remaining fig in his pocket and his dwindling supply of water would not carry him far. Even if he were to somehow make his way back home, what would happen to him? He was still a boy and he feared Langer would force him away again. Then what?

Reaching for his pouch, Joshua drained the remaining warm water down his parched throat. Squinting briefly into the glaring sun, he felt the sting of sweat in his eyes and the oppressive heat soaking his skin under the thick tunic. Facing the road, Joshua began to slowly shuffle back the way he came. Recalling the broken-down well where he and a woman worked to bring up water so many days ago provided the boy with a goal—to simply refill his water pouch. It was not so far ahead. The thought warmed Joshua's heart. Not so much for the critically needed water, but for the happy memory of meeting his first real friend. The one who ran off with his sandal before returning to his side. The well, thought Joshua, was a good place.

The boy's pace slowed as he trudged through the heart of the village with his head hung low and his eyes gazing just a few steps ahead. He was oblivious to the sounds of vendors, barking dogs, and screaming children. Gone was the curiosity and wonder that gripped his attention the first time he traveled this road. His mind now drifted lazily from one idle thought to the next as he moved closer to the well.

Sensing a slight change in the surrounding clamor, Joshua raised his head and casually looked around. Were the villagers frightened about something? Joshua stood and watched as small gatherings formed and lively conversations began. Soon men and women were excitedly pointing, and many began walking with great urgency in the same direction. What was happening? His mind went back to the mob of villagers that pressed in on him and Jesus as they escorted Mother's body.

Joshua was amazed by the spectacle unfolding around him as vendors abandoned their stands, mothers with babies in their arms rushed past, and old men with walking sticks hobbled forward as fast as their ancient bodies would allow. Joshua felt a sudden blow to his back nearly forcing him to the ground. As he regained his footing, a villager offered his apologies as he swept past. "Why are people running?" yelled Joshua to the man who nearly knocked him over.

"The Messiah has come to Sychar," cried the man before resuming his run with the crowd.

How, Joshua wondered, could such an ordinary-looking man have caused such frenzy among these people? As he drew closer to the crowd, Joshua overheard many fevered voices. "The Messiah has not come to the Jerusalem temple where we are forbidden to journey, he comes to us lowly Samaritans at our ancient well," sang out a mother holding hands with her three children as she danced at the rear of the growing throng of villagers.

As Joshua wormed his way through the cluster of sweaty bodies pressing in on all sides, he listened to the bursts of chatter filling the air. "It was a Jew who asked the woman who has known many men for a drink of water," proclaimed one voice. "This stranger must be a prophet for he knew about all the husbands of her past, but he cared not!" said another. "He promised we can all drink living water from him and never thirst again," screamed a woman.[2] The closer Joshua edged to the front of the frenzied crowd, the more exaggerated were their claims.

It was the woman he met at the well so long ago who first caught Joshua's eye. Many villagers had gathered near her in rapt attention as she spoke. "There is the sinful woman who the Jew talked to at the well," said an onlooker.

Joshua could see joy in the woman's face as her hands waved wildly above her head while telling a story of some kind. He gazed at the well where three men stood nearby talking with villagers. One of the men seemed to recognize Joshua and came to him.

"Greetings, Joshua. I am Andrew, the brother of Peter. I trust you delivered the body of Mother to her friends," he said. "You must have loved her very much."

"I did. Is Jesus with you?"

"He is. Rabbi is speaking with the villagers gathered here. His words of truth are bringing them comfort."

"Why do I not see him?" he asked.

"Because he is with the people and it is difficult to distinguish him from the others," said Jesus' companion.

"The villagers are calling him the Messiah. How can this be?" wondered Joshua aloud.

Andrew stared back without saying a word. Just then the scream of a woman penetrated the steady din of chatter. "The living Christ is with us!"

---

2 "But the water that I shall give him shall be in him a well of water springing up into eternal life." John 4:14 (KJV)

Joshua watched in disbelief as a naked woman covered only by a ragged shawl broke from the crowd.

In the same moment he saw Jesus standing on the other side of the well staring back at the woman, her shawl falling to the ground as she lunged toward him. In a commanding voice, this ordinary man cried out words Joshua had never heard. Upon hearing the strange language, the naked woman fell to her knees as the stunned villagers looked on in silence.

"Please cover this woman and help her to her feet," shouted Jesus. "A demon once possessed her, but now she is free."

Silence prevailed as the bystanders gawked at the spectacle playing out before them. Soon two women emerged to cover the unclothed woman who remained on her knees with head bowed before Jesus. Draping a large blanket around her, they held the woman close and quietly escorted her away from the throng of staring eyes.

Joshua remained spellbound as he watched Jesus' face. Shouts of high praise and full-throated accusations came from the restless crowd.

"He is the devil himself," cried the man beside him.

"We have just seen a miracle!" declared a nearby woman, visibly overcome with emotion.

Joshua was knocked to the ground as villagers began to violently push and shove in a desperate attempt to reach Jesus. Hard as he tried, Joshua could not rise as charging feet relentlessly pounded his flesh and forced him down. With no choice but to curl himself into a ball and cover his head with his hands, Joshua squeezed his eyes shut and screamed into the dirt as the brutal stampede raged on.

Joshua's fear of being trampled finally subsided as the terrible sound of feet pounding past his head faded away. Only an occasional bird and the distant bark of a dog could be heard. Joshua did not know how long he remained curled on the ground. Gingerly stretching out his battered legs, he slowly opened his eyes.

But for a pack of dogs sniffing the dirt for remains of food left behind, Joshua was alone. Sitting up, he at once felt a searing pain on the side of his head. His hand came away bloody after gingerly touching his scalp. An examination of his limbs revealed no wounds under his dirt-caked tunic. His head, however, continued to pound as blood oozed from his scalp. Sitting in the dirt, he spat repeatedly to expel the grit from his teeth. Remarkably, his empty water pouch was still slung over his shoulder and the abandoned well was just ahead. As much as Joshua craved a deep drink, he had to wait for the land before him to cease its sickening roll.

With sweat dripping from his brow, Joshua slowly rose to his feet. Struggling to keep his balance, he set his legs and arms far apart and fought to remain standing as the world continued its unrelenting roll. Fearing he was about to fall, Joshua lowered himself to the ground. Just then a strong hand gripped his arm, keeping him on his feet. It was Andrew, the last man he talked to before the world closed in on him.

Without saying a word, Andrew wrapped Joshua's arm over his shoulders and held tightly to his waist as the two carefully crossed the empty grounds to a nearby pepper tree. Upon reaching the shade of its leafy branches, Andrew rested Joshua's back against the trunk and gently lowered him to the ground.

Kneeling before him, Andrew peered into Joshua's eyes and softly lifted the hair near his wound, which bled still. "You have taken a wicked blow to your head, my son," said the man who Joshua dimly recalled was the brother of Peter. "I will remain with you and tend to your wound until it is safe to travel."

"Where did your friends go? What happened here? Did the villagers kill Jesus? Why did they attack him?" came the barrage of questions from Joshua in a weak voice.

"Stay with me, Joshua. Keep your eyes fixed on me," ordered Andrew. Placing his water skin under Joshua's parched lips, he squeezed water into the boy's mouth. Soon Joshua took hold of the skin and swallowed deeply as he stared into Andrew's worried face.

"That's enough for now. You can have all the water you need, my son, for we are only steps from the well, but I must first clean your wound." Andrew poured the remainder of the water directly upon the open gash, sending streams of red fluid down Joshua's face and onto the dirt. "We will need more than water to fix this wound, Joshua. I pray that villagers soon come to the well with their empty pots and I can ask them for help." Removing Joshua's empty water pouch from his shoulder, Andrew stood. "For now, it is you and me, my friend, so we must work together." He then turned to the well to refill both water skins.

"You have not answered me, Andrew. Where did your friends go? Have the villagers taken Jesus away?" asked Joshua with his back slumped against the tree. "Have they killed him?"

Andrew faced the wounded boy who had so many questions. "Rabbi is very much alive, my son. He now meets with the villagers who are begging him to remain in their village. The men have much fear, but Rabbi's words give them peace."

"But many said he was the devil."

"Do you believe that to be true, Joshua?"

After a long pause, Joshua wearily replied. "No, I do not believe this man from Nazareth is the devil. But he surely does magic for I have seen it myself."

"Magic, you say. I see we have much to talk about, but now we must fix your head wound so you can stand firmly on the ground."

"How did you find me, Andrew?"

"Rabbi said to look for you near the well."

"But how could he know where I would be?" asked Joshua.

With his back to the boy, Andrew's words echoed over the ancient well as he lowered the wooden bucket, "We will talk, my son, I promise you."

21

THE WOMEN

As the sun began its steady descent to a cloudless horizon, a pleasant breeze stirred the leaves above where Joshua and Andrew had fallen asleep. One by one, the women of the village made their way to the well with their empty pots and began their late afternoon ritual. Taking notice of what appeared to be a father and son fast asleep under the tree where villagers usually waited their turn to draw water, two of the women carefully approached.

Standing over the two as they continued to nap, the women became alarmed when they saw the boy's head covered in blood. The sound of their urgent whispers woke Andrew with a start, and he looked up into their shadowed faces. Bright rays of the late afternoon sun pierced through the space between the women's heavy cloaks and fell upon Joshua's bloodied face as he continued to sleep. Andrew quickly turned to Joshua's slumped body and shook his shoulders.

Slowly, Joshua opened his eyes a bit but said nothing as he looked on seemingly unaware of his surroundings. "Please help us," pleaded Andrew.

The women lowered themselves to the ground and gently raised the boy's damp hair away from his deep gash. At once they began a rapid dialog and Andrew tried to follow.

The women turned to Andrew. "We must go to our dwellings and get dressings for his wound and fresh cloth to wrap his head. This boy has lost much blood and his head is very hot to the touch. Do not let him close his eyes while we are away. Raise him to his feet if you must," instructed one of the women before they quickly disappeared.

Andrew cushioned the back of Joshua's head with his arm as the two sat together against the tree. He immediately brought his water pouch to the boy's lips and gently squeezed a small amount into his mouth. Andrew spoke soft words of encouragement as he gently coaxed Joshua to take more water. Seeing the boy blink his eyes and begin to swallow more of the water was a hopeful sign to Andrew.

Many villagers had gathered by the well as the sun became a fiery orange ball on the horizon. The men gathered in small groups conversing while gazing at the brilliant sunset. The women silently toiled at the well, raising bucket after bucket of fresh water to replenish their empty pots. Andrew watched as the men occasionally turned their attention to the curious sight of a man and boy resting under the tree. Not wishing to arouse suspicion, Andrew met their gaze with a friendly wave. Soon, however, the curiosity of several of the men led them away from their conversations for a closer look at the strangers.

"What happened to your boy?" asked one of the men as they stood over Andrew and Joshua.

"He was trampled in the crowd today. We now wait for the return of two women who promised to tend to his wounds," replied Andrew as he remained on the ground with his arm around Joshua.

"Are you the Jew who caused such a disturbance in our village?" asked another man.

Before Andrew could respond, the two village women returned holding arms full of supplies. They sharply ordered the hovering men to leave at once so they could care for the boy. As the women knelt before Joshua, the men silently drifted away.

Pressing a hand against the boy's forehead, one of the women softly spoke. "Hello, my son. Can you hear me?" Joshua slowly nodded, bringing a smile to her face as she turned to Andrew. "His head is still very warm, but he looks better. Do we have your permission to do everything we can to treat this young man?"

"You most assuredly have my consent," replied Andrew as he finally pulled his arm from behind Joshua and raised his stiffened body off the ground. Even before Andrew regained his footing, the women were fast at work. A pungent smelling soup was raised to Joshua's lips. Although he promptly rejected it, the sharp aroma immediately opened his eyes wide. After repeated commands by the women to drink, he eventually gave in and took tentative swallows of the strange liquid. While one woman continued to gently administer more soup to Joshua, the other unveiled a long pair of shears and proceeded to cut all the boy's long curly locks from his scalp.

Relegated to mere observer, Andrew looked on with amazement as the women expertly moved from coaxing Joshua to drink the sharp-smelling soup, to cutting away all his hair and gently bathing his nearly bare scalp with an herb-scented water. They applied a thick honey-like substance to his gash before placing a few fig leaves atop the dressing and tying a large cloth around his head.

Darkness had fallen by the time the women finished their work. The expanse of land surrounding the well was now empty of villagers. The barren nightscape gave no hint of the earlier tumult. With only the dim light of a full moon rising in the east, the women quietly set about the task of collecting their supplies. Although Joshua was quiet as he continued to rest against the tree, his eyes regained focus and he curiously gazed at the clumps of sheared hair all about him.

"Your hair will return, my son," said Andrew as he stood over the village women and the boy. "These women have done wonders, Joshua, and they deserve our gratitude." Speaking to the women as they stood, Andrew insisted on filling their empty pots and carrying the fresh water to their dwellings.

"The boy cannot be alone at this time," said one woman. "He must be watched through the night." The other woman placed a small pouch in Andrew's hand. "It holds more dressing for his wound and fig leaves to place on top. Remember to wash the cloth before wrapping his head again." Reaching into the basket, she removed a small barley loaf and a generous chunk of cheese. "You must both eat."

Placing the bread and cheese before Joshua, Andrew proceeded to the well to fill the women's empty pots. When he finished, they set about the task of fixing the filled containers to the long branches that the women would carry on their shoulders, a routine since they were children.

"We must be leaving now, our husbands have been alone with our babies for a long time," said one of the women as she prepared to lower herself to the ground and raise the heavy branch laden with two filled pots. "We will come for our supplies in the morning. Please leave them here by the tree, for I trust you will be gone upon our return."

Sending Joshua their blessings before raising their water pots with audible grunts, the women began their journey home. They did not hear the footsteps of someone approaching from behind as they trudged ahead, but they came to a stop upon hearing Andrew's distant voice. "Greetings, Rabbi."

The women lowered their pots to the ground and quietly listened in the darkness. "Hello, my brother," came the voice. "How is our dear boy?"

"He is doing much better, Rabbi, all because of two village women who gave completely of themselves."

"Please call to them."

"But they are on their way home with heavy pots across their backs, Rabbi."

Seeing the look in Rabbi's eyes brought renewed understanding to Andrew that Rabbi was no ordinary man. Cupping his hands to his mouth, Andrew called to the women. "My friends, please drop your pots and return to us. There is a man with me who you must meet."

The village women looked at one another with concern. They wondered what could be so important about meeting a stranger when the night had grown so long. The women elected to return, but they would not leave their precious pots full of water behind for there were many thieves in the night.

As they drew close, they saw the dark figure of a man walking slowly with the boy they had cared for. Was that a small laugh they heard from the boy? It brought a smile to their faces. The women then saw the familiar figure of Andrew coming to them. "Hello, my friends, I am so pleased you have returned. But it distresses me to see that you have carried your heavy pots all the way back."

The village women said nothing, but silently watched as the boy and unknown man came forward out of the darkness. Joshua spoke first. "I wanted you both to know that I am feeling much better thanks to the care you gave me. I will never forget what you did." He turned to Jesus. "The man beside me is Jesus. He comes from a village I have never heard of called Nazareth. He wanted to meet you."

The women trembled as they looked at each other. "It is you!" one cried. "You are the one who cast out a demon from the unclothed woman today. We saw what happened with our own eyes and we ran to cover her as you commanded." The women's cheeks glistened with tears.

Andrew and Jesus removed the heavy branches off their backs and the women fell into Jesus' warm embrace. Joshua and Andrew looked on as the women clung tightly to Jesus. "You have done wonderful work today and it is my honor to be with you," said Jesus while holding them closely to his chest.

After a time, the women loosened their grip upon Jesus and wiped fresh tears from their faces. "We prayed that someday the Messiah would come to our village, and now the Lord Almighty has answered our prayers."

Eyeing the filled pots on the ground tied to their long branches, Jesus made a request of the women. "Place your burdens upon me and we will walk together."

Andrew quickly came to his Rabbi's aid and hoisted both pot-laden branches upon Jesus' shoulders as he stretched his arms wide around the timber and walked with the women.

"Are you coming back?" shouted Joshua.

"I am," said Jesus. "Will you be here when I return?"

"I will be."

Slipping away into the dark of night with the heavy load upon his back and the village women at his side, Jesus called back. "Then we have an agreement, my son."

22

THE BROTHERS

As the night wore on, Joshua regained his strength, but his impatience grew. He appealed to Andrew for answers. "Why has Jesus not returned to us like he said he would?"

"Rabbi will return as he promised," assured Andrew as he raised a full bucket from the well to replenish their drinking pouches and cleanse their weary bodies. "It would not surprise me if one of the village families pleaded with Rabbi to remain in their abode for the night, for this often happens in our travels."

"Why do you call him Rabbi?"

"He teaches us many truths, Joshua. It is why my friends and I have left the lives we once had to follow him. I was the first. Come, let us sit by the tree again and partake of the bread and cheese given to us by the kind women and I will tell you many stories."

Andrew's offer to tell many stories was enough for Joshua to return to Andrew under the tree. They shared their food as they reclined against the tree. Joshua soon broke the silence, "Tell me of the life you lived before Jesus drew you away."

"I was a simple fisherman, Joshua. Together with my brother Peter and many others, we fished the waters of the Sea of Galilee. It was the only work we ever knew, and we never once dreamed of being called to a different life. Little did any of us know how our lives would suddenly change."

While Joshua listened to Andrew tell his amazing story, he gazed above into the vastness of the dazzling stars as he had on his favorite hill back home so long ago. The endless canopy of lights, along with the luminous moon, was a fitting spectacle for the wondrous words spoken by Andrew.

That men could leave behind all they knew to follow a man they just met was incredible to Joshua. What would possess such men as Andrew to be so drawn to this man they called Rabbi? Joshua was captured by Andrew's words as he told of the multitudes who came to hear Jesus speak. Many simply fell at the feet of this stranger from Nazareth and begged for healing. Joshua's attention was riveted by Andrew's story of an impoverished Galilean villager whose entire body was covered with flesh-decaying sores of leprosy. He cried out in the name of Almighty God for Jesus to make him clean. Andrew told of how Jesus bent down to the suffering man, touched his rotting flesh with one hand, and commanded him to rise. An astonished crowd looked on in shock as the man rose to his feet completely free of the dreaded disease and fell weeping into Jesus' arms.

Andrew continued his testimony unaware that the boy was drifting to sleep. "It is not just these miraculous healings and signs that have brought so many to the Rabbi, but the power of his words. It is like the ancient prophets themselves speak to us through him." Andrew then felt the weight of Joshua's head against his side. Looking down, he could see the boy's chest rise and fall under his tunic. His face, although scratched in many places from the trampling he endured, looked at peace. Andrew slowly removed his outer tunic and carefully bunched it under Joshua's bare scalp as he settled beside the boy and soon joined him in a deep sleep.

It was the sound of men talking from a distance that awakened Joshua. Rising to his elbows, he saw Andrew by the well engaged in a friendly conversation with two other men. The majesty of the night sky was gone, replaced by the gloom of dawn where a light mist hovered over the empty grounds. Sitting upright, Joshua rubbed a hand over his scalp where only a brittle stubble remained. He gingerly pressed on the cloth covering his wound, causing a small burst of pain. As he remained on the ground under the long arms of the tree, Joshua saw another man approach the well. The man was warmly greeted by Andrew and the others. Joshua saw that it was Jesus. As the men continued their early dawn reverie, Andrew looked back at Joshua and saw that he was awake.

Seeing Andrew's enthusiastic wave prompted the others to follow suit, and soon the group of four men were on their way to provide a hearty early-morning greeting to their young companion.

"How are you feeling, my son?" asked Andrew.

"Like I got kicked in the head, but aside from that, I think I am ready to journey again."

Jesus then knelt before Joshua. "I told you I would come back. I am so happy you chose not to leave without me."

"Based on the stories that Andrew told me last night, I thought it would be a good idea to wait for you."

Glancing back at the men, Jesus replied to Joshua with a smile, "At times Andrew can be a very wise man." His wry comment drew laughter from all, including Joshua.

One of the men Joshua had not yet met knelt before him and placed a firm hand on his shoulder. "It is an honor to meet you, young man. My name is Judas. You were very courageous yesterday to have endured such chaos on your own." After a pause, he went on. "People can be unpredictable in the presence of Rabbi, and it is frightening at times." Holding his intense gaze upon Joshua as he stood, Judas offered a small nod before walking away, leaving Joshua with a twinge of unease.

"I'm afraid our brother Judas can be rather dramatic when it comes to describing our fears," said the other man as he sat beside Joshua. I have a feeling you have shown courage many times in your young life. Am I right, my son?" Joshua gave a slight nod to the man before him. "My name is James. You met my brother John, who helped your uncle prepare the body of the woman you loved."

Soon all the men took a place on the ground beside Joshua as Judas passed dried fish and fresh bread from a basket. "It is our good fortune that the fishmonger and baker were getting ready to open when Judas and I walked by their tables," said James.

Jesus then spoke. "Please hold the hand of your brother as we pray. Father, we thank you for the rich bounty you have placed in our laps on this glorious morning. We are also deeply grateful to you Father to see that our young companion Joshua is feeling much better." After a considerable pause, Jesus softly uttered, "Amen."

Andrew spoke up immediately following Jesus' prayer. "May I suggest that we eat this blessed food with some haste for it won't be long before the villagers arrive with their empty pots?"

"Why do the villagers concern you, Andrew?" asked Jesus.

"I have no quarrel with the villagers, Rabbi, but if they see that you still remain in Sychar, they may demand that you stay with them longer." Andrew looked to Judas and James for support, but received none as the two men focused on the meals before them.

"Be anxious for nothing, my friend. If the villagers return before we leave, so be it. Better you enjoy the meal James and Judas have brought to us." With a reassuring pat to Andrew's knee, Jesus turned to Joshua. "Are you well enough to travel, my son?"

Chewing a mouthful of fish and bread, Joshua nodded excitedly before speaking. "I am truly prepared! Please tell me, what is our next destination?" Joshua watched as the men exchanged amused glances at one another.

"We must return you safely to your uncle, my son. We then will gather our brothers, bid you farewell, and continue with our journey to Galilee," confirmed Andrew.

Joshua's heart sank with the thought of being left behind by such adventurous sojourners. "I intend to journey with you," Joshua demanded, but the tears welling in his eyes belied the boldness of his words.

"My dear boy," Judas began, but Joshua cut him off.

"Do not call me that!"

James tried to reason. "It is far too dangerous to join us," he said, glancing at Jesus, "on such an unpredictable journey. I am sorry, Joshua, but I believe the brothers who await our return would also agree."

Jesus remained silent as he studied Joshua's face throughout the exchange. No further words were spoken by anyone. Joshua, who only moments earlier was excited to be in the company of such men, now brooded as he finished his meal. Unable to contain his disappointment any longer, he took hold of his water pouch and abruptly rose to his feet. Feeling that all eyes were upon him, he offered few words before stomping away. "Thank you for the meal. There is no need to see that I am safely returned to my uncle. I can take care of myself."

As Joshua stormed away, Andrew called out. "Joshua, please wait, we will join you."

With his back to the men, Joshua ignored Andrew's plea and continued. He then heard the voice of Jesus. "Let him be."

23

THE STORM

As hurt as Joshua was that the men did not consider him to be anything more than a mere child, he was painfully angry with himself as well. Were his own actions not those of a small boy who did not get his way? And to think he allowed these men to see his tears. How could he be such a fool? These were the discouraging thoughts that darkened Joshua's mind as he put considerable distance between himself and the men. Looking over his shoulder to catch a glimpse of the men before they spied him, he saw that they were readying themselves to leave. He wondered what they would say about him, if anything at all. The thought of returning to his uncle's outpost and bidding farewell to this mysterious gang of traveling men left Joshua in deep despair.

Yet he knew in his heart that he missed his mother and his beautiful sisters terribly. In their presence, he always felt like a king. Maybe it was time to return home, thought Joshua. As he trudged ahead, the idea of returning to the home he loved gained favor in Joshua's mind. Surely, he would not cower before Langer ever again. Not after all he had been through. He was determined to tell Cyrus of his plan as soon as he returned. Although his uncle would try to convince him to stay, in the end, he knew Cyrus would support his decision. Maybe he would persuade Cyrus to join him. Returning home with his mother's dear brother by his side sounded very grand indeed. Journey would love life on the farm. Just thinking about coming home restored his spirits and brought a new spring to his step.

Judging by his surroundings, Joshua knew he had another half day's travel ahead before he reached Cyrus's encampment. He anticipated the excited barks of Journey announcing his return. No longer concerned if the men saw him looking for them, Joshua turned around, expecting to see them trailing behind. But they were nowhere in sight. Did they travel another way? Or maybe, as Andrew feared, many villagers returned to the well and begged Jesus to stay before they got away. One thing was certain: Joshua was alone on this rocky plain. Reaching for his water pouch, he took a long drink while gazing at the billowing clouds forming over the horizon. The towering clouds, he presumed, must have gathered while his mind drifted to dreams of returning to the family he so sorely missed.

Soon a cool wind gust blew into his face as dust raced across the path ahead. Before long, Joshua heard the unmistakable sound of thunder rumbling in the distance, and he knew a storm was coming. His eyes surveyed the barren landscape and saw little in the way of shelter. Spotting a cluster of boulders ahead, Joshua fled for the scant protection of the pile of rocks. It was not the rain that concerned him, but the deadly bolts of fire that shot to the earth from the ominous clouds. Joshua heard many tales of fiery bolts striking down shepherds in fields as they desperately tried to gather their terrified sheep amid a fierce storm. As the black clouds turned day into night, his fears were realized when bolts brighter than the blinding sun streaked across the leaden sky and ungodly crashes from above rattled his very bones. With his back now flattened against the rock formation, the clouds released rivers of water. He braced for the worst the storm had to offer as it pounded down with a vengeance.

Joshua could not control his shivering as the downpour pelted his bare scalp and drenched his blood-splattered tunic that was now clinging to his body like a cold layer of skin. The deadly bolts of fire he so feared struck the ground before him repeatedly, sending bursts of earth into the air and leaving behind the acrid odor of soaked ash. Raising his head to the unrelenting chaos Joshua cried out, "I don't want to die, God! In the name of my mother and sisters, please let me live that I may see them again."

Knowing that his faith in such a remote God was quite weak, but the faith of his mother was strong, Joshua prayed as if invoking his mother, that this invisible God would allow him to live. As the rain continued to batter him, he turned his back to the storm and spread his arms wide across the rock. If I cling to this rock, I will surely survive, he thought.

In time the rain softened and the crashes from the sky drifted further away. Joshua slowly lowered his aching arms from his long and desperate grip of the rock. He turned to face the retreating storm that hovered over the village. Water flowed from his drenched garments as he stood. He gazed on the now distant powerful flashes that no longer posed a danger and took solace in the knowledge that his life was somehow spared. Joshua then patted the rock as a gesture of gratitude before carrying on with his journey to Cyrus's outpost above the Jerusalem Road.

The walk proved to be challenging as the heaviness of his soaked tunic slowed his passage through the dampened terrain. Joshua made a decision. He removed his garments and walked naked upon the lonely land with only the ravens and hares to notice.

The fresh breeze and warmth of the sun felt good against Joshua's bare skin as he slogged ahead. Waving his wet garments high overhead as if they were banners, he hoped they would soon dry enough to dress himself well before entering the encampment. Forging onward, he looked forward to the story he would tell Cyrus of his bravery in weathering the fierce storm on his own. Shielding his face with one hand as the sun glared in his eyes, he failed to notice three men approaching. Not until a single cloud covered the sun did Joshua drop his hand and discover who was directly ahead.

Naked to the world, Joshua stopped dead in his tracks, holding his garments high in the air. To his utter embarrassment and disbelief, there in plain sight stood Andrew, James, and Judas joyfully waving as they saw that their young friend was alive and well.

As Joshua struggled to quickly dress into his still-damp garments, he heard Andrew call to him. "Do not worry about your nakedness, my son. We all have disrobed after a hard rain. It is not a sin to remove soaked garments that cling to your skin. I have seen the Rabbi do this himself many times."

Still struggling with his tunic, Joshua gasped, "How in the name of God did you overtake me?"

"The villagers delivered us in their donkey-driven carts and they traveled a shorter path than yours," said James as he helped Joshua adjust his damp garments.

"Many villagers came to the well as we prepared to leave. It seems word of Rabbi's continued presence traveled fast, and they begged him to remain. This often happens, Joshua," said Judas as Andrew and James nodded. "But there is more we must tell you."

Seeing the somber looks from all three men, Joshua braced for the worst. "What name must I know? Has something happened to my uncle?"

Andrew spoke first. "Your uncle is very much alive, as is the wild dog who hunts for him. But your abode above the road is in ruins from the storm. The fierce wind and rain destroyed everything in its path. Even the hut built of rock and clay barely stands. The wall facing the storm has fallen in a heap and I fear the roof will not hold much longer. I am so sorry, my son."

Joshua hung his head and placed his hands on his knees, unable to stand upright in the face of Andrew's devastating words. "I do not lament for myself, but for my dear uncle who has lost all he ever owned. I fear he may never recover." Rising up, he asked, "Where is the man you follow? With a tone of bitterness, Joshua added, "Surely you feel lost without the man you call Rabbi to guide you."

"He sent us to find you, as your uncle fears you may have perished in the storm. Rabbi now gathers with our brothers who are all lending comfort to Cyrus as they await our return." James placed an arm on Joshua's shoulder and gently spoke. "We are not lost, young man. Although there are many times when we are uncertain of where our path may lead, we are never lost." Looking to Joshua for a response but finding none, James addressed them all. "Let us carry on, then. For there is one thing for which I am most certain: returning with our young friend will be a joyous occasion. What is to follow remains in God's hands."

24

REUNION

ew words were spoken as they journeyed back to where Cyrus's long-time abode once stood. Joshua dreaded confronting all the wreckage. Would Cyrus himself be as broken as the scattered bits and pieces left behind? Joshua feared the sadness he would see on his uncle's face when their eyes met. The thought of Cyrus desperately picking through the scattered ruins as his ever-loyal Journey trailed behind was nearly unbearable. Joshua's thoughts grew darker the closer they came to a reunion. Although he could hear occasional conversation from the brothers, their words were simply sounds passing over like birds of the air. Trudging forward with eyes cast down to the rain-soaked ground, Joshua dwelled on the unfairness of life. He recalled how secure he felt in the shadow of his strong father. Yet without warning, the man he so worshipped was struck down by a wicked viper. Or how he was forced to run for his life from the hideous Langer and flee from the only home he had ever known. And now his poor Uncle Cyrus, who despite enduring a life of hardship, had managed to piece together an existence away from the world he feared, only to see it stripped away without warning. Yes, life is unfair, Joshua concluded. Even the rare, good things in life are not as lasting as they seem. Your family, your home, and even your life can be swept away in the blink of an eye.

In despair, Joshua recalled Andrew's words: "Although we are uncertain of what may happen next, we are never lost." Perhaps Andrew and the brothers had found a way to live in such a harsh world. Then again, the idea of never feeling lost, even when the things you hold dear turn to dust, sounded too good to be true. Clearly, these men had not experienced the life-changing losses he had, Joshua reasoned. When that day comes, as it surely must, they will lose their way just as he and his uncle had lost theirs.

"I see that we are drawing near," announced Andrew as they continued moving.

The words broke through Joshua's melancholy thoughts and for the first time he allowed himself to gaze ahead. Although there was nothing to see yet, the vision of Cyrus looking lost and broken appeared in his mind's eye. Oh, how he dreaded what was to come.

"You have been awfully quiet, my son," noted James, hoping for a reply, but none came. "I must tell you, Joshua, that there have been times in my life when I have trembled in fear of what I was about to face. Only to discover that the monstrous encounter I dreaded turned out to be not nearly as bad as the encounter I created here," declared James as he pointed to his head.

James's effort to offer a measure of comfort brought a hint of a smile to Joshua's face as he gave James a slight nod. Just then came the distant sound of a barking dog. Joshua's heart leapt. "Can you hear that?" he cried.

"Is that the sound of the wild dog your uncle keeps?" queried Judas.

"That is no wild dog barking. That is Journey, the greatest dog in the world!" declared Joshua, prompting a round of welcomed laughter from the three brothers.

Journey's barking grew louder the closer they came, but soon the faint sound of a man's voice could be heard. "Joshua, please tell me it is you," came the far-off cry of his uncle.

"It is me, Uncle Cyrus. I am coming home," he cried with all the strength he could muster, though his voice cracked upon the words "coming home." Joshua broke into a run. He first saw Journey bounding over the tall grass. Then came the wonderful sight of Cyrus with his tunic flowing in the breeze racing behind Journey as fast as his gangly legs could carry him.

Joshua braced for a collision as Journey leapt onto his chest in an overzealous welcome, knocking him to the ground and covering his face with enthusiastic licks. At first the brothers looked concerned as the beast hovered over Joshua, but judging by the sound of his laughter, they saw this was a normal ritual.

Joshua barely regained his footing when there stood his uncle. His garments were torn and muddied, and he was bone-weary. When their eyes finally met, the sadness he had feared was absent. Instead, to Joshua's astonishment, Cyrus was smiling broadly! But soon Cyrus's eyes brimmed with tears.

"Joshua, my dear beautiful nephew. My heart is bursting with joy." He held out his long arms and Joshua buried his head into his uncle's tattered garments. Squeezing his nephew tightly to his chest, the two quietly sobbed in each other's arms while the three brothers solemnly looked on.

"I am so sorry about all you have lost, Cyrus," said Joshua as he slowly pulled away from his uncle's arms.

"It was a matter of time, my nephew. After all, those beds were made of mere sticks and grass. I have been a fool to think my lonely abode would stand forever. Let us return now and we can talk along the way." Nodding to the brothers, they resumed the final leg of this journey to what was left of Cyrus's encampment. With arms linked, Joshua and his uncle led the way as Andrew, James, and Judas quietly followed.

"But what of the hut built of rock and clay? Surely that can be built up again."

"Perhaps, but what then? Will I not still be a lonely man hiding from the world? But enough about me. You must tell me more about the wound to your head." Acknowledging the brothers behind them, he added, "Andrew shared with me how brave you were at the well, but look at this bare scalp; surely there is more to tell."

It felt good to be talking with Cyrus, but Joshua couldn't help but notice that his dear uncle was not nearly as distraught as he expected. If anything, he seemed stronger. Could that even be possible, he wondered. As Cyrus requested, he told the story of the long journey with Mother's body and how the villagers seemed drawn to the presence of Jesus. Cyrus nodded as he listened to Joshua's story of the chaos at the well and how he was nearly trampled to death as the villagers suddenly rushed toward Jesus. He told of the village women who nursed him back to health and of Andrew's magical stories as they lay together under the stars.

Looking behind to see how far back the brothers were, Cyrus spoke in a hushed tone. "How much did Andrew talk about Jesus?"

Without a moment's hesitation, Joshua replied. "Jesus was the center of everything Andrew spoke of." Joshua told of how Andrew left his fishing trade to follow Jesus, how his brother Peter came to Jesus, and how soon there were twelve of them who left everything behind to walk with Jesus. Now, they all called him Rabbi.

"Doesn't that feel odd to you, Joshua, that these men would leave their entire lives behind to walk with this ordinary-looking man who they barely knew?"

"If only you could have seen what I witnessed in the village when Jesus was among the villagers. There were times when the people seemed to lose control of themselves. It's as if he was the answer to their dreams and they could not let him go. Yet there were others who said this man from Nazareth was the devil himself."

"What do you think, Joshua?

After a long pause, Joshua answered his uncle. "I cannot believe that the man they call Rabbi is the devil. Although Andrew told me of the magical wonders he has performed before many, I would not think the men would follow such a man simply to witness his magic."

"So, you believe there is more to this ordinary man?"

"There is something about him, Cyrus, that I cannot explain. People are drawn to this man as a moth is to a flame."

Cyrus slowed his pace, and his face portrayed a man in deep thought as he spoke to his nephew. "I have carefully observed many tricksters who have visited me from the old Jerusalem Road, but this stranger from Nazareth is like no magic man I have seen. He sought me out after the storm reduced my abode to ruins. He witnessed how deeply distressed I was for my loss, and he could feel the worry that weighed on me for your safe return. We then walked together for some time in the empty fields and away from all the destruction." Cyrus shook his head before continuing. "I swear to you, Joshua, in the time that I shared with him, I came to feel a greater sense of peace than I have ever known." Coming to a halt, Cyrus faced his nephew. "It almost frightens me, Joshua, to feel like such a new man."

"Have I ever told you of the peace I feel when I'm lying on the ground staring at the heavens above?" asked Joshua.

"No, nephew, but I have watched you on many nights when the stars glow across the night sky, and I have seen the wonder in your eyes."

The two walked in silence as they neared the storm-ravaged encampment. Joshua finally broke the stillness. "Do you believe the peace I feel when I stare into the heavens is the same peace you have come to know after your time with Jesus?"

Gazing at the waiting brothers gathered by the blaze in the encampment, Cyrus looked to his nephew. "I believe there is only one peace, and it comes from the same source."

"I do not understand."

"Nor do I, my dear nephew." Cyrus saw the brothers now only a stone's throw away. He was hopeful Jesus remained in their midst. As he prepared to join them, Cyrus offered a further thought to Joshua. "I believe the men standing by the fire may know much more of these mysteries than you or I can imagine."

25

CHANGES

It felt odd to Joshua to be greeted with open arms by sojourners who only days ago intruded upon their encampment in the middle of the night. He vividly recalled the moment when Jesus announced that the woman who lay before them was no longer among the living. He would never forget the pain and sorrow that Cyrus and he felt when told by a stranger that Mother was dead. Walking through the wreckage of his uncle's encampment, Joshua now understood that the strange world he had come to know was gone forever.

"How do you feel, my son?" came Andrew's familiar voice as he stepped alongside Joshua.

"I am not sure how to feel, for my uncle has lost nearly all he ever had, and I have no place to go."

"I understand how deeply troubled you are, but my inquiry was about the nasty wound to your head. As for Cyrus, I invite you to see for yourself. It looks to me like he is faring well."

Watching his uncle with the brothers was a sight to behold. The man he knew to be suspicious of nearly everyone was no more. Here instead was a man unshaken by the storm that blew his homestead to bits. This new Cyrus spoke freely with the gathering of brothers as they tended to the vigorous blaze before them.

"I have forgotten about the wound unless my hand rubs across the top of my head and I feel no hair." Turning his gaze from Cyrus and his newfound friends, Joshua assured Andrew, "The wound only hurts when I touch it. My greatest pain is not knowing what is to become of my uncle and me."

"Just as surely as the missing hair on your head will return, so too will your destiny be found. Of this I am certain. For now, let me tend your wound with the healing dressing that the women of the village left for us. We can talk later of the many mysteries and hardships we all must face."

Andrew's encouraging words were comforting to Joshua's troubled soul as they settled against the sturdiest wall of Cyrus's crumbling hut. Joshua glanced toward Cyrus and the brothers huddled by the fire. Cyrus raised his head and their eyes met. The look they exchanged was far from joyous, but it was not sorrowful. As they held their gaze, a look of knowing passed between them. A look that conveyed the harsh reality they now confronted. Deeper still, etched across their faces was the realization that their lives had completely changed. Before turning back to the brothers, Cyrus nodded to his nephew as if to reassure him, "You are going to be fine."

As Andrew applied the dressing to Joshua's wound, he informed his young friend of what had transpired in his absence. He told of the food the brothers purchased in the village with the few coins they had on hand. They all would enjoy a great feast that night and rest under the stars before departing at first light. "Did you know your uncle found many blankets in his hut?"

"Finding more blankets is not my concern," said Joshua. As Andrew gently placed the grape leaves over the pungent-smelling dressing that covered the wound, his young friend continued. "I fear my uncle's strength will vanish soon after you and your friends leave us behind."

"You fear too much, my friend. What if your uncle stays strong long after we are gone? What then will you fear?"

Joshua remained silent as he sat against the wall watching the men by the fire before facing Andrew. "Where is your Rabbi?"

"He is there with the brothers speaking of many things. These are the times we most treasure. Shall we join them?"

"For now, I am content to sit with you and watch from a distance." Staring in wonder as Cyrus easily talked with men who were strangers just days ago, Joshua shook his head. He felt a twinge of disappointment in his uncle as he looked on. "Should my uncle not be mourning all he has lost, and should he not be more worried of what will happen to me?" he said as much to himself as Andrew.

"This change that has come over my uncle is hard for me to accept. It looks as if he is more at home with your friends than he is with me, his nephew." At once Joshua felt a sense of shame for saying such words about Cyrus to Andrew.

The two continued to view the gathering from a distance as they sat against the broken-down hut. Jesus could be seen in the narrow space between the men as he passed from one brother to the next before the fire. Cyrus could be seen engaging in serious talks with several of the men. At times one of them would place a hand on Cyrus's shoulder while gesturing in the air with his other hand as he made an important point. In turn, Cyrus would nod favorably and offer words of his own.

"I told you that we would talk of the hardships we must face and the many mysteries we will encounter in our days. I myself have suffered many hardships in my life. However, in my walk with Rabbi I have experienced more wonders with my own eyes than I can count. I suggest that we look no further than your uncle who now stands boldly among these men," proclaimed Andrew as he held his gaze upon Cyrus. "For here is a man who you say trembled in fear most of his days."

"Life had been very cruel to my uncle; therefore, he trusted no man," offered Joshua in defense of his uncle's fearfulness.

"Yet look at him now, my friend. Is this a man crippled by fear? Does this man look broken after losing to the storm most of what he possessed?"

"Then please tell me. What has happened to my uncle?"

"Your Uncle Cyrus is still the same good man with the same tender soul, but he now knows a greater truth about himself and this life. When we returned after the terrible storm, we could see that most of what belonged to your uncle had been swept away. Rabbi asked the brothers where Cyrus had gone, and they all pointed to the empty fields beyond and at once Rabbi went to find him. After much time had passed, Rabbi returned, and walking beside him with his head held high was your dear uncle. My brothers and I rose to our feet and cheered, for we knew the broken Cyrus was left far behind in that lonely field and a new victorious Cyrus came back." With his eyes still upon the men by the fire, Andrew described the moment Jesus and Cyrus stepped into the washed-out encampment as if he were recalling a dream. "It was a beautiful sight to behold, my friend."

Tossing a stone in the air as he spoke, Joshua sounded unconvinced. "It seems to me that Jesus is very good at casting spells. Just like the one he cast upon the woman at the well. This time my uncle is the one who fell under his magic. Please understand that I am pleased that Cyrus has forgotten his troubles, but I am afraid this spell will lift and the familiar fear and weakness will return to my uncle's troubled soul. By then you and your friends will be long gone."

Rising to his feet, Andrew looked down upon Joshua. "If this is what you choose to believe, then there is nothing more I can say. In my journey with Rabbi, I have seen many people like you, people who do not see the light of heaven even when it is staring them in the face. Your Uncle Cyrus was ready to receive the light and it has lifted him in ways you do not understand. I pray the heavenly light will someday fall upon you." With those final words, Andrew stalked off to join his brothers by the fire, leaving Joshua sitting alone against the wall.

Joshua felt the sting of Andrew's rebuke as he watched him walk away. It is not true what Andrew said about him, he insisted to himself. No, not at all. For Andrew did not know of the many nights when his eyes often brimmed with tears as he became lost in the stars of the heavens. He vowed to tell Andrew of the heaven he knew.

Joshua watched as Andrew joined his friends by the fire in the warm fellowship of their ongoing conversations. He saw Cyrus look back at him in the fading light as he sat alone against the wall of the forlorn hut. Joshua could see that Cyrus was concerned.

Cyrus stepped away from the fire and walked toward the hut with Journey at his side, but halted and waved encouragingly to Joshua to join him with the other men. Cyrus remained standing and waited for a response. Joshua's eyes surveyed the storm-ravaged land, pretending not to notice his uncle's stare. When it became clear that Cyrus was not going to turn away, Joshua finally succumbed to his uncle's request and slowly rose to his feet.

As he made his way up the short rise to the fire, he could see a smile creasing his uncle's long beard. Journey's thin tail wildly wagged in the air. Despite his brooding, Joshua knew that he was deeply loved. He also realized he could not imagine being away from his gentle uncle who now appeared so strong. So why, then, Joshua wondered, did he feel so lost?

The words of James upon finding Joshua after the storm again came back to him. *Although we may be uncertain of where our path will lead, we are never lost.*

26

BY THE FIRE

The anxious thoughts that crowded Joshua's mind seemed to vanish as Cyrus ushered him close to the robust blaze. Joshua could see that the men had built an impressive circle of rocks to corral the fire and he noticed the mountain of debris piled nearby composed of branches large and small. No doubt the scattered remains of his and Cyrus's beds were in that pile of wood, or perhaps they had long ago turned to the ash that now settled at the bottom of the fire pit. Turning back to the west, he saw the setting sun in all its magnificence slowly slipping away. There in the shadows was Cyrus's sagging hut, ready to fall at any moment. Joshua lingered over the sad sight, not yet ready to say farewell. A tug at his tunic brought him around.

There before him was Jesus. "You look good, my son. I know you have been through much. Andrew, James, and Judas told me how brave you were to survive such a storm."

Joshua could feel his face redden when he thought of how the men came upon him in his nakedness. As if reading his mind, Jesus offered words of assurance. "It is not a sin to shed your heavy garments in a fierce storm. For how else can you truly become clean?" He then pointed a finger at Cyrus who was standing tall beside his nephew. "This uncle of yours is about the finest man I have ever met." Gently patting Cyrus on the chest before walking on, he turned to Joshua once more. "He loves you fiercely, you know."

Joshua winced at Jesus' words, knowing the unexpected resentment he harbored toward his uncle for his newfound peace. Joshua stared at the fire as he reached for his uncle's long, bony fingers. "I love you too, Cyrus, but I am so afraid."

Placing a long arm over his nephew's shoulders, Cyrus pulled him closer. "You will be fine, my dear nephew." After a pause, he added, "We will be fine. Of this I am certain." As they held their gaze on the fire, Cyrus's eyes brimmed with tears.

With evening settling upon the men, many chose to recline on the bare ground and quietly take in the wonder of a full moon rising in the eastern sky. Soon the tantalizing aroma of broiling meat wafted over the blaze. As Cyrus and Joshua joined the others seated on the ground, Journey slipped in from behind and nestled between them, softly resting his head on Cyrus's outstretched legs. Idly stroking the resting Journey, Cyrus informed Joshua that the three remaining skinned hares must be cooked that night. "Like the rest of us, I think our friend here needs to recover from the storm before he hunts again."

"But who among them is preparing the feast? For you, uncle, have always charred the meat to perfection."

"It is in their hands, my nephew. The brothers have demanded that you and I do no work. They say the feast is in our honor."

Peering over the flames as they burned high into the night, Joshua could see several of the men fast at work on the far side of the pit organizing the meal. Other brothers, content to lie on their backs, stared into the night sky in silence. Joshua could hear occasional laughter and at times forceful words coming from the brothers sitting together near the fire.

"I do not see Jesus anywhere. Where could he be, Cyrus?"

"I am told by the brothers that he often walks away to be alone."

"Why?"

"I believe he talks with God, who he calls Father."

"How would you know this, Cyrus?"

"Because he did this with me after the storm."

Just as Joshua was about to ask his uncle about why Jesus says "Father," one of the brothers approached, carrying a large wine skin over his shoulder. It was Peter, whose thunderous voice could be heard from all sides of the fire pit.

"It is good to see you again, Joshua. Your uncle has been a generous host to us and we are all very grateful. Please accept this gift of wine that we purchased from your village," said Peter as he withdrew the strap from his shoulder and placed it in Joshua's hands.

Raising the wine skin to his lips, Joshua recalled the rancid wine he purchased from the old villager many days ago. To his relief this wine tasted sweet and pure. With a favorable nod to Peter, he passed the skin to his uncle.

"Thank you for your kindness, Peter," said Cyrus with a slight bow. "As I said to you after the storm, what is mine now can be yours. My plates, though, are mostly broken, and what little food I could store is now washed away; but the blankets left behind from the many sojourners on the Jerusalem Road may be of use to you and your brothers."

Hearing Cyrus recount to Peter all he had lost and what he was now giving away made Joshua wonder how he and his uncle would carry on come tomorrow.

Seeing the look of confusion on Joshua's face, Peter turned to Cyrus. "I am curious to know what plans the two of you have following our departure at first light."

Without a moment of hesitation, Cyrus replied to Peter as he passed the wine skin, "It is in the hands of the Almighty. I trust this as surely as the earth beneath my feet." A knowing look passed between Peter and Cyrus.

Upon hearing Cyrus's words, Joshua nearly slumped to the ground with worry. It was all he could do to not look as stunned as he felt. Although he accepted that his uncle had found a measure of peace following his walk with Jesus after the storm, he was shocked to hear such words being uttered by the man he loved and thought he knew so well. Joshua had no idea what was to become of them. Why was Cyrus unconcerned?

In the midst of Joshua's anxious thoughts, a loud argument erupted between two brothers. Their voices were heated as they sharply disagreed over who they regarded as their neighbor. In Joshua's mind, the argument did not seem worthy of such a vehement exchange.

"I see my fellow Gallaliens have allowed their tempers to explode," said Peter. He quickly handed the wine skin back to Cyrus and attempted to intervene, only to become embroiled in the same argument himself.

The spectacle continued as Joshua and Cyrus looked on while silently exchanging glances. The brothers were engaged in a sharp battle of words over who was a neighbor and who was not. Soon the voice of Jesus could be heard as he emerged from the darkness of the surrounding field. Hearing their Rabbi speak brought an immediate end to the angry voices as Jesus began to tell a story about a man who was walking alone on the Jerusalem Road. He was beaten, robbed, stripped of his clothes, and left for dead.

As Jesus continued with his story, the brothers sat before him as the fire crackled nearby, spitting burning sparks into the night. Lowering himself to the ground, Jesus told of a priest who came along the road, who upon seeing the terribly wounded man walked to the other side of the road. With the brothers all in rapt attention, Jesus then spoke of a man from the highly esteemed tribe of Levites who too walked to the other side of the road to avoid any contact with the man lying in unspeakable pain.

As Joshua and his uncle sat outside of the brothers' circle listening to the story, Joshua recalled the time when sojourners walked a great distance out of their way to avoid facing the young Samaritan who stood in their path. The next words in Jesus' story were truly a surprise to Joshua and Cyrus. To their delight they heard of how a Samaritan man then came along. He did not walk to the other side of the road. Instead, this Samaritan[3] came to the aid of the wounded stranger. He dressed his wounds with oils and bandaged him. He placed him on his donkey and delivered the fallen man to an inn, where he cared for him throughout the night. Joshua carefully rubbed the top of his bare scalp as he warmly recalled how the village women went out of their way to provide him with such tender care.

Joshua wondered what the brothers truly thought of him and his uncle, as several turned their heads around for a quick, nervous glance as Jesus continued with his story about the Samaritan man. What more could this Samaritan man do, wondered Joshua. As if again reading his mind, Jesus told the brothers that this caring man left behind several coins for the innkeeper to tend to the injured man's needs. If that was not enough, he would pay him properly upon his return.

"So, which one among these three men who traveled this road was a neighbor to the fallen stranger?" asked Jesus.

Peter's strong voice could be heard above the rest as he cried out, "The one who showed mercy."

"You answered well, Peter. But most assuredly I say to you all, that if you truly love God with all your heart and all your soul, you need not ever raise your voice again when asked to tell who your neighbors are."

---

3 The Parable of the Good Samaritan. Luke 10: 25 – 37. (KJV)

Upon hearing Jesus' final words, the brothers rose to their feet and exchanged hugs and laughter in a warm display of forgiveness for the harsh words they traded back and forth only moments ago. Soon the slightly built man with piercing eyes, who Joshua knew to be John, stepped before the jubilant brothers to make an announcement. "As we know, our dear brothers, Matthew and Thomas, have been slaving over this hot fire to prepare a mighty feast in honor of Cyrus and Joshua, our generous hosts. Before we partake in this hearty stew, I ask that we give thanks to our Samaritan brothers who have lost so much to this fierce storm. Although, our paths may never again cross, we declare in the name of God Almighty, we will never forget you."

A boisterous cheer rang out among the brothers followed by numerous expressions of goodwill as they faced the uncle and nephew with generous smiles. In turn, Cyrus received their gratitude with joy as he embraced all who came to him. Joshua, though, remained aloof as he stepped away from the commotion and stared into the fire. He was completely unaware that the eyes of Jesus were firmly upon him.

27

TIME HAS COME

The festive meal proceeded in grand fashion as ample portions of charbroiled hare stew and hard crusted bread were doled out to Cyrus, Joshua, and all the brothers. Every plate, bowl, and platter from Cyrus's hut was in use. Although many consumed their meals from broken receptacles, it did not matter in the least as all fed their robust appetites while sitting by the fire. Soon wine skins were shared, adding good cheer to the gathering. Jesus was engaged in lively conversation as he partook of the wine. As the night wore on, Cyrus's musty blankets were held closer, shielding the men against the cooling air.

Unlike his uncle, Joshua did not converse with anyone, choosing instead to be alone with his thoughts. He stared gloomily into the dancing flames. With each sip from the passing wine skins, his eyes grew heavier. His head nodded as he wrapped the dank-smelling blanket around his shoulders.

To Joshua's utter astonishment, he watched his uncle finish the last of his stew and then toss the empty bowl into the fire. A loud cheer erupted from the brothers as they witnessed Cyrus's unexplained act of foolish sacrifice. In a bizarre gesture of solidarity, the brothers followed their host's lead and soon a cascade of broken platters and bowls sailed into the blaze followed by more cheers. Joshua looked on in disbelief as clouds of glowing embers burst into the night sky with the landing of each old wooden or clay plate into the fire.

Joshua wanted to cry out as the strange scene unfolded before his eyes, but seemed powerless to say a word. Urgently turning to his uncle, he saw only a blanket lying on the bare ground. Panic now gripped his heart as Joshua frantically searched in every direction for his uncle.

Squinting past all the smoke and flying embers, he spotted him. Cyrus was standing tall against the black night. His long-bearded face was lit by the fire as he engaged in a lively conversation with a stranger adorned in a flowing gold robe. The two passed a wine skin between them and often raised their heads to the sky and laughed heartily. It was as if Cyrus and the man dressed in gold were long-lost friends. Joshua was deeply hurt by what he saw. It seemed his uncle had completely forgotten he once had a nephew who he dearly loved.

He now heard his own voice screaming across the fire through the dense smoke. "Don't leave me, Cyrus! Please don't leave me alone! Come back to me please!" To his complete dismay, Cyrus never turned his way no matter how long or how hard Joshua cried out.

"Joshua . . . Joshua, wake up," said Cyrus as he knelt beside his nephew, gently shaking him. It pained him to see his nephew stirring on the bare ground so restlessly, even blurting out his name at times. "I am right here, my nephew."

Joshua opened his eyes. Cyrus smiled back reassuringly. "I believe you have been having quite the dream."

Without saying a word, Joshua quickly sat up and scanned the campsite. A thin fog draped the grounds as ghostly figures of men quietly drifted about preparing to resume their journey. The familiar sensation of Journey's cold wet nose touched his face as if to welcome Joshua to a new day. Petting Journey's side, Joshua looked back at Cyrus. "Do you plan to leave with them?"

Clearly hurt by such a question, Cyrus paused before responding to his nephew. "There is no doubt that Jesus and this group of men have filled me with a new strength and even joy. But as to your concern that I may leave with these men, the answer is no. I know you have been through so much, my nephew, but please know this: I would never leave you alone to fend for yourself in this cruel world. Never."

Joshua and Cyrus sat in silence as the men around them gathered their things and, one by one, quietly passed them as they ventured down the hill. The heaviness of the dawn did not call for conversation. Joshua watched as Andrew slowly made his way past, but then halted and returned to where they sat. Crouching down to face them directly, Andrew offered a few words before joining his brothers. "I want you to know how much your friendship has meant to me, Joshua. You are becoming a very fine young man and I pray that you and your uncle discover God's favor as you carry on." As he rose to his feet, a thought occurred to Andrew. "Would the two of you care to escort me and my friends to the Jerusalem Road? We would be honored."

With a shrug of consent, Joshua and his uncle stood and joined Andrew and the line of remaining brothers as Journey dutifully took his place beside Cyrus. The path leading to the Jerusalem Road was barely visible. Few words were spoken along the way. Joshua said nothing and with each step his mind filled with deeper gloom.

A light mist formed around them as all gathered on the road. Joshua stood alone and observed Cyrus silently embrace a few of the brothers before they departed. In recognition of Joshua's desire to be left by himself, many brothers offered a somber nod in his direction before moving on. Soon Cyrus and his nephew were side by side gazing upon the backs of the retreating brothers. Joshua looked up at his uncle and saw that his eyes were moist. Knowing how much the brothers meant to Cyrus, and especially how his time alone with Jesus had effected him, Joshua understood his uncle's tears. He turned again to the road and saw the brothers slowly vanish into the mist.

"I filled your pouch with fresh water from the hidden spring, and here is the same bag you carried over your shoulder when you first came to me. There is one clean tunic inside and the same blanket your mother packed for you so long ago. I also placed a handful of charred hopping bugs in there. I know how much you liked them," Cyrus told Joshua with a soft laugh, though his eyes remained tearful.

Confusion and feelings of betrayal gripped Joshua as he stared at his uncle in disbelief.

"What is this, Cyrus? I do not understand," he cried.

"The time has come, my nephew. Although I have dreaded this day, you must leave me now."

Dropping his water pouch and shoulder bag to the ground, Joshua screamed at his uncle. "What have I done to deserve this? You said you would never leave me alone."

"I am not abandoning you, my nephew; I am releasing you to the world that awaits." Looking back at the fog shrouded road, Cyrus said, "I deeply trust the men who have visited us. They will protect you and I know in time you will be of great service to them."

"But they do not want me. I am but a mere child to them," he protested.

"So, convince them of your worth. One more thing you must know. Jesus is expecting you. Of this I am certain. Please pick up your things, Joshua, and go to them, before I change my mind and hold you back forever."

"But what will become of you?"

"There is something I must do, but please do not worry about me. I will be fine. Besides, I have this loyal beast to protect me."

Cyrus bent down to stroke Journey's fur as Joshua quietly picked up his discarded pouch and bag. Without warning, Joshua rushed into Cyrus's arms, nearly knocking him to the ground. Finally pulling away he looked up with tears and pleaded for an answer. "Will I ever see you again?"

"God willing, my nephew. God willing."

Valiantly trying to shed no more tears, Joshua gave Journey a tight hug around his neck as the loyal beast licked a farewell kiss across his face. "You take care of my uncle, you hear? I will see you again. I promise."

Looking no further at his uncle, Joshua turned to the old Jerusalem Road that had held so much mystery for him and ran. With tears streaming down his face, Joshua ran as hard as he could with nothing but a desolate road ahead. Fighting the urge to look behind, he kept running. But then, without thinking, he turned his head back. Both Cyrus and Journey were gone.

28

AMONG THEM

His chest about to burst, Joshua came to a halt and gasped for air while resting his hands heavily on his knees. His mind was void of thoughts as he panted into the dirt road. Rising, he reached for his water and took a long draw from the pouch. Gazing into the thick grayness ahead, it felt natural to Joshua to again be alone as he traveled into the unknown.

Continuing, but at a slower pace, his mind turned to the brothers and how stunned they would be to see this Samaritan boy coming to them on this dreary morning. What if they turned him away, he wondered. Cyrus's final words came back to him. *Convince them of your worth.* Thinking of his uncle brought sorrow to his heart. So, Joshua began to run again, hoping to leave such sad thoughts behind as he raced to an uncertain future.

The light mist that had accompanied him was no more. Joshua slowed his pace to a steady walk and surveyed the low clouds that seemed to have grown brighter. Looking to the east, the sun weakly pierced through the heavy sky. Returning his gaze to the road, Joshua could see the fog had lifted and there in the distance were the dark hulks of slowly moving men who Joshua knew to be the brothers.

Joshua now felt foolish as he stared at their backs in the distance. How could he have allowed Cyrus to send him to men who wanted nothing further to do with him? The urge to turn around and run was strong. But what then? Cyrus was gone. Standing motionless in the road, Joshua thought of his mother and of the caring woman he called Mother. He imagined their calm reassuring voices speaking to him. *Go to them, dear boy. You are here for a reason.*

Slowly putting one foot before the other, Joshua kept his eyes firmly upon the brothers who remained unaware he was trailing behind. Gradually he picked up his pace and stood tall. Joshua wanted to appear strong and purposeful when they finally noticed that the boy they left standing with his uncle in the dreary morning was coming to them. But doubts played havoc with Joshua's mind as he drew closer. He feared that any sign of weakness detected by these well-traveled men would result in his quick dismissal. Joshua must show only strength. No matter what was said, he could not back down.

Just as he was about to call to them and announce his presence, he saw the last brother in their procession casually turn his head and take in all the distance they had traveled. Joshua stared back and kept walking as the brother, who may have been Thomas, stood still in the road as if he could not believe his eyes. Joshua saw him excitedly call out to his brothers. The men stopped in their tracks and stared back with looks of puzzlement as Joshua continued his advance.

Soon the unmistakable figure of Peter separated from the brothers and marched forward to presumably stop Joshua from coming any closer. Joshua's resolve weakened as he saw the determination in Peter's eyes. His final thought before Peter stepped before him was: please help me, God.

Wearing a warm smile as he approached, Peter placed a hand on his shoulder. "Is there something wrong, my son?"

Trying desperately not to convey his trembling, Joshua replied. "No. Everything is good, Peter."

"Then please tell me why have you followed us?"

"I intend to walk with you." As he said these words, he saw the warmth of Peter's face slightly dim.

Placing an arm around Joshua's shoulder and gently turning him to the road behind, Peter searched for the right words as he walked by his side. "I know you have been through so much, Joshua, but walking with us is just not possible, my son."

Without saying a word, Joshua wrenched Peter's arm from his shoulder and ran to the brothers. This was not how he imagined it would be, as he charged toward the cluster of bewildered faces before him. "Do not allow this boy to take a step further," cried Peter from behind. "He can never be with us."

Joshua watched as Andrew stepped before the others and waited for his arrival. The brother who Joshua knew best looked distraught as he came to a halt before him. Joshua desperately fought to regain his breath while waiting for Andrew to speak. "You know this is reckless, what you have done, my friend." The others looked on in silence with all eyes upon Joshua.

Still struggling to catch his breath, Joshua raised his head to face Andrew. "Is it reckless of me to seek a better life? Is it reckless to leave behind a world of sorrow and pain? Tell me, Andrew, is it reckless to join men such as you and your friends who may be just as reckless as me?"

"Do not listen to him, my brother, for he is just a boy," came Peter's words as he stood with Joshua and Andrew.

"You know that I love you, dear brother, but this is not a mere boy who stands before us. Don't you see that Joshua is becoming a bold young man right before our eyes?" declared Andrew to his brother.

"If he is a young man in your eyes, so be it," replied Peter softly before pausing. His voice then erupted. "But under no circumstance will I walk the streets of Galilee and Jerusalem and be made a mockery of with a Samaritan by my side. He and his people are an abomination in the eyes of the Almighty."

"Then what in the name of God do you propose we do, my brother? Feed him to the beasts who stalk the land?" cried Andrew.

Stepping away as this intense battle of words unfolded, Joshua stood alone, never imagining his mere presence would spark such a confrontation. His uncle had always told him Samaritans were looked down upon by many. He saw that for himself when sojourners avoided crossing his path along the old Jerusalem Road. But never had he witnessed such hatred directed at him, a Samaritan, and it hurt. He recalled the story Jesus told to the brothers of the Samaritan man who cared for the dying stranger when other more important people left him for dead. How shocking such a story must have been to the men he intended to join, and how little he himself understood of the mysteries of this land.

Silence prevailed as Peter and Andrew walked about in front of the brothers trying to cool down after their heated clash. Jesus then appeared holding a long string of twine used for repairs to fish netting. "It seems our friend Jude has not left his fishing trade completely behind, for he still carries this valued material in his bag." Turning to Peter, Jesus placed the twine in his hands. "Use this to bind, Joshua, and then tie him to the bush nearest you and we can be on our way."

Looking at Jesus as if he was staring at a stranger, Peter begged for understanding. "Surely, Rabbi, you do not expect me to bind this boy?"

"What choice do you have, my friend?"

Joshua, terrified like never before, looked back and forth at Jesus and Peter with panic in his eyes. Not a word was uttered by a single brother as the tension mounted.

Peter was first to speak. "Rabbi, you of all men know that I have sacrificed everything to follow you. I left my wife and family behind. I walked away from the only job I have ever known. All that I ask is that I not be put to shame."

"I know the tremendous sacrifices you have made, Peter, and I will never forget. But there is still something that is precious to you that lies deep in your heart."

With hands clenched to his chest as the twine fell to the ground, Peter pleaded before Jesus. "Tell me, Rabbi, what more can I possibly leave behind? Please, Rabbi, tell me what is it that remains."

With hands resting upon Peter's shoulders, Jesus answered with words so soft that Joshua could barely hear. "Your right to yourself, Peter." Pausing to allow his words to penetrate, he continued. "Surrender your very self to me, my dear friend, and I promise, you will never fear shame again."

Joshua did not understand what transpired, but as he watched Peter and Jesus embrace, he sensed that an important moment had passed between them. Fortunately, Joshua's fear of being bound with twine and tied to a bush subsided as he observed the other brothers talking to one another and drinking from their pouches. No one, however, was coming to him, until he observed Judas heading his way. Joshua was grateful to be acknowledged.

"As you can see, these Galileans can become quite angry with one another," said Judas as he stood beside Joshua, observing the other brothers. No one even glanced in Judas's direction.

"Are you not a Galilean, Judas?"

Laughing at the thought of such a question, Judas made it clear how unique he was among the brothers. "I am a proud Judean, my son, and it is because of this that my Galilean friends have chosen me to be their treasurer. They know that if one of them oversaw our scant resources, there would be a battle every day." Laughing once again before turning serious, he queried Joshua. "What is it that you are prepared to do now that you are among us?"

The question took Joshua by surprise. "If what you say is true and I am allowed to be among all the brothers, then I will do whatever is asked of me."

As Judas was about to reply, the voice of John called out to all the brothers. "Although we have not traveled far today, there is a great deal we have witnessed. Therefore, I propose we rest here and consider all that has happened. We have a sufficient supply of food to get us through the night. If we leave before first light, we can be in the land of Galilee before nightfall."

"Go to John now, my friend, before he walks away, and tell him all you are prepared to do."

Without a further word to Judas, Joshua ran to John, calling his name as he drew closer.

John's face was expressionless as he watched the young Samaritan approach. "I will search this land for wood and dry grass to build a fire to keep us through the night," declared Joshua.

John quietly nodded his consent before turning to walk away. He halted as Joshua continued to speak. "I can help prepare the meal if the brothers need my hand, and I will gladly clean up what is left behind so it will appear as if we were never here."

"That will be good," said John before leaving Joshua behind.

As he watched John join the others, Joshua knew that earning his trust would not come easily. Nor would the others welcome him with open arms. Was it not just one night ago when he and his uncle were treated like royalty by these once grateful sojourners? But much had changed since he charged into their world. Except for Judas, he could sense the brothers' resentment of his uninvited presence. Did Jesus even know he was coming as Cyrus proclaimed? Impossible to know, he concluded. For what

Jesus thought and did remained a mystery not only to him but often to the brothers as well.

Joshua's search for dry branches and grass took him far from where the brothers rested. The fear of being abandoned while he carried out this task crossed his mind many times as he drifted deeper into the empty land. But returning with barely enough kindling to start a fire was not an option. So, he searched long and hard with one purpose, to make believers of them all.

The sun simmered low on the western horizon as Joshua dragged a broad limb with a tower of kindling behind. His breathing was labored and his body dripped with sweat as he pulled his heavy cargo. Stacked upon the wide limb were enough branches and dry grass to keep a decent fire blazing through the night. Shielding his eyes from the sun's steady glare, Joshua was exhilarated when at long last he saw the brothers before him. A broad smile crossed his face as he drew closer. "They did not abandon me!" he declared out loud. Soon the brothers were on their feet and running towards him. Yes, Joshua thought to himself, I have proven to be worthy in their eyes, but will they treat me as one of them? That he could not yet answer.

Bartholomew and Matthew, two brothers who Joshua had scarcely talked to, were the first to greet him. They demanded that Joshua relieve himself of the load and allow them to carry the kindling the rest of the way.

"You did well, my friend," said Bartholomew as he enthusiastically greeted Joshua with several slaps on his back.

"Please join the others who will gladly share their wine while we set about building a great fire," said Matthew, as he lifted the heavy burden off Joshua's shoulder.

Observing the brothers a short distance away, Joshua saw Andrew break away and come to him. "Where did you find such a massive stack of timber in this barren land?"

"I have learned much during my life of how to search and gather dry wood. It is one of the few talents I possess. That is why I could make a promise to John that I would return with firewood no matter how long I labored."

The two shared an awkward silence before Joshua spoke again. "Thank you, Andrew, for what you did for me today."

"Although you are my friend, Joshua, you must know that I did not speak those words because of you. It was for my dear brother Peter, who I have loved all my life. As you will see, the men listen carefully to his words, but at times my brother's deepest fears cause him to stumble. Wait for Peter to come to you and you will understand the greatness of this man."

Andrew then joined his friends as they slowly dragged the ample pile of brush forward. It would soon become a roaring blaze.

Before joining the brothers sharing wine from a large sack, Joshua scanned the barren grounds in hopes of seeing Jesus nearby. He was nowhere to be found, nor was there any sign of Peter. Joshua did notice that John and his brother James were walking side by side. As he gazed in their direction, he saw John look his way and shout out to him. "You did well, my son!"

John's recognition of his labors was like a tonic to Joshua's spirit as he made his way to the remaining brothers. Although his body craved water and his own pouch was very low, he dared not ask others to share their own diminishing supplies of the precious resource. Wine, however, appeared to be plentiful and he gladly accepted the skin when it came to him.

Joshua said little as he stood with the men. He preferred to just listen as they discussed matters of great importance. He learned that Jesus was not trusted by the Jewish leaders of Jerusalem and the brothers feared he could be arrested at any time. The thought of Jesus being taken captive by other Jews was hard for Joshua to imagine. "It is why we will seek refuge in the village of Cana, which is near Rabbi's home village of Nazareth," explained Thomas as he held the wine skin to his mouth." He then called upon his fellow brother, Phillip, to tell Joshua what they witnessed at the wedding party in Cana.

"Then you must pass me the wine, Thomas, if I am to tell such an amazing story to our young friend," declared Phillip as the others laughed. As he grasped the wine sack with both hands, Phillip began. "It has been over a year since the night of that wonderful celebration, but I remember it like it was yesterday."

Although the brothers knew well what took place on that fateful night, they relished the opportunity to hear it again from Phillip, the greatest storyteller among them. Joshua followed as the brothers lowered themselves to the ground and anxiously waited for Phillip to carry them back to that miraculous night.

Joshua could see that Phillip was indeed a gifted storyteller. It wasn't long before he too was swept away by the magic of his words. With great drama in his voice, Phillip described how all the men, women, and children of the village had gathered for the wedding party. Jesus and his twelve friends were among the celebrants. Even Jesus' mother, Mary, was among the guests. During this joyous occasion, Mary came to her son with great concern, saying that they were nearly out of wine, and he must do something, or the wedding would become an embarrassment for the bridegroom.[4]

Phillip told of how upset Jesus was with his mother that she would come to him with such a dilemma. Joshua could see the brothers nodding in agreement when Phillip told of Jesus declaring to his mother that his time had not come. Yet Mary continued to plead with her son. Before long

---

4 Water Turned to Wine. John 2: 1-11. (KJV)

Jesus went to the wedding servants who stood by the empty clay jugs that once held wine.

"You must listen carefully, young man," advised Phillip. "For what we witnessed that night will never be forgotten!"

By now Joshua was transfixed by the telling of the story. He learned that Mary instructed the servants to do whatever Jesus said. Phillip lowered his voice to just above a whisper as he described all the servants following Jesus, each holding an empty jug in their arms. Jesus walked the servants to the entrance of the wedding hall where a large wooden vat of water sat next to a pile of wet rags. Joshua was told that this was where all the guests washed their dirt-encrusted feet before entering the wedding hall. Phillip made a point of emphasizing how filthy this water was. He then turned to Joshua and asked, "What do you imagine happened then, young man?"

Joshua sat speechless. He simply shook his head and waited for Phillip to continue.

After a dramatic pause, he proceeded to tell how Jesus directed all the servants to dip their empty clay jugs into the filthy water, fill them to the top, and bring them back to the serving table. As the servants were returning to the table, the head of the wedding party, walking with the bridegroom at his side, came upon them. He ordered one of the servants to fill his goblet with wine.

"I will never forget the look on the servant's face as he frightfully filled the man's goblet with liquid that only a moment ago came from that filthy vat," recalled Phillip. "All we could do was stare at this poor man as he raised the filled cup to his lips."

Joshua then blurted out, "Where was Jesus?"

Looking a bit puzzled, Phillip turned to the other brothers. "Do any of you remember seeing Rabbi at that moment?"

"I think I recall seeing Rabbi walking away as if to say my work is done here," said Thomas as he sat with the others.

"Where Rabbi was at that precise moment was not at all important, young man. The only fact that truly mattered was what happened next. We all held our breath as this man carefully sipped the new wine while staring into the eyes of the bridegroom," said Phillip as Joshua held on to every word.

With wonder and awe in his voice, Phillip delivered the words of the man who had just drunk from the goblet as he spoke in hushed tones to the bridegroom. "Young man, this wine is the most glorious wine that has ever graced my lips!"

Phillip continued the tale. "Raising his goblet high in the air, he then declared in a voice heard by all the wedding guests, 'Our bridegroom has saved the finest wine in all the land for the very last. He is to be praised for such a wondrous gift to us all!' A loud cheer rang out throughout the crowded hall as the bridegroom smiled and bowed before all his grateful guests."

All eyes turned to Joshua for his reaction after hearing Phillip tell the miraculous story. As the brothers raised themselves from the ground, they continued to stare at Joshua and wait for his response.

"If Jesus did indeed turn the filthy water into wine, why did he not announce to all the wedding guests what he had done for them?"

Clearly disappointed by Joshua's question, the brothers shook their heads and gravitated towards the fire that now blazed high into the evening sky. Phillip, though, was curious why the young man would say such a thing.

"What would it have accomplished if Rabbi stood before the wedding guests and proclaimed that the bridegroom did nothing, but it is I who made the wine? Do you doubt that this even happened, young man?"

"I do not doubt that there was new wine for the guests, but I am left to wonder how anything so filthy can be turned into something so good?"

"My son, soon you will see things for yourself that will shake the very ground you walk on. For now, let us join the others by the fire and eat what little food remains."

29

PETER

Although the flames rose high into the evening sky, there was no grand feast to be had. Joshua watched as each brother picked up a small chunk of barely and a handful of fruit. All silently found a solitary place by the fire to consume the modest meal and be alone with their thoughts.

Matthew quietly observed Joshua as he tentatively approached the blanket where only a few loaves and scattered pieces of fruit remained. "Please, young man, don't be shy. You have earned your right to eat tonight," said the brother who earlier had relieved Joshua of his heavy load of branches.

Joshua lifted the smallest portion of hard bread off the blanket, along with a lone fig, and retreated to his own place by the fire. Gone were the robust conversations that Joshua witnessed the night before. On this night there was a chill in the air. The brothers edged closer to the fire with their blankets wrapped tightly over their shoulders and slowly chewed their bread. They wordlessly gazed at the flames.

Joshua too was lost in thought as he sat by the fire. His mind drifted to Cyrus and Journey and wondered where they were on this cool night. He thought of his mother and sisters and hoped that the horrible Langer was no longer a threat to his family. Soon he found himself whispering to the god of the heavens.

It is me again, God. It is foolish to believe you can hear my voice, but there is no one else I can talk to. Please let my family know that I miss them, and that means Cyrus and Journey too. What I hope for more than anything in the world is that everyone is safe. I am on my way to a land called Galilee with a gathering of mostly fishermen who follow a man named Jesus. He says he was sent by his father. All I know for sure is that Jesus has turned Cyrus from a frightened man into a brave man. All the men here call Jesus their Rabbi, but he doesn't act like the rabbi who gave my father's farm to Langer. I am not sure what will happen in the days to come, but I am told that with Jesus, anything is possible. If you can hear me, please tell my family that I am traveling with men who are good, but it is a mystery to me where Jesus will lead us.

Joshua was prepared to say more to his unknown god, but he saw that the flames of the once vigorous blaze were dying down. Remembering the commitment he made to John to be a worthy servant, he made his way to the kindling pile and brought new life to the fire. As he fed the flames, he heard several brothers call his name in recognition of his labors. It felt good to receive such praise, but he dared not acknowledge their words of encouragement, preferring to be seen as a dutiful servant. After building the fire back to its former glory, he quietly made his way back to his blanket.

There were no stars to gaze upon as Joshua reclined. More clouds had drifted in, making the night sky a black void. Lifting his nearly empty water skin to his lips, Joshua drew only enough water to wet the inside of his mouth before tying the pouch closed. How much longer could he go before begging one of the brothers for a draw of their own water? With his blanket wrapped tightly over his outstretched body, Joshua turned on his side and listened to the crackling fire and the far-off cry of a beast. Sleep soon had its way as the flames danced before his closed eyes.

The gentle shaking did not wake Joshua, but hearing his name whispered close to his ear brought him immediately out of his dreamless slumber. There before him Peter was kneeling. Joshua was terrified as Peter motioned for him to rise to his feet and walk. *So this was the end of his time with the brothers. He should have seen this coming. Peter would march him back to the road and order him to never return. All while his fellow sojourners were fast asleep.*

After walking in silence until the glow of the fire was well behind, Peter ordered Joshua to sit with him. Peter handed Joshua his water pouch. "I see your skin is empty. Please drink and satisfy your thirst and then we will talk."

Joshua could not stop shaking as he held the water pouch. He wasn't sure if it was due to the chill of the night or fear of what Peter might say. "Are you sending me away before your brothers rise?"

Peter could only shake his head, before facing Joshua with tears. "I have come to seek your forgiveness. But I understand if you cannot give it at this time, for you barely know me."

The relief that came over Joshua was like no feeling he had ever experienced. "You're letting me stay?" he said with a tremble.

"My son, you needn't seek my permission to stay. For I am but a simple fisherman who is still bound by the fears of this sinful world. I said horrible things yesterday and I am deeply sorry."

"But it is I who forced myself upon you and your friends."

"But it is I who must praise you for doing so. For had you not made such demands, I may never have seen the darkness that still shadowed my heart."

"No one has ever sought my forgiveness before, but as I sit beside you, I feel I am in the company of a good friend."

"You are indeed. If you drink from my water skin to quench your thirst, I will take that as a sign that we can renew our friendship and it will last for the remainder of our days."

Without hesitation, Joshua untied Peter's water pouch and drank until it was nearly empty. Joshua released a loud belch as he handed the skin back to Peter, prompting a laugh from each of them.

"Nothing has pronounced our bond more completely than the sound that erupted from your belly," declared Peter as the two laughed once more.

After a moment of stillness as they gazed upon the glow of the embers in the distance where the brothers slept, Joshua raised a question. "Where is Jesus?"

"That is a question you will no doubt ask many times, as have I and my friends. But rest assured, my son, he is with us, even if at times you cannot see him."

"Why do you follow such a man?"

"There are times I wonder myself why I have set upon this journey where the costs are so high and the dangers so real. Then I realize it is the living Christ who has rescued me, and he alone is leading me to the kingdom of heaven."

"How can Jesus lead you to the stars above where the only true heaven shines down upon us from so far away?"

Peter raised himself off the ground and extended his hand to Joshua as they began their return to the brothers. "There are many mysteries in this land, my son, but very few truths. As you will soon witness, Rabbi is the greatest mystery of all. Yet he walks among us cloaked in truth for all to see, and that is where the danger lies."

"I do not understand."

"The land is filled with powerful men. They watch as Rabbi draws crowds from near and far. Word of a Messiah walking among us has set the land afire, as the sick and the lame, the lost and the broken, all come to Rabbi in desperate need of hope and healing. That is the danger I speak of, Joshua. The powerful see the making of a king in their midst, and he stands as a threat to their very existence."

As Peter spoke, Joshua could not help but recall the frenzy over Jesus' presence in the village where he was nearly trampled to death. He soon felt the comfort of Peter's arm over his shoulder. "What will become of Rabbi and the rulers of this land is uncertain. Little do these rulers understand that what they face is the new Kingdom of God and they will not prevail."

As they approached the campsite, it was hard for Joshua to imagine that the men slumbering before him who followed such a mysterious man could prevail against anyone, much less the most powerful. "Mysteries can be very hard to unravel, my son, such as the mystery of how you have come to be with us," said Peter as he warmed his hands over the diminishing fire.

"That is not a mystery at all, for I was driven from my home by an evil man who threatened to kill me," declared Joshua as he too warmed his hands.

"Young man, I believe you have been running after the kingdom of heaven ever since you were chased from home, whether you choose to believe it or not. Now let us call upon our brothers to arise. The journey to Galilee awaits."

30

ONE YEAR LATER

It was dawn on the Sea of Galilee. The eastern sky was aglow with streaks of deep orange. Joshua sat on the pebbly shore and extended his feet into the fresh water as cool ripples caressed his bare toes. He never tired of watching the ritual of fishermen tending to their nets before putting their boats out for the day. The many vessels returning after a long night on the water, nets full of flapping fish in tow, enthralled him. On this morning he waited for Andrew and his brother Peter to arrive. Perhaps brothers John and James might join them. Together, the brothers had determined that it was time for Joshua to learn the fishing trade. A trade that, until Jesus walked into their lives, had sustained these men and their families for as long as any of them could remember.

In the eyes of the brothers, Joshua was no longer considered a mere boy. Long gone was the ugly scar atop his closely cropped scalp, replaced by curly locks highlighted in red that flowed to his shoulders. Although far younger than the rest, he had proven himself to be of great value. Never, when asked, had he hesitated to carry out the more humbling tasks of washing their garments, begging for alms, and preparing fires on many nights away from their home village of Capernaum. More than being a capable servant, Joshua considered himself to be one of them. He reveled in the late-night talks around the fire where Jesus would tell amazing stories about the Kingdom of Heaven. These talks completely captured Joshua's imagination, and he dreamt that Jesus' tales of such a Kingdom would one day come true. There were other times, however, when Joshua felt he was still an outsider. Especially when the man they called Lord would pull the brothers into a hushed discussion away from Joshua and would cease speaking when Joshua drew near. Little did he realize that it was for his own protection that Jesus shielded Joshua. This is when the rising threats to Jesus' life were openly discussed.

Jesus and the brothers recognized that Joshua still harbored many fears, and they did not wish to cause him greater unrest, knowing how deeply attached he had become to Jesus. It was for this reason it was decided that Joshua would not travel with Jesus and the brothers on the dangerous journeys to Jerusalem where the risks to Jesus' life were the greatest. He instead was called upon to watch over many of the brothers' empty dwellings until their return to Capernaum. Joshua often slept in Andrew's abode during these solitary days, and was frequently encouraged by Peter's family to enjoy meals with them. Spending time with Peter's welcoming family never failed to revive Joshua's soul. It was within this humble household where generous portions of steamy fish stew were served amid the playful antics of their children that he was reminded of his own family so far away.

While the brothers were gone, Joshua also came to know the thriving village of Capernaum. He befriended many vendors and helped them each day to set up shop and to market their goods. This earned him high praise and a few denarii along the way. Soon Joshua was affectionately known among the appreciative merchants as the helpful young Samaritan.

Although Joshua's understanding of Jesus was purposely limited, he was completely in awe of the man he now called Lord. Joshua vividly recalled the first time he entered the outskirts of Galilee and how crowds of men and women flocked to Jesus' side. As the brothers futilely tried to keep the crowds at bay, Jesus often stopped and allowed the people to engulf him as they reached out to touch his garment or desperately begged for healing. In time, Joshua grew accustomed to the large crowds, but wondered at how Jesus could endure such crushing attention.

Joshua came to understand that it was word of Jesus' miraculous healings that drew the sick, the lame, and the curious from throughout the land. He saw with his own eyes how crippled children were brought before Jesus and walked away healed. Blind men cried out to all that they could see after Jesus merely placed his hands over their sightless eyes. Lepers lying by the side of the road begged for Jesus to touch their open sores, and in moments they would rise with skin as fresh as a child's. Because of these signs and wonders, Jesus' reputation grew like wildfire throughout Galilee and as far away as Jerusalem, where the great Jewish temple stood. But among the fevered seekers who now heralded Jesus as the living Messiah, Joshua noticed a growing crowd of religious elders who held Jesus in the deepest suspicion and would confront him with hateful accusations.

Now wherever Jesus walked, he was not only surrounded by people who sought deliverance from their pain but also by those cloaked in religious righteousness who openly confronted him. They charged him with blasphemy and threatened to bring him to justice for his contempt of God's law. This struck Joshua as odd, since never had he known anyone with a greater passion for God than Jesus. But when Jesus declared that he was sent by the Father to proclaim the Kingdom of Heaven, the hatred against him grew nearly out of control.

Now, the Sea of Galilee shimmered in gold before Joshua. The autumn sun crested over the shadowed hills on the distant horizon and bathed his face in the day's early light. His mind wrestled with the confusing mysteries of Jesus, whose mere presence called forth such profound hope. Yet each day Joshua's unease grew as he saw greater numbers of men claiming the sacred law of their forefathers was being defiled by a man professing he alone was sent by the Almighty. *Why*, thought Joshua, *does Jesus insist on inflaming such hatred against him? Doesn't he realize it could cost him his life?*

His worrisome thoughts were broken by the call of his name up the shore. With fishing nets draped over their shoulders, Joshua delighted in the sight of Andrew and Peter coming his way. He could see that the two brothers were well liked by the other fisherman as they walked along the busy waterfront, waving and laughing with men they had probably known all their lives. Joshua rose as they approached in good cheer, ready for a great day on the water and a chance to reacquaint themselves with their old way of life.

"Today we are going to teach this young farm hand how to fish," declared Peter with a big smile.

"But first, we must carefully examine the seaworthiness of our old boat which has sat on the rocks for so long," cautioned Andrew.

"I have looked in on her from time to time when we have returned home with Rabbi. I can assure you, dear brother, she is ready to sail," said a confident Peter.

As they passed by all the working boats, Joshua saw an overturned vessel tucked away well beyond the water line. Sand and pebbles had drifted against its side and old palm fronds leaned forlornly against the overturned hull. "Is that your boat?" asked Joshua, hoping to be told differently.

"She may not look like much now, my son, but wait till we put her out to sea, and you will discover what a true glory she is to behold," said Peter with great pride.

"Are not John and James joining us?" Having never been in an open boat, Joshua could feel his unease growing as he watched the two brothers turn the boat upright. Several sand crabs skittered away as their hiding place was suddenly removed.

"Yes," confirmed Peter. "But if they do not arrive soon, we will have no choice but to carry on without them."

Hoping to delay the expedition longer, Joshua offered a thin excuse "Should we not wait for our good friends?"

Placing the old netting inside the stern along with a smelly sack of fish parts, Peter turned to Joshua. "Young man, the fish will not allow us to wait for the appointed hour."

As Peter pushed the worn-looking vessel toward the water, he heard the voice of his brother.

"Here they come!" shouted Andrew as he waved at the approaching pair. "Please hurry, or I fear my brother may leave without you."

Joshua saw the two laughing upon hearing Andrew's warning. Peter stood muttering to himself as John and James finally arrived.

"What's all the rush, Peter?" asked John.

"The fish are growing impatient with us." Peter's comment drew a laugh from all as they joined him in pushing the worn vessel out to sea.

"Jump in, Joshua, and grab the oars. The rest of us will follow," said Andrew.

One by one the brothers piled in as the boat rocked from side to side. Unsure what exactly to do with the oars, Joshua was relieved when Andrew sat beside him and took command.

"It's very simple, Joshua. We just sit facing the shoreline and push the water back with the oars and then we lift the oars out of the water like this and do it all over again until we find a spot to cast our nets. Once you learn to become a master rower, you are halfway to becoming a true fisherman."

"What is the other half?"

"Learning to go where the fish are," interjected Peter. "We must trust the gulls to guide us to the fish. This is what made me such a superior fisherman, my son. I allowed the gulls to lead me to the treasure."

Joshua could see the knowing glances of bemusement shared between the others as Peter expounded on his fishing prowess. As Peter continued, Joshua considered the present moment. It was truly peaceful gliding atop the sea as the blue waters sparkled in the morning sun. Gazing at the distant shoreline as the day lazily unfolded, he understood what made these men devote their entire lives to the sea. But as the aged bones of this vessel creaked and groaned with each rolling swell, Joshua looked to the others for reassurance that all was well as they rowed further out to sea.

"We have been doing this all our lives, Joshua," said Andrew as he sensed their young friend's growing unease. "Truthfully, we are probably more comfortable out on the water than we are on the land. Isn't that right, my brother?"

"You may well be right, Andrew," said Peter as he took a moment to dreamily scan the sea in all directions and gaze at the gulls circling high above. "Welcome to our true home, Joshua, here in the middle of the mighty Galilee. Let's cast our nets here and allow these old boards of the sea to carry us into the glorious catch that waits for us below."

Instead of the well-practiced tossing of the net upon the water, James and John now wrestled with something at the bottom of the stern. "Is the net caught on the old wood?" asked Andrew.

"We have a giant leak back here!" cried John as he and James began to desperately bail water with their hands.

Seeing the panicked looks on all the faces of these lifelong fishermen immediately brought Joshua to a level of fear he had never experienced.

"What do we do?" screamed Joshua.

"Everything possible, because our lives depend on it," declared Andrew as he threw the large bag of fish parts overboard. "Anything we don't need we throw into the sea to lighten our load."

"Throw out the fish nets, Joshua," yelled Peter while furiously rowing back to the shore.

Joshua saw the pile of nets at the stern where John and James continued to bail water at a feverous pace. Nearly falling overboard as he unsteadily made his way to the stern, Joshua fell face first into the submerged nets. With great effort, he strained to pull the heavy netting out of the cold pool of water and heave it over the side. Gasping for air, Joshua peered into the sea below and watched the netting swirl into the depths. To his amazement, he observed this heavy pile of old netting magically transform into a broad underwater canopy. It then slowly rose to the surface and gently spread itself out over the sky-blue waters of the Galilee. The brothers never saw their once-treasured nets drift farther behind as they fought feverishly to save themselves from sinking into the depths of the Galilee.

Joshua quickly turned his attention to Peter and Andrew, who each gripped a single oar and were furiously rowing through the water looking as grim as he had ever seen them. "Are we going to die out here?" cried Joshua. No response was uttered and then came a glorious shout from the stern.

"Throwing out the heavy nets has tremendously helped our cause, men," declared James. "Unless this old boat gives itself completely to the sea, there is a very good chance we're going to make it back to shore."

James's declaration prompted a hearty cheer from all aboard as Joshua nearly wept with relief.

"Joshua, please go to the bow and have a seat. Then our mighty vessel will be in perfect balance for her last voyage home," said Peter with a tinge of sadness in his voice.

As Joshua viewed the shoreline come closer, a silence fell over the boat. Now out of the imminent danger of sinking, Peter, Andrew, John, and James stared off across the sea. Gulls would occasionally swoop in, but quickly flew off when they discovered there were no fish aboard this vessel.

"So, Joshua," came the voice of Andrew from behind. "What did you think of your first day of fishing?"

At first there was silence as the crew considered the question posed by Andrew. But soon everyone on board, including Joshua, broke into uproarious laughter at their sorry situation.

Turning to face the brothers, Joshua solemnly cast his opinion. "If it is all right with you fine men, I have decided to stick to farming." More laughter followed his pronouncement.

"When did you arrive at this rather unsurprising decision?" asked a bemused John.

"The moment I realized that no matter who you are, the sea can swallow you into its depths without a care."

Joshua's dark assessment cast a pall over the brothers, who only a moment ago were making light over their hapless circumstances. The only sounds were the cries of gulls as they swooped past and mocked the boat as it returned with not merely empty nets but no nets at all. As the shoreline approached, Peter and Andrew relied on the current to bring them in and only dipped an oar into the water for occasional steering. The leaking water had risen to nearly ankle depth, but bailing had been all but abandoned as the cold water sloshed from stern to bow in rhythm with the gentle swells.

Still perched at the bow, Joshua gazed upon the daily commerce of Capernaum unfolding before him. As fishmongers actively bartered on the shore, he observed three camels packed high with boxes led by turbaned drivers.

"What are those camels carrying?" asked Joshua with his back to the brothers.

"Spices mostly," said Andrew. "They're on the way to Jerusalem from Syria."

Joshua scanned the busy shoreline for anything of interest as the sea-laden boat barely floated above the waterline. "Wait! Is that the Lord I see?" shouted Joshua excitedly, pointing to the spot where they pushed from the shore at dawn.

"Where?" demanded Peter. "I see nothing but your waving hand."

"He's right there sitting under the tree where your boat used to be."

"Oh yes, it is indeed the Lord," said Peter as he and the brothers began to wave enthusiastically. "I wish He didn't have to see us this way as utter failures."

Andrew then placed an arm over Peter. "It's all right, my brother. We could have died out on the sea today. I much prefer that we are living and ready to greet the Lord, even if we are wet and weary, and without fish."

31

THE WAY

U nlike many joyous occasions in the past when Jesus had returned to the brothers after being away for a considerable time, this reception had a different feel. In silence, Peter and Andrew pulled the broken vessel from the water as John and James pushed from the stern until the boat was well above the shoreline. The four men heaved the water-sodden boat over on top of the stony ground as sea water flowed back to the shore.

As the brothers sheepishly avoided Jesus while they tended to the fallen vessel, Joshua ran to greet the Lord with open arms.

"How did you know where to find us, Lord?"

"I was told Peter and Andrew carried fishing nets from their abodes. But I am curious what brought you here, Joshua?"

"The brothers wanted to teach me how to fish." Turning to see the four laboring over the boat, Joshua added, "but it did not go well."

"I can see that," said Jesus as he walked to the men. "My friends, the work of this boat is finished. Be glad that it brought you safely home. It is now time to leave the past behind and never look back."

Each brother quietly approached Jesus and was quickly drawn into a strong embrace from their Lord. "There is nothing to be ashamed of my friends. Leaving the past behind is hard and I know how fond you are of your former life, but the Kingdom of God is now upon you and your lives are no longer your own. The glory that awaits is beyond your understanding. Trust me when I tell you that the day is coming soon."

"We truly welcome the day your Kingdom reigns over all of Israel, but dear Lord, how long must we wait? It seems your enemies are drawing near and we see no soldiers by our side," lamented Peter.

"Your faith is weak, Peter. You still seek hope from the world, where only death awaits. I beseech you, my friend, to make up your mind. Do you belong with this tattered boat or are you with me and the angels of Heaven who will lead you to life everlasting? In the name of my Father who has sent me to this fallen world, I demand an answer from you Peter," thundered Jesus.

Joshua stood in silence with Andrew, James, and John as they witnessed Rabbi deliver a fiery rebuke to Peter. Given his deep love for both men, he was terribly unsettled by the moment. Joshua trembled as he desperately hoped that Peter would respond with a strong declaration of his faith to the Lord.

Although clearly shaken by Jesus' words, Peter held his head high and stared directly into the face of the Lord. "From the moment you called me from my working boat, my arms filled with nets, I knew that my life would never be the same. Dear Lord, I know without question that I am standing before the living Messiah."

As he often did with the brothers, Jesus placed both of his hands upon Peter's shoulders for reassurance and delivered a command that was linked to a promise. "Then, my dear friend, be the man I intend you to be, and you will see life everlasting."

A sense of relief came over Joshua as he watched Peter and the Lord embrace. Looking beyond them at the shoreline to the noisy exchange between traders and fishermen, not a soul took notice of the encounter between a lifelong fisherman and a man who claimed to be the living Christ.

Stepping before the others, Jesus produced a barley loaf and a handful of figs from inside his cloak. "I trust that you are hungry after your difficult day on the sea. Let us gather under the palm and break bread while we talk of where we go from here."

With the mood relaxed, Joshua felt free to ask questions of Jesus. "Where have you been, Lord? For days I have sought you, but you were nowhere to be found. There are times that I worry that your enemies have taken you away."

"You should never fear for Rabbi, Joshua," advised John as he pulled a piece from the barley loaf before passing it on. "We know the dangers that exist all around us, but your worries, my son, do not help the Lord as he carries on in these evil days."

John's words felt like an unfair rebuke to Joshua. He knew at times the brothers were dismayed when he expressed his fears, but giving voice to his anxious thoughts often eased his worries, especially when it came to what he considered Jesus' unwise and at times foolish actions.

"John, you must understand that the young man's worries will never hinder what the Father has called me to do." Looking to Joshua, Jesus continued, "Young man, do not allow your fears to overtake you, for nothing good will come of it. I say to all of you once again, the Kingdom of Heaven is here; therefore, we must face the path set before us with complete abandon, for there is glory to behold."

"Please, Rabbi, tell us what path is set before us now. Surely you do not intend for us to journey to Syria or Egypt, where you are unknown," said Andrew.

"I am the only true way,[5] Andrew. Surely you must know this by now. Trust in me as we walk this perilous path together. There will come a time when all the world will know of my Father's Kingdom, but many will choose not to enter, for them there is only death." Jesus paused as he gazed intently at Peter, Andrew, John, and James before again speaking. "My Father again calls me to Jerusalem. I appeal to you, my friends, to follow me to this great city on the hill. We will celebrate the Passover together and I will glorify His name. A glory that will last day upon day forever."

Before any brother could speak, Joshua broke in. "Dear Lord, I have faithfully looked after all the brothers' dwellings when you have journeyed to Jerusalem in the past and I have earned coins for the treasury while you all have been in this great city which my eyes have never seen, yet . . ."

"As you wish, my son," said Jesus, cutting Joshua off before he could say another word.

"But you did not hear what I was about to ask."

"Oh, I most assuredly did. I say that the time has arrived for you to come up to Jerusalem and see what the Father has called me to do. But you must gather your courage, my son, for the enemy is near and there is no escape for the faint of heart."

"But if there is so much danger awaiting you in this city, why must you go at all?" protested Joshua.

The brothers looked on in silence as Joshua continued his questioning of Rabbi. Although they did not truly understand when Jesus spoke of his Father, they knew without a doubt that their destiny awaited them in Jerusalem. They were prepared to follow the Lord no matter what the cost.

---

5 Jesus saith unto Him, "I am the Way, the Truth, and the Life: no one cometh unto the Father but by me." John 14: 6 (KJV)

"Let me ask you a question, my son. If your father, who you loved, gave you a command, would you choose to ignore his request?"

"Never, my Lord, for my father always knew what was best."

Jesus said nothing further, knowing the young man realized he had answered his own question.

"Lord, I propose that we prepare to leave at the break of dawn in ten days' time," said Peter.

"So be it," said their Rabbi.

There was much discussion among the brothers as they walked away from their fateful meeting under the palm tree by the dilapidated boat. A sense of renewed energy prevailed as they excitedly made plans for notifying the others and gathering the necessary supplies. The brothers knew the challenges of preparing for such a journey. They expected that large crowds would be drawn to Jesus as word spread of his sojourn to Jerusalem. They also understood that at any time riots could break out if the religious elders continued with their growing charges against the Lord for what they considered to be his blasphemy of the sacred texts. Perhaps the greatest unknowns of all were the potential actions of Jesus himself. Chaos might come from Jesus' words alone. Many times the brothers had witnessed the confusion caused when Jesus changed course and sought a destination known only to him. There were potential life or death consequences facing the brothers as they followed Jesus. Still, in their hearts and minds, they would not have it any other way.

As Joshua kept pace alongside the brothers, he too shared in the excitement of the journey ahead and called on each of them to tell him more about the stunning temple that rested high on the hill. But as the brothers continued their walk through the bustling village of Capernaum, Joshua became aware that Jesus was no longer with them. It would seem that during all the steady banter, He had simply slipped away.

It took the remainder of the day for all the brothers to learn of Jesus' plan to again journey to Jerusalem. As these men, known by the villagers as Jesus' closest friends, moved across the city collecting supplies, word traveled fast that Jesus would soon be on the move. In the coming days, Capernaum brimmed with excitement as the streets overflowed with men, women, and children who intended to journey with their Messiah.

Although Jesus was nowhere to be found, his presence was everywhere as followers in the thousands gathered on foot and in donkey pulled carts, awaiting word that Jesus was beginning his journey to Jerusalem. Day and night, cries of hope could be heard throughout the village from countless pilgrims who claimed that Jesus would rescue them from their lives of destitution.

Standing in the doorway of Andrew's humble rock-and-timber dwelling on the night before their departure, Joshua quietly watched as a noisy crowd began to swell on the street below. Although he had not seen Jesus in days, he fervently hoped that the Lord was near and His journey would begin as planned. He feared the patience of these weary-looking pilgrims was wearing thin.

The plan had seemed so simple as Joshua heard John and Peter explain it to the other brothers. On the appointed day, they would gather with Jesus in front of Peter's abode at the earliest hint of dawn. They each would carry a skin of fresh water, a blanket, and enough food to sustain them for the next two or three days. Knowing their food and water would be depleted well before coming into Jerusalem was not of immediate concern to the brothers. They understood that traveling with Rabbi called them to cling to their faith for whatever may lay ahead.

Joshua could no longer watch as the crowd steadily grew outside Andrew's door. Turning away, he walked deeper into Andrew's dwelling where his friend's snoring penetrated the dark space. He wondered how

Andrew could sleep so soundly while just outside his door the world seemed ready to come apart. To ease his anxious mind, Joshua again examined the items he would carry.

Having counted everything for the last time, Joshua gave in to his fatigue. He stretched out on the empty sleep pallet adjacent to Andrew and covered himself with the blanket he would take on the much-anticipated journey. The sound of Andrew's snoring nearly blocked out the chaotic noise from outside, giving Joshua a sense of sorely needed calm. For if Andrew could sleep so deeply at a time like this, perhaps he could allow his own heart to cease its pounding.

Joshua felt a hand on his shoulder and immediately opened his eyes. Andrew's whiskery face was staring from above. "The time has come, my friend. We will go to my brother's house where the others will be gathered," said Andrew with the sound of sleep still in his voice.

Sitting up, Joshua asked the only question that mattered to him. "Has the Lord returned?"

"He has indeed. My brother was here only a moment ago to tell me Rabbi is now with us and ready to begin our journey." Andrew was silent as he stuffed his belongings into his pack. He then met Joshua's eyes with a sobering gaze. "You know, my son, that you do not have to make this journey. For you have nothing to prove to any of us."

Joshua raised himself from the sleep pallet and faced Andrew with a forceful look. "There is nothing that will keep me from following the Lord on this journey. Although I live in constant fear of what may happen to him, at this very moment I have never felt so alive."

"Then we best be on our way, my son, for the Lord awaits."

32

"THEY HAVE NO FOOD"

S tepping into the pre-dawn darkness, Joshua remained several paces behind Andrew as they made their way to the congested road below. Joshua observed that many of those along the road slept on the bare ground with only thin coverings to protect them. He forced himself to look away from the carts overflowing with people, their disfigured limbs over the sides, unable to walk and struggling to sleep.

Although deeply moved by the dire circumstances of so many, he pretended not to notice as they silently passed. To keep from staring at the countless despairing faces, Joshua busied himself with his blanket, always wrapping it tighter around his shoulders to fend off the sharp chill of the damp air. He wondered how this unending swarm of men, women, and children could endure much longer without seeing the man they fervently believed would be their king.

Andrew looked behind and motioned for Joshua to come beside him. As Joshua approached, he placed an arm over his shoulder and spoke just above a whisper. "Do not say a word when you see Rabbi and our friends outside my brother's dwelling. Most of these people would not know the Lord if they saw him. Peter will be watching for us as we walk past. We will keep walking and they will quietly blend in with the others and follow us from behind."

"How will we know if they are following us?" asked Joshua.

"I promise you, it will not take long to know that the Lord is in our midst."

Just as Andrew predicted, Peter stood only a few paces ahead with the brothers. Although Joshua could not identify Jesus as he and Andrew walked past, he did observe a look of recognition between Peter and his brother. Joshua's long-awaited journey to Jerusalem was underway.

He wondered what his family would think of him if they could see him now. Here he was, the boy who felt so lost after the sudden death of his father, now leading the way to Jerusalem with the man many believed to be the future King of Israel following behind. Never could he have imagined such a thing happening to him. It did not seem so long ago that he walked side by side with his father as they tended to their goats. All he ever wanted then was to grow into the man his father was and work their farm together. How his life had changed, thought Joshua.

Looking behind, he saw Andrew talking with several men. Seeing Joshua staring at him, he offered a slight wave as if to say, keep moving. Gazing further behind, Joshua could hardly believe what the first light of day revealed. Stretching as far back as he could see was a congested line of sojourners all slowly moving forward. Most of them were on foot, including countless children who ran alongside the endless procession. He observed women with babies wrapped close to their chests. Still others were crammed into carts. Those traveling in carts were the sick and the crippled who were unable to walk on their own. Yet these were the ones who possessed the deepest convictions. With unwavering faith in the man they believed was their Messiah, they clung to the desperate hope that they would be healed by the mere touch of his hand.

Joshua continued to trudge ahead, but now many surrounded him along the path. As the sun burned off the early morning chill, he removed his blanket and stuffed it in his satchel. He took a portion of his barley loaf to satisfy his growing hunger. A woman with two young children saw Joshua's bread. She gently placed a hand on Joshua's arm. "Can you please spare a piece of your bread for my children?" she softly pleaded.

"Did you not come prepared for such a journey?" Joshua sharply replied.

"We have traveled from far away and I have nothing more," said the woman.

Joshua could feel his resentment rising as he reached into his pack and broke off a sizable piece for the mother and her children, leaving him with only the small piece. Upon receiving the bread, the woman silently bowed and quickly retreated with her children. As Joshua resumed his pace, he felt a tap on his back. Quickly turning around, he was stunned to see an old woman who was the mirror image of Mother. The woman spoke no words as she gazed upon Joshua's face. He immediately reached deep into his satchel and retrieved the remaining piece of bread, placing it in her outstretched hands.

"Wait, I have more," he said while turning away to pull a fig from the bottom. Joshua held it out at once, but the old woman was no longer there. Spinning in every direction as crowds passed him by, he saw no one who looked like Mother. Holding the lone fig in his hand, he realized he possessed no more provisions than most who were on this journey. The thought of the woman who resembled Mother brought a smile to his face.

Although his food was nearly gone and Jerusalem remained impossibly far away, he had a deep feeling that this was where he belonged.

Looking back again, Joshua saw that Andrew was straining to make his way through the crush of people and come closer to him. Judging by his expression, he could tell something was wrong. Finally coming alongside, Andrew spoke in a low voice that Joshua strained to hear. "They have no food. Most of these people have been walking for days and they have little to eat or drink. They cannot go on like this much longer or things will get very bad."

"What can we do?" asked Joshua.

"I want you to go back until you see my brother. Rabbi will be nearby. Surely, they know that these people will starve unless something is done soon. We must have a plan before nightfall. I will let others pass and wait for you, Joshua. Now go, we have little time."

"But what if they are nowhere to be found?" asked Joshua as his fear began to mount.

"Trust me, you will find them. Now please, be on your way."

Joshua had not taken notice of the narrow canyon when he was moving forward near the front of the procession. But now he struggled to move against the flow of sojourners as they made their way through the tight passage. Frantically, he looked for any sign of Jesus or the brothers. The air was sour as he squeezed between men and women who had been traveling for days. Panic rose in Joshua's chest as he recalled the day he was trampled to the ground as villagers rushed toward Jesus at the well. Struggling to breathe, Joshua pushed people out of the way as he fought for air. He was soon stopped by two men who threw him down hard.

"Have you gone mad?" shouted one of the men with a knee to Joshua's chest. A cluster of onlookers quickly gathered.

Looking terrified at the thin-faced man who hovered over him, Joshua gasped. "I am frightened by crowds."

"Then this is not the place for you to be, young man." Removing his knee from Joshua's chest, the man continued to hold Joshua to the ground with his outstretched hand. "Why do you run the other way?"

"I am searching for a friend. His name is Peter, and he is with the man you call Messiah."

Turning to those who closely gathered, the man said with a laugh, "This frightened young man says he is looking for the Messiah." Derisive laughter followed as they mocked Joshua lying on the ground.

"Listen here, young man, we are all searching for the man who performs the signs and wonders, but he is nowhere to be found. Don't insult us with your lies, for my patience is wearing thin," said the man holding him down.

"Get on your feet, Joshua," came a familiar voice.

"Peter, is that you?"

Stepping before the onlookers, a strong arm reached down and roughly shoved the man away.

Pulling Joshua to his feet, Peter delivered a command. "Never let anyone hold you down, son, never."

"How dare you shove me aside!" declared the man as he prepared to confront the stranger.

Peter grasped the man's tunic and pulled him close. "Trust me when I tell you, I am not a man you wish to quarrel with." With a swift shove, he released the man's tunic.

The man stared back at Peter as if he were thinking of confronting him further, before thinking better of it and vanishing back into the crowd.

"Thank you, Peter," said Joshua as the two edged their way forward with the rest.

"Why was that man holding you down?"

"I was moving against the crowd through the narrow passage in search of you and the Lord and I panicked. That's all I want to say about it."

"As you wish, Joshua, but never forget what I said to you."

Joshua nodded but said nothing more, feeling ashamed that Peter had to come to his aid.

"Now, why were you seeking Rabbi and me?"

"Andrew sent me to tell you that most of these people have nothing further to eat or drink. Surely the Lord does not want these sojourners who have traveled so far seeking his blessing to perish along the way."

"I can assure you, Joshua, that the Lord knows the danger that exists for us all."

"Where is the Lord?"

"Rabbi and our friends have left the road to gather in an empty field behind us. It is what I have come to tell you and my brother. Let us find Andrew and go quickly to the field where the Lord and our friends await."

"But what will happen to these people who hunger and thirst?" Joshua cried.

"They will persist," assured Peter.

"But what of their hunger?"

"That, young man, is in the hands of the Lord."

33

HEAVEN
AND EARTH

Walking alongside Andrew and Peter, Joshua was the first to speak. "If many die on this journey, will it not be the fault of the Lord?" Silence followed as the three moved further away from the Jerusalem Road toward where they hoped to find Jesus and the remaining brothers. Meanwhile, the throngs of sojourners wearily kept to the road and continued to trudge ahead, driven by the belief that their Messiah was coming to them.

"There will be those who will say that the man who claims to be King of the Jews has led many to their death. But these words will be spoken by Rabbi's enemies," said Peter.

"I am not ready to say that many will die on this journey," said Andrew. "Let us not forget that the Lord is with us, Joshua." Pointing to a green field of grass in the distance, he cried out, "I think I see them! It must be the Lord, as many people are leaving the road to gather by the cluster of trees amidst the grass."

"If there are trees growing, then there must be a spring nearby," declared Joshua. He broke into a run. With his back to the brothers, he joyfully shouted. "I'll tell the Lord you are right behind me."

As Joshua drew closer, he saw that the once-small gathering was growing rapidly as people left the Jerusalem Road in massive numbers. He feared that Jesus would soon be in danger if they thought that he had caused the widespread hunger and thirst.

As Joshua entered the fray, he could not believe his eyes. There before him were countless people holding pieces of fish as they walked past. Many others were spread out on the ground sharing loaves of barley and a bounty of dried fish with their families.[6] How can this be? wondered Joshua. Surely this is a dream.

Standing still in the midst of this unbelievable sight, he saw John providing fish and bread to a mother and her children. "John, what is happening? Where in the world did all this bread and fish come from?"

Smiling as he saw the incredulous look on Joshua's face, John tried to explain. "There was a young lad who brought several cooked fish and a few loaves of barley to Rabbi." As John spoke, he placed a generous portion of fish in Joshua's hands, saying, "You must eat too, my son."

"This cannot be real," insisted Joshua as he placed a tiny piece into his mouth and slowly chewed. Realizing at once that what he tasted was true, he gazed across the field in wonder as more people continued to come to this magical space to be fed. Turning again to John, Joshua said, "Who could ever know there was such magic as this?"

"This is not magic, my friend, but the work of the Lord."

------

6 Feeding The Four Thousand. Mark 8:1-9 (KJV)

Pleading to John for an explanation he could understand, Joshua begged, "Surely there is more you can tell me."

"When it comes to the Lord, not all things can be explained. But this you must understand: with the Lord all things are possible. I urge you to walk around and see for yourself the beauty all around you and know that it is all from the hand of the Lord." John stepped away from Joshua and vanished into the crowd.

Joshua remained still as he slowly ate the fish that John placed in his hand. He wondered why he did not feel the joy that was so abundant all about him. He thought of his mother and how wonderful it would be if she were here with his sisters. Uncle Cyrus and the mighty Journey also came to mind. He could see his uncle being overjoyed and Journey romping happily about with a large fish protruding from his mouth. Joshua understood the reason for his lack of joy in the midst of this wonder. He was not with the people he loved most and therefore was unable to share the beauty that was before him.

As Joshua suffered his self-pitying thoughts, a man who looked vaguely familiar approached. "I may be wrong, but are you not the young man I pushed to the ground and held down on the crowded road so others could have a good laugh?"

After a pause, Joshua held his head high and said, "What if I was this young man you speak of?"

"Then I owe you a very sincere apology. I was wrong to have acted in such a way and I beg for your forgiveness."

Stunned by such an outward act of grace, Joshua was quick to respond. "I of course accept your apology, but please understand I too was causing a bit of mayhem on the road."

"No need to explain, for I was truly at fault," said the man. "But I must ask, who was that man who came to your defense?"

With a self-conscious smile, Joshua replied. "A very protective friend. His name is Peter."

"I must admit, he was quite impressive." Facing Joshua closer, he continued. "A friend like that is truly hard to find. You are a very lucky man." He then broke off a generous portion of his barley loaf and handed it to Joshua. "Please accept this bread as a token of my apology. Be well, my friend."

As the man was about to leave, Joshua placed a hand on his shoulder. "Thank you. May we meet again someday." With a friendly nod, he turned and walked away.

With his spirits lifted by the unexpected encounter, Joshua set off to explore the wonders that surrounded him. As he wandered about, he felt a growing connection to the countless strangers he passed. Many greeted him like an old friend. Children bumped his side as they played and chased after one another with screams of delight. But for Joshua, the most extraordinary sight of all was the abundance of fish and bread enjoyed by thousands of joyful men, women, and children leisurely spread across the grassy plain.

Seeing that his water skin was empty, he strolled to the distant palms where he hoped to find a pool of fresh water. Along the way he marveled at the never-ending scene of good cheer and welcoming smiles. As he drew closer to the palms, he saw that the crowds grew thicker, and his expectations rose that water was nearby. But there was something else in the air that Joshua could not help but notice. Where there was laughter and lively conversation before, a hush now fell over the crowd. Faces no longer showed joy but rather a sense of being held by a spell. At once he knew he was near the Lord.

Joshua made his way to a nearby palm by the clear spring and filled his water skin. He noticed that from this position he could easily gaze upon Jesus. It was the first time he had seen Jesus since the day he announced to the brothers from the banks of the Sea of Galilee that they would journey to Jerusalem. Looking much the same in his worn garments, Joshua watched as Jesus sat upon a large rock and spoke softly to the gathering before him. Although Joshua could not hear his words, on occasion Jesus would rise and place his hands on the shoulders of some listeners. Joshua had no doubt that lives were forever changed as those fortunate few came away in tears of joy following an intimate moment with their Messiah.

Unable to remain hidden any longer, Joshua gradually worked his way to the front of the quiet assembly. Any moment he would be face to face with Jesus and he grew anxious. But as soon as their eyes met, he felt his heart melt as Jesus swept him up in a welcoming embrace.

"My dear Joshua, it is so good to see you," declared Jesus.

Struggling to speak as he stared at the ground, Joshua finally raised his head and asked a single question. "Is this Heaven, Lord?"

Jesus studied his face. "What do you see around you, my son?"

"I see people at peace who no longer hunger or thirst. But my Lord, how can this be?"

"I have been sent by the Father, Joshua. I am the Bread of Life."[7]

"I wish I could understand your words, Lord."

"I promise that one day you will know far more, but the time has not yet come. What you see all around you is but a glimpse of the world to come. Please take heart, Joshua, for the Kingdom of God is close at hand."

Joshua was about to speak again, but felt a hard push to his back. Spinning around, he faced a frail old man whose eyes had no color. A young woman held tightly to his arm.

"I'm so sorry, my father cannot see what lies directly ahead." In that moment, Jesus came from behind and gently placed his arms around the

---

7 And Jesus said unto them, I am the bread of life: He that cometh to be Me shall never hunger; and he that believeth on Me shall never thirst. John 6: 35 (KJV)

blind man's head and held him closely to his chest. Knowing his time had passed, Joshua walked away, listening to the intimate sounds of the man's weeping and Jesus' comforting words. The time had come, thought Joshua, to seek out the company of the brothers. This had been a day like no other and he was anxious to be among them.

As the day grew longer, Joshua wondered how it might end. There were still countless people everywhere he gazed, enjoying the glorious day. *How long will they remain? Will Jesus lead them back to Capernaum or are we all to endlessly bask in this land of plenty?*

He caught a glimpse of Peter and Andrew not far ahead. Andrew carried a large woven basket into which he and his brother tossed the boney remains of fish cast aside by the multitudes. "Greetings, my friends," said Joshua. "Have you ever witnessed anything like this before?"

Joshua saw a look pass between the brothers before Andrew replied. "We have indeed. It was some time ago when an even greater multitude of followers gathered by the Sea of Galilee to hear the Lord. Then, as now, an abundance of bread and fish was provided to the hungry before we crossed the sea." Looking to Peter, Andrew asked, "Is there more you wish to share with Joshua?"

"Perhaps another time, my brother," said Peter as he picked up fragments of fish and placed them in the basket. Looking to Joshua, he continued. "There are many stories where the Lord has opened our eyes to things we never before imagined."

"Like this day?" asked Joshua.

"Like this day indeed. But now, my good friend, there is work to be done, for the glory of this day will not linger much longer.

Needing no further encouragement, Joshua joined the brothers. They continued the humbling task of collecting the remains of fish that lay scattered upon the grass throughout the lush field.

As the brightness of the glorious day began to fade, Joshua saw that many placed their collection of bones into the baskets as well. Over time, Joshua caught glimpses of all twelve brothers who had separated into pairs, carrying a basket between them. He looked on as they not only filled their baskets with fragments of fish but also carried on fruitful conversations, often ending with warm embraces.

As the sun began its fiery decent, soft clouds the color of faded roses billowed high in the western sky. All who had gathered from villages throughout Galilee and beyond and had celebrated their newfound abundance now toiled as one to clear the field. A sense of contentment and peace fell upon those assembled as they labored, knowing the Messiah and future King of Israel had walked among them.

Taking it upon himself, Joshua carried the overflowing baskets to the edge of the spring where Jesus once sat. Here he emptied each basket to form a growing pile and returned them to the brothers. By the time the first stars began to glitter, Joshua had built a pile of bones far beyond the size of any man. Inspired to set the pile ablaze, he told the brothers of his plan. He received their enthusiastic support as they neared completion of cleaning the field.

Returning to the spring, he saw that fallen palm fronds had been added to the pile and, as planned, a small blaze drew the multitudes to the brilliant display. By nightfall, the hill of discarded bones and palm fronds had transformed into a towering blaze sending countless embers into the darkness, where they vanished into the glittering heavens.

Joshua watched from afar as many drew close to the fire and simply gazed at the mesmerizing flames. He was soon joined by all the brothers as they too were captured by the spectacle of such a majestic blaze against the blackness of the night.

"Where is the Lord?" asked Joshua of the brothers as they lay on the grass nearby.

"He has walked far from this crowd where he can be alone and pray," said John as he spread his blanket next to his brother James.

"But what will happen to all these people who followed him to this place?"

"They are already moving on," said James as he reclined with his out-stretched hand holding his head above the ground. "Many will return to their villages with stories of the signs and wonders they witnessed on this day. By the first light, most will have deserted this field, but you can be assured they will leave with peaceful hearts, for many have been healed and all have been truly blessed."

Stillness fell upon James and Joshua as they gazed upon the spectacle before them. Joshua broke the stillness. "What happened here today, James?"

"I am not sure I can say, my friend, but of one thing I am most certain: We are in the presence of God."

As the far-off hum of countless conversations continued, Joshua finally gathered the nerve to ask his good friend a question that had been on his mind for a long time. "Do you believe that Jesus is God?"

James sat up and faced Joshua. They stared at one another for some time before James offered a response. "Rabbi has often shared with us that he has been sent by his Father. Although there are those who wish to kill him when they hear him speak this way, I choose to believe this with all my heart, Joshua. It is why I will follow him to the end of my days."

"No matter what happens?"

"No matter what."

James lowered his head to the ground and pulled his blanket up to his chin. "We all have questions, my friend, and I believe those will never end. But now, you must rest, for I know you are as weary as I am. You can also trust that Peter will be shaking us all awake before there is even a hint of the coming dawn." James turned his back to Joshua to signal that their nighttime talk was finished.

For the longest time, Joshua sat and stared at the distant flames as the brothers, now all his dear friends, lay fast asleep. He finally laid his head on the soft grass and thought of the night that Mother spent her last day on earth laying on his bed of sticks at Cyrus's lonely outpost. He vividly recalled her constant foretelling that "I Am is coming." His last thought before sleep had its way came with a whispered laugh to himself. *I Am is not coming. I Am is here.*

34

THREE MONTHS LATER

As he walked along the main road of the tiny village of Bethany in the early morning, Joshua looked down at the new sandals gracing his well-traveled feet. They felt perfect, thought Joshua, wondering who left them beside the old, tattered pair that his uncle had lovingly crafted for him. It could have been anyone since he had often complained that it was easier for him to walk barefoot than try to squeeze his feet into sandals he had so long ago outgrown.

Joshua never imagined that the journey to Jerusalem would take so long. It had been a challenging trek since that impossible day when thousands of Jesus' followers on the verge of starvation were fed an abundance of bread and fish. He was told many times by the brothers that to follow Rabbi often took courage and incredible patience. Now he understood the true meaning of their words.

Many days they found themselves in villages far off the road to Jerusalem where men and women clothed in rags would beg Jesus to bless them and their children. It was in these desolate villages where Jesus seemed most at home. There, next to a fire, he would joyfully tell stories of the Kingdom of God late into the night to eager, uplifted faces. As time passed, more people joined Jesus and his friends on the road. Among them was a diminutive woman named Mary. She was accompanied by other women who clearly adored Jesus.

As Joshua continued his walk through Bethany, he fondly recalled the time he was introduced to Mary as they departed one of the nameless villages.

"Joshua, there is someone who would like to meet you," said Andrew.

Coming to his feet, Joshua saw a tiny woman who he noticed once before now standing beside Andrew. She wore a faint smile as she nodded to Joshua.

"Her name is Mary. She is Rabbi's mother," said Andrew.

"It is my honor to meet you," said Joshua as he nervously bowed before her.

"It is indeed a pleasure to know you, young man. May I ask you a question?"

"Of course, anything you wish."

"How did someone as young as you come to journey with my son and his friends, for they are so much older?"

Sharing a glance with Andrew before responding to Mary's question, Joshua answered her. "I believe I forced my way into their good graces."

"Where is your home, my son?"

"I come from a farm outside a small village in Samaria."

"So, you are a Samaritan?" she asked.

"I am indeed."

"But you are so young. I am sure you have family who miss you terribly."

"As I miss them."

"Yet here you are."

As Mary was about to leave with Andrew, Joshua stated, "So, I under-stand you were with your son at the wedding when he turned the filthy water to wine."

Facing Joshua, Mary replied, "I was indeed." After a pause, her face broke into a broad smile. "It was a truly wonderful wedding." She walked a few steps away before turning back. "We must talk again. Until then, be well, my son."

As Joshua walked through the village, he understood what a privilege it had been to have special time with the mother of Jesus. He wished he had asked more questions. Since that unexpected visit, Mary often disappeared into the many people who surrounded Jesus wherever he walked. Joshua went generally unnoticed by the newcomers as they sought out the company of the brothers.

The growing flock often retreated from Jesus during the times he was confronted by religious authorities. Two days ago, a high-ranking temple official clothed in a clean white tunic traveled from Jerusalem with his guards to charge Jesus with the crime of blasphemy and arrest him. However, the official's deep hatred for Jesus grew quickly out of control. As the temple priest drew his angry tirade to a close, he paused and without any provocation spat into the face of Jesus. He then calmly turned to his guards and ordered them to bind "this so-called Messiah."

Joshua was beyond stunned to witness such a vile act against the one he treasured above all others. In the next breath, he heard the undeniable roar of Peter as he lunged forward and brought the temple priest crashing to the ground. This prompted the guards to furiously descend upon Peter and pry him off the priest. Pulling him by the hair with one foot pressed into his back, one guard swiftly drew a long knife from his tunic and placed it against Peter's taut neck. The other guard looked to their temple official and waited for his command.

"How dare you put your hands on me?" cried the priest as he rose to his feet and urgently brushed the dirt from his once-spotless tunic. Approaching Peter, he delivered the order. "Finish him."

A voice that made the ground tremble shouted out, "In the name of the Father of Heaven who has sent Me, release this man!" commanded Jesus. Ignoring the official's demands to "do no such thing," the guards, shaken by Jesus' powerful command, abruptly backed away from Peter. Turning to the priest, Jesus spoke directly. "Trust me when I tell you, you will have your time with me. But now you must go."

Joshua did not move as he watched the temple official slowly turn to the villagers, who stood by in stunned silence. Many covered their mouths in shock as he cursed them. "This man who you so adore is a liar and a fraud. One day you will know, my friends, how blind you have been. And when that day comes, may you feel the shame you so richly deserve." Looking no further at Jesus, the priest walked away in the direction from which he had come as the guards marched behind him.

It was clear to Joshua that the confrontations with Jesus were becoming more threatening as they drew closer to Jerusalem. He sensed a growing discomfort among the brothers. He was deeply troubled to see the men he so admired now uncertain of their walk with Jesus. One time when seeing

James visibly upset as he walked alone, Joshua approached and pleaded with him to share his grief. As they walked together, James finally spoke to his young friend. "Rabbi is saying that he will soon be going to a place where we cannot follow. But that he will send someone to help us."

"Surely he will not journey alone," wondered Joshua.

"Ever since that day when Rabbi called upon me to leave everything behind and follow him, I knew with all my heart and soul that He was the one. Yet now he says the day is coming when He will leave us behind, and it breaks my heart."

"What do you believe is causing the Lord to talk this way? Do you think He is about to die?"

As James contemplated his reply, the only sound came from their slow steps upon the narrow village road that meandered through Bethany. Finally, James responded, "I have never heard Rabbi speak of his own death. But I do know when He began to tell of going where we could not follow."

Joshua came to a stop. "Please tell me."

"Soon after we encountered the Romans in Jericho."

Just hearing James speak of Jericho and the Romans filled Joshua with dismay. Not for the obvious danger they faced, but for the hope that seemed to spill from his soul on that fateful day. *He vividly recalled entering the large village of Jericho and seeing Roman solders for the first time. It felt like they were waiting for Jesus and his gathering to arrive. Joshua was spellbound as two guards adorned in shiny helmets and glistening body armor came out of nowhere atop majestic dark horses. They promptly circled them as they approached the village.*

Joshua's eyes fixed on the golden handles of their swords that slapped smartly against their sides. They looked down in disgust at the gathering of weary men and women dressed in worn garments and slowly shook their heads. He remembered Andrew's urgent words as he spoke under his breath,

"Stop looking at them and do not say a word. If they address you, simply nod your head and stare at the ground."

As the Romans, atop their horses, took pleasure in scattering the crowd in every direction, he heard them speak sharply in a foreign tongue. No one responded. Slowly the guards laughed as they stared down at Jesus who had stepped forward from the frightened assembly. In a voice filled with mockery, one guard spewed words that were understood by all. "So, you are the King of the Jews." Turning to his fellow soldier, he declared, "Behold the King!" Joshua fought to keep his eyes cast downward until he heard them ride away and the sound of their derisive laughter faded into the noise of the village.

On that day, for the first time since Joshua began his journey with the brothers, a seed of doubt was planted in his soul.

35

GLORY
AND TERROR

Without question, Joshua's favorite hour in Bethany was after everyone was down for the night. Spreading his blanket atop the highest slope in the village, he gazed in awe at the shining temple that towered so high above the city of Jerusalem. After all this time listening to so many tales of this magical city, he could scarcely believe that it now lay before him. The majesty of the temple captured his soul. Never had he viewed a building so impossibly massive, nor had he gazed upon something so brilliant against the darkness of the night. For Joshua, the temple was by far the most beautiful sight his eyes ever beheld.

When Jesus spoke of the Kingdom of God, surely he must have been speaking of this glorious sight, thought Joshua. Why else would Jesus be leading so many here? Soon we will enter the heavenly kingdom rising above Jerusalem and be delivered into the wonderous mystery that awaits us all. But why then, he thought, do so many authorities of Jerusalem and this magnificent temple despise Jesus? For some time, Joshua had witnessed the venomous looks Jesus received from religious leaders who savagely confronted him with outrageous charges. Now at the outskirts of this magical city, it felt that a breaking point was coming.

As Joshua wrestled with his disturbing thoughts, his eyes were diverted below to a small figure carrying a torch. It seemed late to Joshua for someone to be walking alone outside the village. The longer he gazed at this figure, it became clear that the carrier of the torch was coming to him. But who could this be, he wondered. The figure cloaked in a dark tunic was too small to be one of the brothers. Was it an older child coming to him for help?

Joshua rose to his feet to receive the unknown caller, but as the torch illuminated the person's face, he knew at once the identity of his mysterious visitor.

"Mother Mary, what an honor it is to be graced by your presence." Knowing that a visit from the mother of Jesus at this late hour was highly unusual, he asked, "Is everything all right?".

"All is well, my son. But I have come to you to share a disturbing dream I had tonight about you."

Trying his best to convey calmness in the face of such an admission, he invited her to sit and recount her dream to him.

"It was not a long vision, but it upset me so that I felt I should come tell you about it right away."

Joshua remained silent and waited for Mary to tell of her dream as the beat of his heart quickened.

"It was late at night and dark like it is now," Mary began. "There was not a star in the heavens nor light from the moon. Out of this black night I heard a scream and then I suddenly saw your face. Your face was all that was before me. Tears streamed from your eyes, and it frightened me to my bones to see how terrified you were. This vision upset me so that I woke up and cried out your name; then I realized it was nothing but a dream. I tried returning to sleep but it was hopeless. I knew I must rise and seek you out on this very night."

Joshua and Mary were silent following her telling of the dream. Sitting side by side on the hilltop, they gazed at the shining temple rising before them in the distance.

Breaking the stillness, Joshua asked. "How did you know where to find me?"

"I saw you make your way to this hilltop as the sun was going down this evening." Maintaining her gaze ahead, Mary continued. "It is quite beautiful. I understand why you have chosen to be alone here at night. I am sorry if my dream has caused you to despair, but I felt I must share it with you."

"Thank you, Mary. There is no need to be sorry. I just wish I knew what such a vivid dream could mean for us both. Perhaps we will never know. It is, after all, just a dream," said Joshua as he tried to show calmness to the mother of Jesus.

"That is true." Rising to leave, Mary posed a question as she pulled her torch from the ground. "Where do you believe dreams come from, Joshua? Are they from God or do they come from within us?"

Pushing himself up to extend a proper good night to Mary, Joshua replied. "I do not believe God bothers with our dreams. He leaves those sorts of things for us to figure out. But surely you know better than I, Mother Mary."

"I asked Jesus that very question when he was but a young boy, and do you know what he said?"

Joshua silently shook his head.

"He said I believe everything is from God, every single thing." She then turned away and proceeded down the hill.

"Good night, Mary," said Joshua. "It was an honor to visit with you once again."

Raising her torch higher, she called back. "Good night, my son. Thank you for allowing me to share my dream. Let us pray we can both sleep as dawn will be coming soon."

"Mary?" he called.

Stopping, she looked up. "Yes?"

"Do you ever worry about him?"

"A mother never stops worrying about her child, no matter how old." Resuming her walk, she called back to him. "Those new sandals seem to fit you well."

"It was you!"

"No, my dear, it was my son. He asked that I leave them by your old sandals that you outgrew."

"But what will Jesus wear?"

Joshua stared at Mary as she resumed her walk and waited for her reply only to hear her call out with some motherly advice.

"Please try to sleep, my son. Passover is nearly upon us and we will all need our rest to prepare for the feast."

Joshua remained standing as he watched Mary's torch reach the bottom of the hill and wind through the village until she was out of sight. Although her dream of him was truly unsettling, he was now in awe of the sandals that graced his feet. To think that only the day before they were worn by Jesus himself. As he unrolled his blanket and prepared to sleep, he carefully removed his sandals. With newfound reverence he closely examined each one before hiding them under his blanket.

Gazing up at the countless stars, his arms beneath his head, Joshua made a promise to himself. He would do whatever possible to find Jesus at first light and thank him for the gift. He knew with absolute certainty that a day would not pass that he would not treasure these precious sandals.

The morning sun shone brightly on his face, prompting Joshua to pull the blanket over his head and roll to his other side. It had taken him a while to settle into sleep after Mary's late visit. Now his body longed to remain tightly wrapped inside the blanket a while longer. But Joshua's mind churned with Mary's words. Her disturbing dream, however, seemed to have lost its haunting power. Rather it was her telling him to get his rest because Passover was coming, and he needed to prepare a feast. "Is that what Mary said?" he wondered as he pulled the blanket over his head. He could not precisely recall her words.

As Joshua drifted in and out of sleep, he thought of his father who he knew was Jewish. Still, he could not recall a time when his family observed the traditions of his father's Jewish ancestors. His mother was not a Jew, yet she often said the prayers she learned from her Jewish friends in the village. Although half asleep, he could vividly remember his mother praying alone late at night. But Joshua had learned nothing at home about celebrating Passover. It wasn't until he heard the brothers share stories of their own Passover celebrations that he realized this was something very special. Jesus clearly felt the same way.

As scattered thoughts about what little he knew of Passover rambled through his sleep-clouded mind, he vowed to learn more about the sacred day and the feast he was expected to prepare. If there was a chance this morning, maybe, after thanking him for the sandals, he would ask Jesus to teach him more about this celebration. And that's when it hit him, like a bolt of lightning!

In a single motion, Joshua threw the blanket off and sat up with his eyes wide open and peered at the village below. His first thought was how quiet the village seemed. Squinting at the sun that was now well above the horizon, he felt immediate shame, knowing he had slept far past the time he would normally join the brothers at the break of dawn. He quickly stuffed the blanket into his pack and took a long drink from his water skin. He paused for a moment as he slipped into his priceless sandals before hurriedly making his way down the hill to the village. Again, he was struck by how empty the village appeared. Where were all the followers of Jesus who had returned in large numbers as they drew close to Jerusalem? Where were the brothers?

Something, he feared, must have happened to Jesus.

"Andrew!" he cried. "Peter, James, John where have you gone?" Joshua stood in the middle of the empty road and listened to his cries echo through the vacant village. Turning wildly in every direction, all he noticed were a few old men walking gingerly in the distance and a pair of aged women gathering scattered eggs across the road in the shadows of a low-slung building as chickens poked in and out of an open door.

"They're all gone, son," said one of the women as she rose from collecting eggs. "They went to Jerusalem early this morning." Adding calmly, "It was quite a sight to behold. The man who everyone calls the new King of Israel was sitting grandly atop a donkey. He was near the front when they all headed out."

"How could they leave me behind?" he cried, as much to himself as to the egg collectors.

The woman set her egg basket on the ground and with hands on her hips examined the distressed young man in the road. "Is your name Joshua?"

Leaping across the road to her side, he nearly shouted in her face. "Yes, it most certainly is!"

"I think I heard your name being called by some of the men before they left," she said while bending down to retrieve her basket.

"Do you know a woman named Mary?" he asked.

Joshua's question brought the hint of a smile to her face. "There are many women in this village named Mary, my son. But I do know that a large group of women left for Jerusalem well before the new King and his adoring followers left the village."

"Why would they depart before the Lord and the others?"

With a look of surprise, the old woman replied. "Don't you know? They have gone to prepare for the Feast!"

"Yes, of course," said Joshua under his breath. "The feast."

36

THE MULTITUDES

Joshua found himself walking alone and brooding over his misfortune. Learning that everyone he had come to love and admire had left him behind was deeply hurtful to him. Yet who could he really blame but himself? He simply was nowhere to be found when the time came for Jesus and the brothers to lead the followers into the Kingdom of God. But maybe they truly intended to walk no further with him. Perhaps, he lamented, they saw him as unworthy to enter the gates of Jerusalem as one of them. Yet the old woman from the village said they were calling his name! It was this last encouraging thought that Joshua clung to as he joined the long line of weary pilgrims.

They must all be journeying to the temple for the Passover, he assumed. The atmosphere seemed festive as many families played instruments and sang to their God. Others walked beside goats and lambs that were to be offered as a blood sacrifice to cleanse them of their sins. Joshua had heard of this custom, but failed to understand how the blood of animals could relieve one of their sins.

Joshua kept his thoughts to himself as he swiftly moved through the procession. He desperately hoped to find the brothers before they disappeared into the city of his dreams. His mind continued to dwell on his darkest fears as his pace quickened. *What would happen if he never saw the brothers again? What if Jesus journeyed where no one could follow, as brother James mournfully told him not long ago?*

Joshua heard a thundering sound from somewhere ahead. Was it the roar of a wild beast, he wondered as he stood still in the road. Then the sound came again, and he saw the look of amazement on all the pilgrims' faces.

"Did you hear that?" he shouted. "It is the hail of many followers across the land, for Jesus is entering Jerusalem!"

"You speak of the Messiah," shouted a man traveling with his family.

"The new King of Israel has come to lead us all," cried another.

"It is the Lord," declared Joshua as he broke away from the procession and ran as fast as his legs could carry him. The sound of pounding feet followed close behind and the roars ahead grew louder. In the excitement of his pursuit, he barely noticed that the city of Jerusalem had risen around him. Nor did he see the many branches and garments that he trod upon as the thickening crowd forced him to push past bodies in his relentless effort.

Casting his gaze beyond the masses before him, he stared in wonder at the great temple towering above. No longer did Joshua hear the continuous cheers and praises from the crowd. Transfixed by the glistening gold walls that climbed into the clouds, Joshua felt that he was standing in the shadows of the glorious Kingdom of Heaven.

Feeling the constant push from behind, Joshua again pressed forward. A narrow gap appeared amidst the crush of bodies before him. He rushed ahead to catch a glimpse of what lay just beyond. In that moment, he was nearly overcome by what his eyes beheld. There, with his back to him, was the figure of Jesus. His head was slightly bowed and his arms rested gracefully at his sides. The donkey carrying the Lord stepped ahead with ease, unperturbed by the surrounding commotion. Joshua saw the brothers keeping pace with the Lord as they walked beside him, drawing ever closer to the broad steps of the temple.

Before running ahead to joyfully greet them, Joshua paused for a moment to take in the remarkable sights and sounds before him. He marveled at the throngs of people who showered the Lord with blessings. Many he saw had tears in their eyes as they cried out to their Messiah and future king. He warily gazed up at the Roman guards in their shining armor as they rode past atop their royal mounts while casting looks of mild amusement upon the frenzied crowd. But the sight that truly unsettled him was the line of men in long robes who glared down from the summit of the temple steps. Although Joshua could not see their expressions, he knew for certain they had not gathered to welcome Jesus to their glorious temple.

His sense of foreboding was quickly broken by the call of his name. "Joshua, you are here," came a familiar voice. Soon, Brother James wrapped his strong arms around him in a fierce embrace that nearly lifted Joshua off his feet. "I feared that you were lost to us, my son! Come quickly, let us tell the others!"

In that moment, Joshua knew in his heart that he would never be abandoned. He had friends for life that loved him as much as he loved them. But now he struggled to keep pace with James while carefully slipping through the tight cluster of adoring followers who cried out a chorus of praises as they threw fragrant flowers before their Messiah. Joshua anticipated his joyous reunion with all the brothers who stood only steps away at Jesus' side.

But in that moment the world shifted. In the blink of an eye, the feeling of celebration turned to one of desperation. Joshua could only stare as panic gripped his heart and his breath quickened. The brothers were overcome by an advancing mob wanting more from their Messiah than merely to adore his presence. With countless arms reaching out, they lunged forward as one for a chance to clutch a piece of Jesus' garment as he sat calmly upon the animal that had delivered him from Bethany to the grand steps of the temple.

Chaos erupted in every direction. The chorus of praises quickly turned to screams as Joshua fell to the ground and struggled to breathe. His mind did not comprehend the pandemonium overhead. He braced himself on hands and knees, his only thoughts centered on frantically getting air into his lungs.

"Get to your feet, Joshua," came a distant voice. "You must fight to raise yourself or you will be trampled in the street!"

Was that James who called to him, or could it have been someone else? All that was certain was the sharp smell of dirt and rock that filled his head as he drew blessed new breath. With newfound strength, Joshua rose to his feet. Looking ahead he could scarcely believe his eyes as he gazed in wonder at the peaceful sight before him.

The overzealous worshippers he feared would tear Jesus apart now gently rested their heads against their Messiah and his animal. He stared in awe as Jesus placed his hands upon each head and spoke softly in words only they could hear.

"There you are," said James, as he stepped before Joshua. "Where did you go? I thought you were right behind me."

"I was until the crowd near Jesus became unruly and I fell to the ground. Did I hear you call to me?"

Looking at Joshua with curiosity, James replied. "It was not my voice that you heard, my friend. But we must go now, before I lose you again."

"Please tell me first what happened here."

"People were hungry, Joshua, and Rabbi fed them. Surely you have witnessed this before." James then pulled Joshua by the arm and together they pressed forward.

Soon Joshua was greeted by the brothers with many cheers and embraces. He was overjoyed to be with them again, but uncertain if the brothers knew where Rabbi would lead them now that they all stood before the temple. Despite the seeming chaos that surrounded him, Joshua real-ized he was no longer afraid. He struggled to get to where Jesus remained atop the donkey amid the congestion of followers. Although only steps away, a crush of adoring followers were still reaching out to the man who would be their new king. Joshua was stunned when the Lord greeted him with a smile and dismounted the donkey and handed him the reins.

"It is good to see you, my son. Please walk this gentle animal away from the crowd and a young lad will come to you and take the reins."

Holding the reins loosely in one hand, he looked to Jesus. "Will I see you again, Lord?"

"You will indeed. Trust with all your heart, and you will find me." Placing a firm hand on Joshua's shoulder, Jesus closed his eyes. When he opened them, he gave Joshua a reassuring nod, turned, and walked away. Before he vanished into the crowd, Joshua saw that the Lord's feet were bare.

"Where are you taking the donkey?" cried Andrew from above the crush of people between them.

Joshua called back to the brother he cherished. "The Lord told me to take the animal to a young lad who will find me away from the crowd."

Andrew was silent as countless people passed before them, but he held his gaze upon Joshua. In a voice much softer than before, he offered a brief message to his dear friend. "See to it that you return to us, my son. We will be waiting."

"I will find you and I will trust our Lord with each step." Following Joshua's words, the two broke their gaze and went their separate ways.

37

A HIDEOUS HILL

Joshua wondered if he would ever break through the horde of pilgrims pressing in from all sides. He never realized that this festival called Passover would attract such a multitude to the temple. But as he led the donkey through the never-ending throng, he heard distant calls that were surely for the Lord. "The Messiah has come" and "The King of the Jews will save us all," came the faraway cries. It warmed Joshua's heart to hear such words.

Pausing, Joshua came back to the donkey and spoke softly as he gently rubbed her brow. He hoisted himself up to gaze beyond the cluster of people surrounding him. What his eyes beheld was beyond his imagination. The golden walls of the temple shone as powerfully as the sun on the masses of people swarming below. "Surely this is the Kingdom of God!" said Joshua to himself. As far as he could see there were people. But there was a space in the other direction where the crowd pressed no further.

He knew at once that this was where he would find the lad that Jesus had spoken of.

"Girl, I believe we are on the right path," said Joshua as he got off the donkey, keeping the reins in hand. The animal appeared thirsty, but he had no water. "We are almost where we need to be girl, I promise. Please stay with me." It was then that the thirsty donkey lowered herself to the ground, unwilling to go further without water.

"Can somebody please help me?" cried Joshua. "My donkey needs water!" His desperate plea was met with silent stares as people walked past. Joshua cradled the donkey's head in his lap and continued to beseech the crowd. "This is the animal who carried the future King to the city. I beg of you, don't walk by and let her suffer!"

Soon a boy and his father approached and held out their filled water skin. Joshua poured a small portion of their water into his empty pouch and thanked them. Carefully placing the skin under the donkey's nose, he quietly rejoiced to see her slowly lap up the water. In time others offered water as well. Soon the donkey raised her head and stared at the gathering. Following several blinks of her eyes, she abruptly stood on all four legs to the sound of boisterous cheers from the many onlookers.

Seeing that the donkey had her fill of water, Joshua looked into the skin and found that some remained. Trying not to notice the floating spittle, he raised his head and quickly consumed the remainder in three large gulps before trudging ahead. Joshua saw that the crowds were thinning as he led the donkey forward. Then suddenly there was nobody, just he and the donkey walking alone upon a barren landscape. Looking behind, he gazed again at the temple looming powerfully in the distance and the endless multitudes swarming below its towering pillars.

Joshua tread further into the desolate surroundings with his eyes keenly fixed ahead for any sign of the lad that Jesus promised would be waiting. He heard a distant call and soon a boy waving his arms emerged from behind a rock formation in a hollow below. The donkey brayed loudly, and Joshua knew at once that this was the lad.

"Greetings," said Joshua as the boy approached.

"Shalom to you. My name is Benji. How has my girl been treating you?"

"She hasn't given me any trouble at all. But she probably needs food and more water. I'm Joshua." He placed the reins in the boy's hand and watched him climb upon the animal. The boy was truly happy to be reunited with his donkey and he leaned down to kiss the top of her head.

"Does she have a name?" asked Joshua.

"Her name is Baby. I was in the stable when she was born. No one else calls her that but me," said the boy as he patted her soft fur. "I should go now. My mother and father will worry if it is dark and I have not returned."

"I understand, but I must ask you a question before you leave. What are they building on that hill?

The boy turned to see where Joshua was pointing. "The hill is called Golgatha," said the boy. He turned back to Joshua with a solemn face, "It is where the Roman guards take their prisoners to die on a cross. You must not be from the city, or you would know of Golgotha."

Gazing at the top of the hill, Joshua finally replied to the boy, "I am from a small village like you, but mine is much farther away."

"So, you are here with your family for the Passover," said the boy from atop his donkey.

"I know very little of the Passover, for I am a Samaritan. But I am traveling with men who know much of this Passover, including the man who journeyed here on this donkey of yours."

"Is he the man my father says will be the new King of Israel?" With eyes opened wide, the boy waited for an answer.

Joshua nodded with a smile.

"So, Baby has delivered a new King to the Temple of God! That is very good," said the boy as he patted his donkey again. Then he began his journey home.

After watching the boy and donkey trot slowly away, Joshua returned his gaze to the hill called Golgotha. With the sun descending, he could see the silhouettes of two men on horses and before them the shape of a cross. Pinned to the cross was the figure of a man whose head turned violently from side to side. *They are watching him die*, thought Joshua, his eyes fixed on the grotesque scene. He heard the sickening cries of agony drifting down from the hill and it was more than he could bear. Joshua had seen dying before, but never had he witnessed torture. It was all he could think of as he trudged his way back to the multitude gathered before the temple.

Soon surrounded by throngs of joyful Passover pilgrims, completely unaware of the hideous execution occurring just beyond the temple, Joshua was comforted. Many took pity on him and offered food and drink when they saw how hungry and bedraggled he was in his stained threadbare garments. Joshua expressed gratitude for the surprising outpouring of generosity.

With renewed strength, Joshua wondered how he would ever find the brothers again amidst the teeming sea of strangers. Although it was night, the temple glowed with a fiery light. Again, Joshua was held spellbound as he gazed at the majestic building shimmering gold against the black sky. No longer was he haunted by the revolting scene of death at the hands of the Romans. "This is the Kingdom of God that towers above me," said Joshua to himself. "It is here where I will be reunited with Jesus and the brothers. For only beyond those shining pillars will my journey come to a glorious end!"

Driven by a clear purpose, Joshua forged his way through the crowd intending to climb the grand gateway to the temple. Seeing no temple guards waiting at the base of the temple, Joshua bounded up the stairway and did not look back. His heart leaped with anticipation as he neared the summit. To his surprise, he observed many people running down the temple steps with looks of despair and confusion. By the time Joshua reached the top of the steps, he was stunned by the chaos before him.

People were running in every direction. As Joshua stepped through the towering pillars, he was nearly run down by a herd of oxen charging by. The vast open space that spread before him all the way to the towering walls of gold was a sight to behold. Joshua's attention was diverted by the odd sight of livestock running wild across the temple court. Men holding whips chased after them as the sounds of their cursing echoed off the temple walls.

Something has gone terribly wrong, thought Joshua as he quickly lowered his head to dodge a flock of doves taking flight. *What had happened to this Kingdom of God that he had dreamt of for so long?* Trying to make sense of the chaotic scene surrounding him, he looked down at his sandal-clad feet, the same sandals that were once worn by Jesus, and he let out a gasp. There upon the marble floor were coins, not merely a few, but a countless number of coins scattered across the vast porch of the temple.

Seeing a man on his knees desperately hoarding coins into a basket, Joshua bowed down and begged for an answer. "Sir, what has gone wrong here?"

Looking up at Joshua as he swept coins into his basket, the man screamed at the top of his lungs. "The man who everyone is hailing as the Messiah and the new King of the Jews has attacked our temple and destroyed the Passover!"

38

JUDAS

Shaken by the man's words, Joshua wandered aimlessly about the courtyard in stunned disbelief. He gazed at empty animal pens with open gates and row upon row of wooden tables tossed on their sides as if ravaged by a storm. He found it impossible to accept that Jesus was to blame for such mayhem. Joshua offered to help vendors who scurried about trying to re-establish order to their Passover business, but was continuously waved off. "Keep away from them," shouted a nearby temple guard. "This is the business of the temple and the money changers who work for us. If the Passover is to be saved it will be only us who will do the saving," he declared before joining a Roman guard corralling loose animals.

Where have the brothers gone? wondered Joshua as he desperately searched for any sign of them. Surely, they can explain what has happened to this glorious temple. As the money changers frantically gathered Jewish shekels and Roman denarii off the floor, Joshua noticed a group of men in long robes who appeared detached from the present disorder. They were speaking to a man dressed in a ragged tunic. From the back, he resembled one of the brothers, thought Joshua. He continued to fix his eyes on the men in long robes as they conversed with this man who was clearly not one of them. Then the man in the ragged tunic turned around and walked away. The robed men watched him leave. Joshua could not believe his eyes!

"Judas!" he cried. "It is me, Joshua!"

Judas momentarily stopped and looked the other way before turning to face Joshua as he excitedly approached. "It is very good to see you, Judas. Do you know what has happened to the temple?"

Judas, looking at the attempts to restore order, paused before addressing Joshua. He chose his words carefully. "I know that you love Rabbi dearly, as do I, but you must know that money means nothing to him. What he did in the temple today wreaked havoc on the business of the Passover."

"But why would the Lord do such a thing? I know how he treasures the Passover and this glorious temple," asked Joshua.

"As I told you, young man, Rabbi does not know money, nor what it takes to preserve this mighty house of God." Placing a hand on Joshua's shoulder, he added. "The world can be a very complicated place, my son. Someday you will understand."

Joshua could feel his anger rising as Judas spoke to him as if he were a child. "Who were those men I saw you with?"

"It is not your place to question me regarding to whom I speak." As Judas turned to leave, Joshua pulled at his tunic. "How dare you lay a hand on me?"

Verging on tears, Joshua cried out, "Why do you speak to me like this, Judas? I thought you were my friend."

Looking impatient with Joshua, Judas offered a final response. "Whether we are friends or not does not matter now. If you must know, the men I was speaking to are priests of the highest order in the temple. They did not take kindly to Rabbi behaving like a madman as he turned over countless money tables and whipped opened pen after pen of sacrificial animals that were to be sold to the highest bidder." Moving closer to Joshua, Judas spoke in a hushed tone as if describing a marvel. "You cannot imagine the enormous sums of money that come into this temple during the festival. For Rabbi to shout, 'They have turned *my house into a den of thieves*'[8] was utter blasphemy to these men of God!"

"But what could you offer these men? Are you not just a simple man who follows the Lord?" he wondered aloud.

Judas's face darkened as he stared back at Joshua. "You had best be on your way, young man. It is not safe for a Samaritan such as you to be on your own in this Temple of God."

Joshua felt the hurt from Judas's clear threat. "Where have the others gone?" he demanded.

With a sigh that sounded false to Joshua, Judas went on. "I am afraid they have scattered far and wide, leaving me to pick up the pieces as they have done so many times before." He then backed away. "You must go, my son, for the temple guards may be watching you as we speak."

"I am not your son," said Joshua in a trembling voice.

Judas responded with a shrug and turned his back. Joshua stood still and watched Judas walk away. He soon vanished amid the frenzied activity of guards and venders working to restore order so the fruitful business of the Passover animal sacrifices could resume. For a moment, Joshua considered following Judas, but quickly recalled his threat of the temple guards and instead made his way back to the pillars.

Standing at the summit of the temple, Joshua gazed into the night. A sea of pot fires spread below as pilgrims huddled in small gatherings and waited for a sign that the temple was again open. For now, Roman guards atop horses and authorities of the temple blocked their passage. As Joshua

---

8 And said unto them, it is written, My house shall be called the House of Prayer; but ye have made it a den of thieves. Matthew 21: 13. (KJV)

descended the massive steps, he was joined by others who shared looks of disillusionment as they retreated from the upheaval above. *Where have you gone, Lord? Where are you, my brothers?* These were Joshua's only thoughts, as loneliness and uncertainty clutched his heart like a cloak.

Passing by the guards unnoticed, he slipped into the pressing throng and proceeded to make his way. But Joshua's steps slowed. The weight of a solitary question nearly killed him. *Where was he to go?* The thought stopped him in his tracks.

Long into the night, Joshua searched the vast grounds outside the temple walls for any sign of Jesus or the brothers. Searching the countless faces of families gathered by fires and of those who wandered as restlessly as he did proved fruitless. Growing more desperate, Joshua resorted to asking strangers if they had seen the man who many called the Messiah. Many laughed in response to his inquires; others simply shook their head in silence. He struggled to fend off his growing fatigue as the night wore on. Hope of ever seeing the men he loved sank with each stranger's denial. Yet he carried on.

"Did I hear you asking about the Messiah?"

Joshua stood still, unsure if the woman's voice was real or if his weary mind was playing tricks.

"Are you looking for the one who is to be our King?"

Joshua spun around so quickly he nearly fell. Looking up, he saw a man and a woman smiling at him with eyes full of curiosity. "Yes, I am looking for this man and his friends. His name is Jesus. Please tell me you have seen him."

"My wife and I did see the man you speak of as he entered the city riding a donkey. We cried out to him as he strode past, and I believe he saw us. But I'm afraid we have not seen any sign of him since."

Joshua's shoulders slumped upon hearing the man's words. As he turned to walk away, the man reached for his arm. "You look troubled, my friend. Is there anything we can do?"

"Unless you can lead me to Jesus, I'm afraid there is nothing you can do."

"My name is Jacob, and this is my wife, Sophia. We have come from afar with our families to celebrate the Passover, but also to see the man who many tell us is the Messiah, soon to be crowned the King of the Jews."

"You look hungry and tired, my son," said Sophia as she placed her hand on the young man's shoulder. "Come spend the night with us, where our families have gathered away from this crowd. We have food and a safe place to rest for the night."

Raising his head, Joshua could see these were people who meant him no harm. "My name is Joshua, and for many seasons I have traveled with Jesus and his friends. But I have lost my way in this multitude, and I fear I may never see them again."

Seeing Joshua's despair, Jacob offered words of assurance. "Surely you will find him near the temple but perhaps not on this night. The temple is closed for some reason. Rumors are spreading that Jesus himself is responsible. Why would the man who is to be the new King wish to prevent us from entering this glorious temple to purchase an animal for our sacrifice to God? There must be an explanation."

Joshua remained silent, not wishing to share what he knew.

"Tomorrow is another day, and the temple will no doubt be open to us then," promised Sophia. "Until that time, please come rest with us and our families on the Mount of Olives and tell us more about the man who will soon be our King."

39

THREE NIGHTS LATER

Nightfall was approaching as Joshua sat with the families of Jacob and Sophia. From their position on the Mount of Olives, he observed the temple glow brighter as the sun slipped from sight and the towering torches of the temple bathed the golden walls in fire-light. Gazing around where he sat, Joshua watched a myriad of cooking fires twinkling against the darkness as the aroma of broiled meat wafted through the air.

This was the night of the long-awaited Passover meal. Through the course of the feast, Joshua learned of the Israelites' escape from slavery in Egypt. With rapt attention, he listened to how these ancestors sacrificed a lamb and spread its blood against the walls of their homes so that the Angel of Death would pass them over and slay Egypt's first-born sons instead of their own. It was a story that Joshua did not fully understand. He realized that the shedding of the blood of an unblemished animal to honor their faith in God and devotion to their ancestry made Passover a treasured event in the lives of these pilgrims.

With the celebrated feast drawing to a close, Joshua watched as Jacob and Sophia's families packed up their belongings for the long journey home. Gazing across the hillside, Joshua could see that nearly all the families on the Mount of Olives were preparing to leave. Joshua wondered if Jesus and the brothers were doing the same. His mind searched for an answer.

Where have you gone, my friends?

Since arriving on the Mount of Olives, he searched for any sign of Jesus and the brothers. Rumors of Jesus gathering with pilgrims throughout Jerusalem or on the Temple steps sent Joshua chasing from one end of the city to the other. But each time he arrived at the rumored location, he found nothing but more strangers and further rumors of Jesus' whereabouts. Returning to Jacob and Sophia's family gathering on the hill, exhausted and heartbroken, he resolved to continue his search in the morning. A glimmer of hope remained that they were still here.

"You are welcome to journey with us in the morning," said Jacob as he handed Joshua a cup of wine before sitting beside him.

"Thank you, my friend. You have been very kind to me, but I must continue to search," said Joshua as he gazed at the activity below. Watching the families gather their belongings into baskets, he noticed a large group of men that stood out from the rest. They appeared to be trudging up the hill as one.

Seeing Joshua jump to his feet with his eyes fixed below, Jacob asked. "What do you see?"

"I am not certain, but they could be guards from the Temple."

"Why would Temple guards come to the Mount of Olives? There are only poor people here!"

Joshua was silent as he stared at the men drawing closer. The numerous cooking fires flickered upon their ornate garments as they steadily marched past families who quickly scampered out of their way. The flames illuminated the face of the man in front and Joshua knew at once that the gates of hell had opened and Judas was leading the way.

Joshua shook with anticipation as Judas and the guards marched through their gathering, leaving cookware and the remains of the Passover meal scattered in their wake. He saw that Judas's eyes were locked ahead as he and the guards steadily ascended the Mount of Olives.

"I must go now," announced Joshua.

"I'm coming with you," demanded Jacob.

"No, you are not!" Joshua then embraced Jacob for the last time and turned to leave. There, facing him, was Sophia holding a blanket. "The nights are cold, my dear; you will need this wherever you are going." Joshua quickly tied the blanket around his shoulders and kissed Sophia on her forehead before bounding away. "May God be with you, my son," were Sophia's last words to Joshua as he charged into the night.

Keeping a measured distance behind them, Joshua's heart pounded with the knowledge that Judas and the guards were coming for Jesus. *Surely there will be a confrontation, but what could he do to stop them?* As they approached the summit of the Mount of Olives, he watched as the guards paused at a lone cook fire to light torches. Joshua crouched behind to avoid their watchful eyes as he desperately searched for a way to warn Jesus and the brothers. *If only he knew for certain where they were.*

With fiery torches held above their heads, the guards resumed the pursuit into a dark grove of olive trees. Joshua ran to one side for a better look at where Judas was leading them. Joshua was completely unprepared for what followed.

Jesus emerged from the trees looking as if he was expecting this intrusion. Directly in his wake were Peter, John, and James, stunned to see guards with torches. Judas stepped forward and kissed Jesus on both cheeks. The guards quickly descended upon Jesus with ropes. Peter rushed to confront a guard and swiftly disarmed him of his sword. In a single motion, he nearly separated the guard's ear from his head. As the guard howled in agony, Jesus came forward, placed his palm upon the guard's head,[9] and the ear was restored. Jesus turned to Peter and quietly rebuked him. The guards then seized Jesus without a struggle and led him away.

Joshua was mortified. Jesus had just been arrested and all he did was watch from a distance. No longer able to bear the shame, Joshua burst from the shadows and charged after the guards. Hearing the pounding footsteps behind them, two of the guards turned and seized Joshua. He twisted and pushed against the men with all his strength, sickened by the thought that his foolishness could cost him his life. In the middle of the fierce struggle, Peter's long-ago words came back to him: *Never let any man hold you down again.* Screaming at the top of his lungs, Joshua pulled with all his might against the strong arms of the guards. He pulled so hard he felt his tattered outgrown tunic rip apart. In an instant he lifted the blanket from his neck and broke free from the guards.[10] Dropping the tattered garment and blanket, the guards gave chase. Unable to catch Joshua, they gave up and simply watched the young man wearing sandals and nothing more as he raced deeper into the darkness of the olive groves.

Joshua kept running even when he knew the guards had halted their chase. Soon, gasping for air, Joshua could flee no further. It was only after taking cover behind the thick trunk of a tree that Joshua felt the deep cold of the night against his bare skin. Wrapping his arms tightly around his pounding chest, he started to shiver uncontrollably. Joshua knew he must keep moving. Remembering a cave near where Jesus was taken, he lowered his head against the night wind and forced himself to run again.

---

9 And one of them struck the servant of the high priest, cutting off his right ear. But Jesus answered, "No more of this!" And touched the man's ear and healed him. Luke 22:50-51 (KJV)

10 And there followed Him a certain young man, having a linen cloth cast about his naked body: and the young men laid hold of him: and he left the linen cloth, and fled from them naked. Mark 14:51-52 (KJV)

Joshua had never experienced such cold, and never had he felt more alone. He did not weep for himself, for tears would do him no good. He only sought shelter to hide his nakedness and seek protection from the cold. Finally, he saw the cave and without hesitation Joshua slipped into the dark opening. Mercifully, the air was less cold. Gingerly he stepped further in and the air became warmer and heavy with the scent of olives. In the darkness he stumbled upon an object the size of a farmer's wagon, covered by a thick cloth. He tore away the covering and recognized the familiar shape of an olive press. The fabric smelled of olives and dampness. Joshua shook it once and quickly wrapped himself. Exhausted, Joshua lay on the floor of the cave and was asleep in moments.

40

BROKEN BREAD
AND WINE

Dawn

The sound of approaching footsteps woke Joshua at first light. Terrified that the guards had returned for him, he buried his head deep under the musty covering. Then came the voices of two men as they entered the cave. The talking ceased as footsteps drew closer. Joshua trembled under the thick cloth, knowing at any moment he would be discovered and dragged away.

Joshua tried not to breathe as he sensed their hovering presence. Suddenly the thick cloth was torn away. The startled men jumped back as they gasped at the sight of a naked young lad curled on the floor. So taken aback were the men that they quickly replaced the covering over Joshua's shivering bare body.

"We mean you no harm," said one of the men. "We are simply here to harvest ripe olives for the press."

"Please tell us why you are here," said the other man. "Does the pile of garments we passed on our way here belong to you?"

"Yes," came Joshua's muffled reply. "Can you please return them to me?" He then heard the sound of one man retreating. Joshua was overcome with relief, knowing these were not guards coming to take him away. Slowly he pushed his head from under the covering and saw a wrinkled old man with hands on his hips staring back.

"My brother and I have been harvesting olives in this garden for many years, but never have we seen a man sleeping next to our gat-shemanim," declared the man as he pointed to the olive press. "Let alone a naked one!"

The other brother, looking like a twin of the first one, returned holding the frayed blanket and the remains of Joshua's torn tunic. Joshua raised a bare arm to receive the bundle. "Thank you." He raised himself from the floor and covered his body with the blanket. Examining the torn garment, he quickly tossed it aside.

"You have asked me why I am here, and I will tell you. But you may not believe what I have to say." The old men remained silent and waited for Joshua to continue. "Temple guards came to this garden last night and arrested the man who many call the Messiah. I was here with this man, whose name is Jesus, and I tried to prevent the guards from taking him away. It was foolish and I failed. In my struggle with the guards, my garments were ripped away and I fled into the olive grove. Your cave was my shelter through the cold night."

The old men looked at one another and then back at Joshua. "We have heard of the man you speak of. Many say he will be the new King of Israel. But if what you say is true, and the guards have arrested him, you must go to the jail near the Temple. There he will be held in chains until a trial," said one brother.

"How do you know these things?" asked Joshua.

"We are old, young man, and there is little we have not seen."

"How will I find this jail you speak of?"

"Continue down the Mount of Olives and you will see it near the Sheep Gate of the Temple," said one of the brothers. "As you proceed down the mountain, you will also see that the pilgrims have departed now that the Passover has come and gone. Look for garments that may have been left behind, for you cannot go far with only a blanket over your body."

Joshua nodded silently as he tied the blanket over one shoulder. He gratefully accepted a drink from their water skin and a small portion of bread before leaving the cave.

"One more thing, young man." Joshua stopped and faced the old men. "Never forget about the Romans we all bow to." One of the men stepped out from the cave to make sure Joshua understood the importance of his words. "The most important men of the Temple collaborate with the Romans whenever money and power are at stake. You will be wise to keep that in mind."

Joshua retraced his path through the olive groves hoping to see any sign of the brothers, but it was obvious they had fled following Jesus' arrest. Surely, he assumed, they will be near the Temple jail where Jesus was being held. Making his way through the trees, he finally broke through and again cast his eyes upon the massive temple looming before him. No longer did it hold any trace of majesty and glory against the dark morning clouds. To Joshua, the temple was now a barrier, even a foreboding presence.

From the top of the Mount of Olives, he could see that it was just as the old men described, a near empty hillside with only abandoned items and the smoldering ashes of lifeless cookfires. Joshua trudged down the hill still clad only in a blanket, searching for anything that could pass for a suitable garment.

After some time, he managed to find grimy inner and outer tunics, still damp with the morning dew. Tossing off the blanket, Joshua quickly wrapped himself in the garments, which smelled of smoke and sweat. He continued in the direction of the Temple jail.

Midday

Gazing at an unadorned building made of large stones, Joshua thought it must be the jail. Although it rose two levels above the ground, it was dwarfed by the high walls of the Temple. He questioned the wisdom of entering this place where Temple guards might recognize him as the one who escaped from their clutches just the night before. In the midst of his uncertainty, a Temple guard emerged from the stone building holding a thick chain. Joshua watched as the guard wrapped the chain through a large loop by the door before securing the chain with a long spike and walking away.

Joshua immediately sprang ahead to intercept the guard. "Kind sir, may I ask you a question?"

The guard halted.

"Can you tell me when the man named Jesus will be released from your jail?"

Looking puzzled, the guard offered Joshua a curt response. "Young man, the jail is empty. Our prisoners were released to the Romans some time ago." The guard turned to leave.

"Was Jesus among them?"

Irritated with the questioning, the guard replied while walking from Joshua. "If you're speaking of the Nazarene who caused so much trouble, I can tell you with certainty that he never was brought to my jail."

"Then where is he?"

The guard remained silent as he walked away.

"Please tell me where they have taken my Lord," cried Joshua.

"The priests delivered him to Pilot." Turning to face Joshua, the guard gave a warning: "Say no more or I will unlock the jail and throw you in."

A feeling of dread crept into his heart as he watched the guard disappear. Jesus was not where Joshua expected him to be and the brothers had simply vanished. Again, he was alone.

Who was this man named Pilot, he wondered as he shuffled along the temple wall. Seeing a gathering of people not far ahead, Joshua decided to approach them for a small drink of water. Maybe he could ask them about Pilot.

"Pardon me, but could I bother you for a drink of water? I am a stranger here and I seem to have lost my family," said Joshua.

They carefully examined the young man in soiled garments before eventually offering him a water skin. "You can keep it," said one of the men.

After taking a long drink, Joshua expressed his gratitude before posing a question to the gathering. "Do you know where I may find a man named Pilot? I am told my friend is with him."

Joshua's question prompted them to mutter among themselves. A woman came forward to ask the name of his friend.

"His name is Jesus." Seeing the sudden alarm on her face, Joshua could feel his heart sink as he waited for a reply.

"Young man, Pilot is the Roman Prefect of our land." The woman looked deeply into Joshua's eyes as he stood still before her. "I am sorry to tell you that Pilot has sent your friend to Golgotha to be crucified."

Joshua's first reaction was one of disbelief. Surely, she was mistaken. For Jesus is the one they call the Messiah and soon he will be their King.

"No, that cannot be true," said Joshua as he shook his head before the woman. "You are wrong!" he screamed.

The woman watched with great sorrow as his eyes filled with tears. She pulled him tightly to her chest as he was wracked with deep sobs.

Dusk

Joshua arrived at the top of Golgotha gasping for air. A Roman soldier approached on a horse and harshly ordered him away. Joshua saw in the distance three men hanging from the hideous crosses. The soldier did not let Joshua pass, but pointed to an area away from the crosses where other witnesses stood. As he drew closer, he hoped against hope that Jesus would not be one of the three.

Not raising his head until he reached the cluster of onlookers, Joshua tentatively looked up. It was him. There, nailed to the middle cross, hung the naked blood-soaked body of Jesus. The man he loved more than life itself.

Nausea gripped Joshua, and in an instant he dropped to his knees and heaved what little remained in his stomach.

Coming to his feet, Joshua numbly stared at the cross. Guards lazily stretched below the lifeless body of Jesus. Not far from the guards were three women draped in garments that covered their heads. As if not able to bear much more, one of the women turned away from the cross and faced the onlookers. It was Mary, the mother of Jesus. Her face was ashen. She met Joshua's eyes over the distance that separated them. Tilting her head to the side, she seemed to offer Joshua her heart in the midst of such crushing sorrow. She turned away and rejoined the women. As the sun slipped closer to the horizon, Joshua broke his gaze from the broken body of Jesus. Feeling empty and forsaken, he numbly walked down the hill of Golgotha, a heartbroken young man with no hope.

Nightfall

The streets of Jerusalem were far less crowded now that the Passover celebration was over, and life had returned to its normal pace. It was along one
such street that Joshua sat upon a vendor's stoop. His head was covered
by his dirty garments as he presented his cupped hands to all who passed
by. Drifting in and out of sleep, Joshua barely noticed when coins were
dropped into his outstretched hands. Aroused by the sound of a cart rattling by, Joshua saw he had accumulated enough coins for a modest meal.

Rising to his feet, Joshua set about in search of a food vendor open
at this hour but all he could find were wine merchants who offered broken
pieces of bread with a purchase of wine. Securing his skin of wine and a
small bag of bread pieces, Joshua sat in the doorway of a vendor's closed
shop. Despite the numbing effects of the wine, the haunting vision of Jesus'
body hanging from a cross was all Joshua could see as he fell into a stupor.

Dawn

"Get up! Get up! You must leave at once," barked the vendor as Joshua lay
snoring before his doorway.

After much shaking and cursing, Joshua finally awoke and was
quickly on his way.

Stumbling along the street, Joshua heard the shouts of vendors filling
the air as he dodged out of the way of oncoming carts pulled by donkeys
and men. Although Joshua had no idea where to go, he moved on as if he
had a destination. Soon the sickening thoughts of yesterday returned with
overwhelming clarity, nearly causing him to retch.

Up ahead the sun shone upon the road, although it seemed too early
for the road to be so bright in the grayness of dawn. Squinting into the
light, Joshua saw the outline of a man approaching. There was something
familiar about the way he walked that caused Joshua to pause in the middle of the street. Coming closer, the light appeared to vanish as the man

stepped before him and smiled. Upon seeing his face, Joshua was terrified and turned to run.

"Do not be afraid, Joshua, it is me," came the words of Jesus.

With tears flowing, Joshua struggled to control his shaking and speak. "How can this be, Lord? I saw you with my own eyes and you were dead on the cross." He looked to the sky and cried, "This cannot be real!"

Jesus firmly gripped Joshua's shoulders. *"Look at me, son. The world is broken, but I have overcome the world."*[11]

Joshua felt his strong hands and slowly met his steady gaze.

"You are a warrior, Joshua."

"I am not a warrior, Lord, for warriors do not cry," Joshua meekly protested while brushing tears from his cheeks.

"Oh yes, they do, my son. They cry and they roar, for the Kingdom of God is upon them." Releasing his grip, Jesus stepped back. *"Soon I must go, but I promise with all my heart that one day we will meet again. Until that day, please know that you will always live in me, as I will live in you.*[12] *For you, Joshua, are my warrior."*

Joshua lowered his head as he felt the tears returning. The air was still as he looked down on the street. Not even the sound of vendors could be heard. When he raised his head, Jesus was gone. Turning to the once-noisy vendors, Joshua could see that they had all ceased preparing for the business of the day. They now stood as statues staring back at the stranger in the street with looks of wonder on their faces.

"He lives," whispered Joshua softly to the silent vendors. With a raised voice he said it again, "He lives." To his utter delight, he saw the

---

11 These things I have spoken unto you, that in Me ye might have Peace. In the world ye shall have tribulation: but be of good cheer; I have overcome the world. John 16: 33. (KJV)

12 Abide in me and I in you. John 15: 4 (KJV)

vendors begin to nod as he repeated the words and embraced one vendor after another. Joshua then ran into the middle of the barren street and lifted his face and arms to the sky. With tears of elation streaming down, he roared for all to hear. "HE LIVES!"

EPILOGUE

It was before dawn when Journey restlessly paced in the barn. I rose from my sleep pallet to look around. The family was still fast asleep in the main house. I listened for any nervous sounds coming from the goats or chickens but there were none, and I was relieved. All was still in this wee hour of the morning before the world awakened.

I gave Journey a few gentle pats to his side and assured him it was just the wind before falling back on my pallet and returning to sleep. No sooner had I drifted away when Journey stuck his cold wet nose on my face and forced me to sit up. There he sat, just staring at me, whimpering. When I asked if he wanted to go outside, he ran in circles and barked. I knew then, there would be no more sleep.

Outside the air was cool and still. Journey started to bolt up the hill but somehow, I managed to hold him back. If there was a wild beast lurking somewhere, I did not want Journey to be his next meal. After all, the old boy was not nearly as fast as he used to be.

Gazing up the hill near the site where we buried Langer, I saw the dark shape of a young man. As I stared in silence, tears filled my eyes as I realized my dear nephew had come home.

Journey easily broke away from my grip and bounded up the hill. I cried out to Joshua and waited in the silent dawn for his reply. And then it came as Joshua let loose a wondrous roar from the top of the hill and Journey joined in, howling happily at his side. In moments, my sister and nieces ran from the house dressed only in their thin night garments. Before long we were all laughing and crying. Never in my life had I felt such joy!

ACKNOWLEDGEMENTS

For many years I have been intrigued by the unidentified boy who flees the Garden of Gethsemane after Jesus' arrest. This account is only told in Mark's Gospel, 14:51-52. Over time, this provocative scene slowly grew into a story idea that I pondered for longer than I can remember.

One day I finally got the nerve to say out loud what I had long wrestled with. Over coffee with a trusted friend, Rich Kasten, I presented my tale of a runaway Samaritan boy who chases Jesus to the cross. Rich, who is a true renaissance man and devoted member of the renowned Lake Avenue Church of Pasadena, California, where I too attend, was my first test. After patiently listening to my long-winded idea inspired from a single New Testament verse, Rich declared that my story sounded truly compelling! That was all I needed to hear.

Over the next year or so, I shared my work in progress with a trusted few. Among them was Rich, who always kept my eye on the prize. My wife, Maureen, is a woman of such immense talent that, at times, it takes my breath away. Maureen took on the daunting task of scouring through each chapter with a red pen as she embarked on the heroic mission to save me from myself. Although this was an excruciating experience, I always knew I was in loving hands.

I also shared this developing story with my sister, Sharon. Throughout my life, Sharon has been my touchstone. Of course, she would be with me every step of the way.

For years now, my wonderful son has urged me to write a book. In fact, he never stopped with this plea to his dad. So here it is, Matt, my book. Although it may not be the one you had in mind, I hope it makes you proud.

Finally, it must be said that from the day I first sat down to write this story and each day since, I have felt the comforting presence of God right beside me. So, thank you, Lord, for gently guiding me on this most unusual journey that I pray continues for the rest of my days.

ABOUT
THE AUTHOR

A Chicago native, Schuyler as a teenager always dreamed of becoming a radio and TV talent. His aspirations led him to Hollywood where he trained as a broadcaster. He began his career as a country music DJ and news reporter in the Southwest. Ultimately he became a TV news anchor in Dallas. In time, Schuyler moved to Los Angeles, where he worked as a television news correspondent. This eventually led to a decades long high-profile career in crisis management, political consulting and speech writing. Most recently, Schuyler turned to publishing, founding a family-oriented magazine in Southern California. Inspired by the Gospels, "The Young Samaritan" is his debut novel. He currently lives in Pasadena, California with his wife Maureen.